Fledgling

Natasha Brown

DEDICATION

To my family, who supported my dreams; my mother, who helped tutor me in prose, my daughter, who displayed the strength and inspiration for my story, my son, who is one of my biggest fans, and my husband, who's my #1 fan.

Read a **Lost Chapter** of Fledgling after finishing the book! Check the last page of the book for your special code to access the extras!

CHAPTER 1

Sterile white walls surrounded Ana once again. They provided a form of anesthesia, a cocoon that left her comfortably numb. She sat on the examination table, her hands folded on her lap. Even though she was eighteen and technically an adult, she might as well be six years old again. Totally powerless.

"Good thing we don't pay Dr. Wilson by the hour." Her mother sighed.

Ana glanced over. Her mom was busily fidgeting with her watch. Permanent worry lines creased her otherwise attractive features, making her appear far older than she was.

"Mom, you should know by now that it always takes longer than you expect. Nothing moves quickly here." Ana gripped the edge of the padded table and shrugged. A long strand of dark hair slipped over her shoulder.

A sharp knock announced Dr. Wilson, a tall man with glasses. "Hello ladies, I'm sorry I'm running late today."

Ana's mother, Melissa, jumped up, almost knocking her purse onto the floor. She hurriedly shook the doctor's hand.

"Hello, Melissa," Dr. Wilson said. "Nice seeing you again."

"Hi, David. It *was* only the other week we were here. Only difference is, I don't have a job now." The strain on Melissa's face was evident. "Layoffs."

Dr. Wilson frowned. "I'm sorry to hear that. Any hope for a new job?"

Melissa shrugged. "Well, my sister talked to my old boss and she thinks I can get my job back at Clark Bend Bank."

Ana shot her a glare, which she conveniently avoided.

"Eva won't be happy about leaving her friends, but she's resilient," Melissa said. "But I'm not so sure about dragging Ana to Idaho. What do you think, Dr. Wilson...is it too risky?"

Dr. Wilson adjusted his glasses. "It couldn't hurt going down to a lower altitude. More available oxygen could make

Ana a bit more comfortable."

Ana wondered if they would notice if she stood up and left the room, but instead, she tapped her toes together in a nervous rhythm.

As if reading her mind, Dr. Wilson turned to face her. "Oh, Ana, didn't mean to ignore you. How are you feeling?"

His familiar frown was probably one of the first things she saw when she was born. Why did everyone always have to feel sorry for her? She was sick and tired of it. She wasn't pitiful, like a stray dog. Or was she? Ana stared into his eyes and saw the answer.

"I'm okay."

"Baby, weren't you complaining about shortness of breath?" Melissa glanced at her. "You *were* having problems the other day with carrying the laundry upstairs."

"How is that different from three weeks ago?" Ana whispered.

Dr. Wilson nodded sympathetically and sighed. "Things don't look good. I know you don't want to hear the word transplant, but I'm afraid that *is* where we're going. Your heart is hardening much more rapidly now, and I'm worried you're approaching congenital heart failure. At this rate, you might only have a few months."

Silence fell. With each breath Ana took, she counted away the seconds she would never get back. Each breath closer to surgery, or worse.

Dr. Wilson breached the quiet room with his softened voice. "Although moving may be a bit of an adjustment, it could give you a little more time in the waiting game. When you're placed on the transplant list, it could be a day or a year. Idaho doesn't have any transplant centers, but Washington does, and I know the division chief at Seattle Children's Hospital. Where was it in Idaho you were thinking of moving?"

Melissa cleared her throat and answered, "Clark Bend in

northern Idaho. It's not too far from Seattle."

"Well, it's up to you ladies. But I would support the move. As long as Ana takes it easy. No carrying heavy boxes or arm chairs. And as long as you get right in to the cardiology department." He grinned and squeezed Ana's shoulder.

His wire rimmed glasses gleamed from the florescent lighting, and Ana's reflection stared back at her blankly. She was having a worst case scenario kind of day. Then she considered it was more like a worst case scenario kind of life.

Her mother caught her eye. Worry was written all over Melissa's face. Ana knew her mom only wanted the best for her, and it had just gone from hard to worse after the layoffs. A job with insurance was necessary. With no family nearby, going through a transplant would be a challenge. Melissa needed her sister's support.

She never had the leisure to make decisions based on what she wanted. Always handcuffed without a choice. A choice would imply there was more than one option, and there never was. Not in her case.

As her doctor told her mother all about the state-of-the-art facility in Washington, Ana dropped to the floor and slipped to the window. Her long, pale fingers tightened into fists, and she closed her eyes tight. She was tired of the constraints of her body and the never-ending fear that plagued her. She hated her heart. It always ruined everything. Peering from the third story window down to the cars driving past on the streets below, she wished she could trade places with any anonymous, normal person. Boring would be great. If her biggest problems were cars and boys, she would be overjoyed.

Normal. Was that too much to ask?

CHAPTER 2

Ana shifted her weight on the backseat of her mother's Honda. The worn leather groaned in protest. She yawned, which drew her mother's attention.

"How're you holding up back there?" Melissa looked back through the rearview mirror.

"Fine. Just tired of sitting," Ana said, arching her back to stretch.

Long strands of chestnut hair fell loose from her ponytail, whipped by the gust from the open window. *Each hair so free.* A ribbon of jealousy wove its way around her chest and squeezed the air from her lungs.

"We're almost there, shouldn't be much longer," her mother said.

Ana rested her head against the window and watched the passing scenery in silence. Evergreen forests shrouded the mountains with dense growth, and fields of butter yellow grasses waved in the breeze. The postcard landscape would have soothed her nerves at home in Colorado, but with each passing mile she felt more and more isolated and alone.

On the passenger seat was a haphazard pile of food wrappers, magazines, and a lumpy pillow that had seen better days. Ana's reprieve from navigating for her mother up front provided only a fleeting break from those watchful maternal eyes. As she glanced up at the rear-view mirror, she noted the familiar creased frown her mother wore when she didn't think Ana was watching. Always under surveillance.

"Clark Bend's only a little further ahead. We'll be able to stretch our legs as soon as we get to the house." Her mother changed her frown into a strained smile.

The flash of sun glinting off a metal sign caught her attention.

"Welcome to Idaho...thanks," she mumbled.

"What's that, baby?" her mother asked from the front

seat.

"Nothing," Ana said.

Ana didn't think Idaho looked any different than Montana, from where they had just traveled through. The same mysterious dark river curled alongside the highway for what seemed like hours. As it grew wider, she knew they were drawing closer to town. Its source, the Lake Pend Oreille was just beyond Clark Bend, a place Ana remembered from her childhood.

Melissa switched off the radio. "Hey, girls? You want me to drive by your schools real quick?"

Ana glanced over to her twelve-year-old sister, Eva, who folded her arms and glared out the window. The whole trip Eva had made her position clear – she was angry about being ripped away from her friends.

"No, we *definitely* don't need to do that." Eva spat.

Ana also had no interest in seeing her new school. A pain in her chest made her flinch, and her heart sputtered. Heat radiated from her face down to her fingers as she thought about the inevitable gawking she'd receive on the first day at school. She drummed her fingers on her leg and shook her head, as if the action could shake her fears free. She tried convincing herself it was an opportunity for a fresh start, but it was a hard sell.

How was it a good thing to be in a new school at the end of her senior year?

Ana grasped the silver chain around her neck and admired the gift her mother bought her along the way, a charm of a regal bird with wings outstretched. If she could pick an animal that represented freedom, it would be a raptor. She would give anything to fly away and be free.

Ana's gaze fell on her sister, who was squirming in her seat. "Eva, you okay?"

Eva's eyes crinkled in a frown. "I've gotta *go*." She tilted her head to the side and squinted at her mom through the rearview mirror. Her tangled brunette hair tumbled over her shoulders.

"Hey, Mom. I don't think it can wait–better pull over." Ana knew her sister had a very weak bladder, and when she said she had to go, it was best to listen.

"Can't hold it, Miss D?"

"Ugh, I hate going outside," Eva rolled her eyes. "And Mom, I'm not six anymore. Stop calling me that. I'm not a *diva.*"

"Sorry, D. Better safe than sorry. There's a turn-out just ahead." Melissa drove a little further and pulled off the road.

Eva groaned as she wrenched open her door and edged toward a clump of tall grass near a grove of trees.

"Hey, Ana, would you mind getting out and keeping an eye on her? Your sister isn't at home in the wilderness like you are."

Ana nodded and slipped outside, walked slowly around the back of the car and sat on the bumper. She could see some movement behind the trees to her left, and she heard a loud snap followed by a startled yelp.

"You okay, Eva?"

"Yeah, this tree is grabbing at me. Give me a minute. Any cars coming?"

"Don't worry sweetie, I can *barely* see you. I haven't seen a car in a bit."

Ana grabbed a stalk of long grass that rose up at her feet and twisted it around her pointer finger. Movement from the field on the opposite side of the highway caused her to look up. A tuft of red fur flashed from between some bushes. She squinted and tried to find it again but couldn't. After another moment of waiting the small furry creature crept out from under a log and paused.

Ana sucked in her breath. It was a fox. The patch of white fluff on its chest made her imagine how silky soft it was. She wondered what it would feel like to run her fingers through its fur. As she mused, it darted across the field and dipped out of view down a slope. When it came back into her line of vision, it leapt up a hillock into the air. It arched down and when it was nearly to the ground, a large bird swooped up and flew into the air. The dying sunlight allowed her to discern the pointy 'horns' of an owl who appeared unsteady as it rose through the sky. Ana soon lost sight of it behind the tall trees.

She searched the ground for the fox and couldn't find it. It had disappeared.

Whatever, Ana. You're tired.

Was her mind playing tricks on her? The fox was probably hidden in the grass.

"Well, that's better, but now I have a scrape on my arm."

Startled, Ana turned to face her sister, who had a twig snagged in her hair. With a snicker, she reached out and removed it from Eva's head.

"Did you go sightseeing, Eva? I wasn't sure if you were walking to the house," Melissa said as she started the engine and slowly pulled back out onto the road.

"I didn't want anyone to see me," Eva said sulkily.

"From space?" Ana said.

Eva combed her fingers through her ratty hair and seemingly grew more agitated with every knot she found. "I can't wait for a shower."

Ana nodded in agreement and touched Eva's arm. "I'll let you take the first one – promise."

Her sister shot her a grin, and Ana returned her attention out the window. After a couple of minutes, a ditch in the road jolted the car. She noticed a dust covered road sign. They were close now.

As if on cue, her mother gave both girls a meaningful smile. "Alright, here we are. Home sweet home."

They drove past a field of tall grass and turned down a gravel driveway. Before them was Grandma Jo's home. It had been over five years since they last visited. And it wasn't a happy memory. Funerals were never happy.

Dull windows peeked out from behind low branches in a grove of fir trees. Modest sized to begin with, the house was dwarfed by the tall evergreens that surrounded it. The cheery pastel blue paint and the bare flower beds that lined the walkway begged for attention. The lush surroundings were a little overgrown and needed a good pruning. Ana's thoughts soured. It was familiar, but it wasn't home. Not hers. The last person who lived there had died.

The silence in the car was broken when Eva slid outside before the engine turned off and started up the front walk.

Her mom got out of the car to stretch, but Ana sank further into the leather seat. Her lids dropped shut for a moment until Melissa said, "Hey Ana – you coming? Don't you want to come in and say hi to your aunt and uncle?"

Ana's eyes flicked open, and she noticed the maroon sedan parked beside them in the driveway. She reached for the door and took one last breath before pushing herself out of the car. She sauntered up to the front stoop where her mother and sister were and waited for the onslaught of emotion.

Before Melissa could reach for the door, it swung open. Aunt Tera burst out and embraced her sister.

"Oh my, you girls are gorgeous!" Their aunt gushed. "Why, you are simply *stunning*, Ana. Just *look* at your beautiful figure."

Aunt Tera winked and lifted Ana's arms to point out her curves. Ana extracted herself from her aunt's grip to wrap her arms around her waist, trying to conceal herself.

Aunt Tera turned toward Eva. "And you! Eva! My...you're so graceful. Like a ballerina!"

Eva giggled and embraced her adoring aunt. It was clear she enjoyed the attention.

After fussing over her nieces, Aunt Tera gave her sister a

warm hug, and the two of them chatted about the road trip. Arm in arm, they sauntered inside. Aunt Tera's tight curls bounced around her cheery face, and Ana heard her say in an undertone, "I am so happy you're here and not a minute too soon. Jace is getting back into fishing, and you know how much I can't stand the smell of his gear, and not to mention eatin' fish. Thank goodness I have someone else on my side when it comes to picking dinner…"

Ana shook her head. Things hadn't changed much. Her aunt was still the same boisterous woman she remembered. Ana had always tried to spot the similarities between her mother and aunt; it was like a game. She studied Melissa's short brown hair and thin features and compared them to Tera's curly red hair and round face. *Nope, nothing*. But as they snickered together, Ana noted something – the laugh lines that framed their lips were like parentheses.

"You all must be so tired and hungry! Don't worry, I made you spaghetti. And we'll be out of your hair after dinner. We don't want to tire you all out." Aunt Tera's gaze lingered on Ana, and she squeezed her shoulder.

As they sauntered into the house, a voice boomed in greeting. "Welcome home!"

Thick as a trunk, Uncle Jace's form towered before them with open arms. He got to Melissa first, then Eva. Last of all, Ana was wrapped in a bear hug that took the breath out of her. She freed herself from his grip and rubbed her sore shoulders.

The sweat stained band on Uncle Jace's fishing hat indicated it hadn't left his head for a very long time. Ana wondered if he would be able to remove it if he tried. Then she figured it was probably better staying where it was. She guessed he still had blond hair underneath after she spied pale locks poking out, like saplings searching for light. Always eager to tell a new story or joke, Uncle Jace's blue eyes twinkled as if unable to hold back a laugh.

"Jace, you're just a big kid!" Melissa said, shaking her head.

"And that's why we never had any… he keeps me busy enough keeping an eye on 'im." Aunt Tera winked at Eva.

The smell of spaghetti hit them, and their stomachs growled like wild animals.

Aunt Tera heard their bellies. "For heaven's sake, let these ladies eat! They don't want to stand around while there's perfectly good food in the other room!"

As they were shepherded into the kitchen, Ana immediately noticed the smell of the old menthol cigarettes that grandma used to smoke. Wait, how was that possible? She had always hated that smell. One more thing to make her feel at home.

They popped their tired, hungry bodies in front of the old kitchen table set for five. A huge yellow bowl of spaghetti, a basket of breadsticks, and fresh Parmesan cheese beckoned from the table.

"You're the best, Aunt Tera," Eva said.

Uncle Jace chuckled and answered, "She made enough to feed an army!"

Ana heard Aunt Tera mutter under her breath that spaghetti leftovers were better than eating fish for the next week, and she snickered as she sat down next to Eva.

"Now, I wasn't sure what you were bringing here with you, so I went ahead and brought some extra towels and kitchen utensils. I've never really bothered going through anything of Mom's, so you should have just about anything you need here – you know how she couldn't get rid of anything." Aunt Tera paused to grasp her sister's hand. She hurriedly wiped a tear and continued. "So, Mel – Danny over at the bank is expecting you on Monday. He's got everything set, and he seemed a touch eager to see you again too."

Melissa shook her head and shut her eyes. "I hope you weren't encouraging him, Tera. You know how he used to annoy me. That man just doesn't know when to stop talking."

As Ana removed her napkin from her lap, her aunt turned with a serious expression and asked, "So Ana, when's your doctors appointment? Where was it...Spokane?"

Ana exhaled, disappointed she wasn't able to avoid the question. "Yeah. It's in a couple weeks in Spokane. It's not too far a drive, right?"

"Yeah. Although it depends on how fast you drive. If you go slow like Jace over here, then it'll take longer."

"Hey, now." Uncle Jace defended himself.

Aunt Tera exchanged a glance with her sister and blinked at Ana. "So, you feeling any better since you got here? I know it's only been, well, less than an hour now, but Mel says we're at a lower altitude than up in Denver. That's supposed to help you... right?"

"Yeah, that's what the doctors tell us," Ana said. "I haven't noticed anything yet. Still kinda soon. It's been a long day though. Hopefully I'll start feeling better."

"If you come fishing with me, I bet you'll feel great! Some fresh air and sweet silence – nothing like it." Uncle Jace smirked as he tore through a breadstick and mopped the extra sauce on his plate.

Aunt Tera patted Ana's arm. "There should be some real nice kids in town for you to make friends with. I bet they won't care a thing about your heart condition."

"I wasn't planning on telling anyone," Ana said and stood up so fast her cup almost tipped over. Hoping to end the conversation, she collected the empty plates and set them in the sink. Her delicate fingers reached under the faucet, and the stream of warm water glimmered over her skin like a translucent glove.

Aunt Tera stood and stopped her from washing the dishes. "Oh sweetie, you don't need to do that after the day you've had! Why don't you go rest on the couch?" Tera shooed her. "Oh, and Jace parked the old van out near the shed – the keys are just there on the counter. It should get you to school and back."

Ana reluctantly lowered the dish back into the soapy water and wandered into the living room.

***

Her aunt and uncle drove down the gravel driveway and waved goodbye. Ana sighed. She imagined herself a tornado survivor. And it wasn't even over yet. She still had to unpack. Then there was school on Monday. How was this better than staying in Colorado?

"Alright, the movers will be here any time now. Are we still agreed on who gets which room?" Melissa said to the girls.

Ana and Eva nodded. Every summer when they visited in the past, Ana had stayed in her mom's old room, a small, dark space with slanted, low ceilings. Eva naturally gravitated towards the large, airy room that once housed Aunt Tera's belongings. There was no need for discussion.

Eva climbed onto the living room couch and plugged her nose as she reached for the large retro TV remote. "Pew, this couch stinks. I wish we hadn't sold *our* couch. Mom, did you bring the disinfectant, or some odor-eating spray?"

While Eva and their mom discussed their cleaning plans, Ana's anxiety level peaked. She needed to get out of the house and see the sky. It was getting dusky out, but she thought she remembered how to find her way to her special place.

Ana slipped on her jacket. "I'm going outside. Let me know when my stuff gets here."

Melissa frowned and looked out the living room window. The sun set behind the trees.

"I don't know, baby," she said. "It's getting cold out, and you've had such a long day already. Can't it wait until tomorrow night? I'd rather you stay inside and rest."

"I'm going," Ana said with a glare.

Ana turned around and headed into the kitchen. She wrenched open the cupboards in search of a flashlight. When she finally found one, she tossed it onto the white tiled countertop. No surprise that after so many years, it was out of batteries. Ana shrugged. She didn't really need a light anyway. She was at home outdoors and always managed to find her way through the dark. Nothing frightened her when she was in the wilderness, especially when she went star gazing. Under the infinite sky, all of her problems seemed so insignificant.

She breezed through the back door and wandered out onto the small back deck. A dense grove of trees and rocky outcroppings encircled a small lawn with one great pine in the center. Ana noticed a discreet trail that led away from the yard and grinned. It was still there.

The trail was barely noticeable, but she knew where to look. Berry bushes and scrub grew across it from disuse. She shifted them out of the way as she moved her delicate body through. Sounds from the forest inhabitants warmed her ears and she knew she wasn't alone.

Ana enjoyed the terrain – it was a close cousin to her beloved Colorado. Rolling mountains cloaked with deep jade evergreens and grassy valleys seemed to offer her a figurative olive branch in friendship. The only thing missing was the occasional white bark of aspen, but she could adjust to the welcoming landscape. A brisk smell met her, and she decided it must have recently rained. She paused, and breathed in the scent like a wine connoisseur tasting a bouquet of flavor.

She meandered on and headed toward an opening up ahead on the trail. Her heart thudded as she pushed herself forward into the dying rays of the sun.

A panorama appeared like a watercolor, with wilderness that stretched as far as the eye could see. Before her was the perfect surface to star gaze. An immense flattened granite stone reached over the grassy fields. In the distance, beyond the meadow, the wild green wilderness was split by a dark river.

Ana stepped onto the dark granite and slowly lowered herself on the rock. She stretched flat on her back and closed her eyes. Her special place in Colorado reached out to her in memory. Hidden in the pines, she discovered a small field behind their home and had convinced her mother to drag a metal lounge chair there so she would have a place to lie down. When she didn't want to talk to anyone or was in one of her moods, she went there to unwind under the night sky. Her silent companion, Orion, guarded her from the painful thoughts that crept into her mind whenever it was quiet and dark. His bright constellation lit her imagination and pointed the way to his wintry friends: the Great Dog, Taurus the Bull and the Twins.

For the first time in days, she allowed herself to breathe. The constant, hidden fear and depression that clawed at her soul burst out in the form of salty tears. Curled into the fetal position, she began to sob in silence. She rarely allowed herself the freedom to break down, because it tired her. She didn't like feeling sorry for herself.

As the sky overhead turned a deep blue, stars began to glimmer and pulse and sing their nighttime overture. Ana traced the constellations in her mind and soothed her agitated heartbeat to a slower rhythm. The tears dried but she continued to gaze into the abyss.

Something rustled in the meadow, and she caught sight of a lithe dark form. As she traced the small animal's movement through the grass, she remembered the time. From the safety of her rock, she pushed herself up a little too quickly. Blood rushed out of her head and made her dizzy. Ana knew better than to do that, but she was tired and couldn't think clearly. Before she turned away, she glanced over her shoulder to look for the silent nighttime visitor, but concluded she must have scared it off.

She was alone again. What a familiar feeling.

CHAPTER 3

Morning sunlight filtered in through Ana's window as she slipped on her favorite pair of jeans and a green t-shirt. After she noticed the pines sway outside her window, she grabbed her winter jacket and wandered into the bathroom to brush her teeth. Her bedraggled reflection gave her a start. She reached for her comb. Tangled, knotted hair wasn't the first impression she wanted to make. She smoothed out her long dark tresses before flicking out the light.

Steam curled from Melissa's cup of coffee and reminded Ana of home as she walked by it to the fridge. Her mother picked it up, took a sip, and then smoothed out the lines of her business jacket.

"How do I look?" Melissa asked.

"You look great, Mom – as usual."

Melissa shook her head. "Yah, well. Are you nervous?"

The syncopated rhythm of Ana's heart returned. She swallowed the lump in her throat and forced a smile. "A little. I can't wait for tonight – when it's all over," Ana said and smirked. "How 'bout you?"

Melissa looked at her. "I'm a little nervous too...but excited." She gave Ana a hug and cleared her throat. "How are you holding up after unpacking yesterday? Not too tired?"

"No worries, Mom, I'm fine." Ana stretched, her body slow to react. She thought about all of the boxes she unpacked the previous day and was thankful it was almost done.

Eva breezed into the kitchen wearing her favorite purple dress, with her hair in a tidy ponytail. She seemed a little restless but wore Ana's contagious grin. The girls hugged their mother goodbye and headed out to Ana's inherited van.

The banana yellow paint on the VW camper made her flinch. It was her Uncle Jace's pride and joy, maybe fifteen years ago. Now it was just a weathered milk carton with wheels. There was no way to go unnoticed in this vehicle, which was why Ana was so focused on getting to school early to avoid the rush.

"C'mon Eva, let's go – hurry up."

Eva yanked open the door with a screech and climbed in. She whipped around and stared at the table and seats arranged in the back. "Cooooool. A sink too – that's *awesome*."

Ana shook her head and grumbled to herself as she started up the loud engine. It blustered to life, and they rolled down the driveway.

Once on the highway, Eva flew her hand like an airplane out the window while Ana tried to relax. It eased her jittery stomach to see her sister's amusement.

She reached the middle school, parked and walked with Eva into the office. The receptionist smiled and escorted her down the hallway filled with kids. As Eva was led away, she turned to give Ana one last hesitant smile. Ana blew her a kiss and turned out the door. Although Eva was unhappy about the move, Ana knew her sister wouldn't have any trouble making new friends. She never did.

The high school was a couple blocks away and before she knew it, she was in the parking lot. She pulled into a secluded spot at the back corner under some pine trees in an attempt to be inconspicuous. She hoped her yellow van would blend in. No such luck with all the shiny cars around.

She walked up the front steps past groups of milling students. The brick building's boxy appearance seemed cold and rigid. She bit the inside of her lip nervously. With one last deep breath of fresh air, she passed through the large wooden doors.

CHAPTER 4

Chance glanced out the window at the morning sun crowning the plains to the east. Bird song filled the forest canopy above. With no neighbors for miles, the solitude on the mountainside was peaceful.

Chance lifted his bare arms over his head in a long stretch and groaned. Another monotonous school day. Only a few short months more until he graduated. Thank God.

He dropped to the wood floor and began doing pushups.

A light knock came from his door.

"Come in," he said.

The door cracked open. Niyol's soft brown eyes focused on his grandson. "Chance, do you have time today after school – or will you be working?"

Chance lifted himself to his feet. "Kenny's expecting me, but I'm free afterwards."

"Alright, I will see you then."

"Thanks, Grandfather."

The door slipped shut with a click. Chance pulled on a black t-shirt, grabbed a pair of faded jeans and ran his fingers through his thick hair before he darted downstairs. He sniffed the air, closed his eyes, and stalked into the kitchen.

"Morning." He leaned in and kissed his mother's smooth bronzed cheek while she cooked breakfast, inhaling the smell of eggs curling up from the pan. Her long black hair was pulled back into a low ponytail. She turned and gave her son a hug.

"Good morning, Chance. Grandfather was looking for you – did he find you?"

"Yeah."

"Your father wanted me to ask if you were planning on hanging out with the guys at all today?"

Chance flexed his fingers, annoyed. Why did she always have to start out the day the same way? Did she really think he would give her a new answer today? "No. I only need to be at Kenny's for an hour or two... so I'm gonna head out with grandfather after work."

His mother frowned but kept her eyes on the frying pan. "Well, I'll be on shift tonight so I won't see you, but your dad should be around after he closes up the shop."

Chance patted his stomach and peered over his mother's shoulder. "Mmmm, smells good. I'm starving."

"One more minute, then you can eat. Why don't you grab your things while you're waiting?"

In the living room, he retrieved a bag from a brown suede couch and glanced up at a wide tapestry featuring a large angular bird that hung from the wall above it. A bright column of light from the skylights above illuminated the weaving, and gave it a bright airy glow.

When he returned to the kitchen, his mother was scraping a large pile of eggs onto a plate. He accepted it and within seconds, wolfed it down. He deposited the empty dish into the sink and threw his bag over his shoulder.

"Thanks for breakfast, Mom. See you tomorrow." Chance called over his shoulder as he sauntered to the front door.

Sunlight glinted off the glossy black paint of his classic Chevy truck. He dragged his fingertips along the side, in a tender caress, before he jumped in.

He roared down the mountainside, a dust trail in his wake. As soon as he turned onto the highway, he sped up and grinned at the speedometer needle as it climbed above seventy miles per hour. Once he reached the valley, he sighed and reluctantly edged his foot off the accelerator. Buildings scattered the landscape, interspersed with evergreens and naked deciduous trunks with the bare beginnings of spring buds.

Chance pulled into the school parking lot and headed to the back corner. A space was available near a stand of evergreens, and he parked beside a bright yellow camper he had never seen before. He laughed to himself, jumped from the cab and locked his door. It could definitely use a paint job. To top the list.

He strode up the front steps and disappeared inside as the bell rang.

CHAPTER 5

Ana's eyes adjusted to the darkened hallway. The school office was immediately to her left. A receptionist sat at a tidy desk perpendicular to the door. She lifted her head and smiled at Ana. Her tight curly hair hugged her head in gray ripples, which made Ana think of fresh sheared wool.

"Hi, I'm Ana Hughes...it's my first day."

"Oh, hello. That's right. I have your file here somewhere." She opened a drawer then placed some papers in front of Ana. "Alright, this is your schedule. Your first class is calculus with Mr. Morrisy. His room's just down this hall, fourth door on the right. This paper..." She placed it in Ana's hands. "You need to have all of your teachers sign. Return it back to me by tomorrow morning. Any questions?" Her softened blue eyes seemed to contradict her leathery skin.

"No, I think I'll be fine." *Hopefully,* she thought.

Ana accepted the sheets and skimmed over her schedule.

"Good luck!" The receptionist called after Ana as she walked to the office door, her feet slowing the closer she got. Ana reached for the knob and turned with a flinch. "Thanks."

Jitters returned to her stomach as she thought about being stared at. The further she walked down the corridor, the more her cheeks smoldered. She was unable to tear her eyes away from the cracked linoleum floor. If only she could shrink away or become invisible.

Students filed into the hallways and moved in different directions. A few heads turned Ana's way, but no one acknowledged her. She tried to focus on where she was going and kept her eyes straight ahead. Thankfully, she found the room the receptionist directed her to without needing to ask anyone.

As she opened the door, she took a deep breath, and told herself that everything would work out. *In just seven hours the worst will be over.* She walked in and spotted the teacher, standing behind his desk. She handed him the form to sign as he handed her a book and directed her to an empty seat at the front of the class. *Oh, no, not the front…*

The class was full, and only a few students continued to filter in. Some of them gawked at her and whispered to their neighbors. Ana's cheeks scalded. She slid down in her seat and wanted to disappear.

A girl to her right had a kind face and wore glasses. Her blond hair was pulled back into a loose ponytail. She turned and grinned at Ana. The welcome appeared genuine, so Ana returned a timid smile back.

"I'm Laura, Laura Wegler. You're new here?" The girl leaned over to talk to Ana in a low monotone.

"Yeah, I just moved this weekend. My name's Ana Hughes," Ana whispered back.

"Nice to meet you," Laura said before she turned her attention back to the front of the room as the bell rang.

The last people darted through the door and shuffled to their seats.

Mr. Morrisy cleared his throat and announced to Ana's horror, "We have a new student in class. Her name is Ana. Please join me in welcoming her to our school."

Scattered clapping and a couple guffaws echoed through the back of the room. Frozen with fear, she focused on a crack in the linoleum floor in front of the teacher until he continued. "Alright people, open your books to page 171. We'll be discussing the Chain Rule today."

Class passed slowly for Ana. The material they reviewed was new. She struggled to keep up with the lesson, which only frustrated her, since she prided herself on her school performance.

At the end of class, she approached the teacher and said, "Mr. Morrisy, This is past where my class was, are any tutors available?"

"Actually, Laura's at the head of the class. She might be

willing to help you out." He motioned over to the girl who sat next to her.

Laura overheard this while she flung her backpack over her shoulder. She walked up to Ana and said, "You need some help in calc? I'd be happy to help."

Ana sighed in relief. "Thanks, Laura, that'd be great. I promise I'm a quick study – this just isn't a subject I've reviewed yet."

"No problem. So – you need help finding your next class?"

They walked out together and into the busy hall.

"That'd be great." Ana read her schedule aloud. "I have US History with Ms. Walker."

"Ohhh – sorry. She's a crab. If you sit with *adoring* eyes on her the whole time, you'll become a favorite though. Her room's just up those stairs, first door on your right."

"Great – thanks for the heads up."

"Hey, Ana...I normally sit out at the patio with my friends under the trees during lunch. You can join us if you'd like."

Laura's invitation seemed to be offered in earnest. Ana was relieved to have someone to sit next to and accepted. "Yes – thanks. There's nothing worse than sitting alone on your first day. I'll look for you – see ya."

When lunch period finally came, she was relieved to walk onto the open patio. Groups of students milled around and stared at her as she walked by with her head down. She scanned the landscaped concrete courtyard until she saw Laura beneath a tree at the far corner with some friends.

Ana walked towards her, careful to keep her eyes on the ground, anxious Laura's sentiment had changed since calculus. Laura looked up and waved her over. Relieved, Ana sat down beside her and her friends in the cool shaded grass.

The chatty girls frowned at Ana at first. Laura smiled at Ana and made the introduction. "This is Ana. She's new here."

A chorus of hellos welcomed Ana, then they turned back

to continue their interrupted conversations.

Laura greeted Ana warmly. "How's it going so far? Met anyone?"

"No – to be honest I've been trying to avoid being noticed. I take my time settling in." Ana smiled, and lowered her eyes. "The day's dragging on. I'm just trying to get through it without incident."

Laura shrugged. "I'd say in a week you'll be old news, and they'll be busy staring at someone else."

Ana felt more eyes on her than she was comfortable with and stared down at the grass again. She said, "I guess I can do a week."

CHAPTER 6

Chance leaned against the school fence, as he stared across the courtyard. His friends were laughing and punching each other in a mock fight. Their taunts fell on deaf ears – he wasn't paying any attention.

"Hey Chance – what's up, man?"

Chance turned to his friends. They snickered at him and his sinewy body tensed. "What?"

"Um, whacha staring at? I asked if you were gonna be at the shop today?" One of them asked.

The guys turned and followed Chance's gaze to a tall pine tree that rose from the edge of the patio. A group of girls sat below it.

"Yeah... I'll be at work after school. Kenny needs me to clean his office and put away a shipment of parts." Chance acted like nothing happened but failed to ignore his friends' sniggers and lurid comments. Anger surfaced and he snapped. "What's the problem?!"

He pushed away from the fence and made it shake and shudder as he stormed toward school. He only hung out with the guys because it was easier that way . He would prefer being alone and not listen to their dribble. Days like this made it hard to remember what his reasons were for being friends with them. His mother was concerned he wasn't social enough, or had any friends anymore, so he made an effort. Graduation wasn't far off. If he could make it until then, he wouldn't have to keep up appearances any longer.

Voices called after him while he walked away.

"Hey, wait, man! We're just fooling around!"

"Come back!"

Chance flung his bag over his shoulder as he passed through the courtyard. His attention pulled back to the pretty girl he noticed from across the grounds. He'd never seen her before.

Long dark hair fell around her face and she seemed preoccupied with hiding behind it. Her eyes remained down, but he thought he caught a glint of green.

Whatever, he thought. Girls were the furthest thing from his mind. He wouldn't complicate his life any more than it was already.

A pretty face was just a distraction. A distraction he didn't want.

He pushed through the door to his next class and settled into the darkness. The bell rang a moment later, and he heard people shuffle into the building. He dropped his bag beside his seat, then removed the camera his mother bought him after she had encouraged him to take a class more creative than mechanics. She said he could learn all he needed on the job from Kenny and he might as well get a little culture. He figured it would be an easy class to pass, so he went along with it.

Students filed into the darkened classroom, while their teacher sat in the corner and appeared to be asleep, but Chance knew he would be on his feet by the start of class.

Everyone settled and Mr. Frisk rubbed his eyes and rose to his feet as expected.

The door opened once more and light streaked across the dark room. A figure stood and hesitated before approaching the teacher. It was the new girl.

Chance's eyes bore into a white sheet that hung from the wall in front of him. As she walked past his seat, he caught the scent of pine and rain. He crossed his arms and exhaled the smell from his lungs, but the fragrance lingered.

***

Ana wandered up the steps in search of the photography class. Her legs grew tired by the time she reached the top stair and she paused to catch her breath. People blew past her as she clung to the rail. It was a constant reminder that she was different. Of course, she hadn't always been so worn down and unathletic. She yearned to be normal like the rest of her classmates. Their ability to climb a mountain or think about a limitless future was something she envied.

Everything she had, she appreciated. Family meant everything to her and she didn't want or expect more. She liked things simple. It hurt less that way.

She eyed clouds moving through the skylight as she neared her door. With one last doleful look, she walked into the darkened classroom.

Dazed, she stood in the doorway and waited for her eyes to adjust before she moved forward. A shaft of light was provided by a lamp clamped to a desk in the corner of the room. There, Ana spotted the teacher, who appeared to have just woken, his hair smashed to the side of his head and his clothes wrinkled. He waved her over to his cluttered desk.

She handed him her form. He grasped it in his stubby hands and signed it. As he handed it back, he smiled a warm creased grin and directed her to an empty chair.

Ana sat down and tilted her head forward to shield her from the humiliation of being drawn out yet again by another unabashed teacher. With great relief, she soon discovered that he had no intention to introduce his new pupil. Instead, he began a slideshow from a projector pointed at a white sheet that hung on the wall.

Darkness soaked into her, and she was comfortable for the first time that day. In the quiet dark, her heart made its own unique rhythm as though it were ready for a performance at center stage.

"Alright, listen up. We'll be reviewing shutter speeds and apertures today. Please direct your attention to the next series of slides."

Her eyes adjusted to the gloom as she stared at the slideshow. Some of the images seemed remedial to her, so she let her eyes venture across the room.

To her side, she noticed a lean figure a couple seats away. Slouched back in his chair, his coppery hand supported the side of his head. Thick dark hair appeared to have grown out from a haircut and fell in waves around his sinewy hand. His athletic build made him appear quite tall. She realized a little too late she was staring – the darkness offered a false sense of security. The object of her curiosity turned to meet her gaze, and she snapped her attention back to the slide of a babbling brook as her cheeks and ears flushed.

"Notice in this image, the movement of the water is much clearer than the previous image? Can anyone venture a guess at why they're different and why this image looks better?" The teacher's voice broke Ana's disorientation.

Her attention was drawn to someone shuffling in their seat, and she glanced to the side. The boy stared right back at her. Her eyes flashed back to the projected image on the wall, and her cheeks flushed with warmth.

After her surprise settled, determination filled her. *Ana, you have no interest in guys. They are only trouble.* She shook her head with disgust, angry at herself for being affected by good looks. Mr. Frisk continued the lecture on proper shutter speeds, and Ana put all her attention on him, resolving not to turn back again. When the lesson was over, the teacher switched the lights on, and fifteen pairs of eyes blinked in surprise.

"We'll practice shutter speeds today. You have until the end of class to pair up and take pictures on the grounds at school. I wish to see some of your experimental imagery in tomorrow's class. Oh – and I would appreciate it if you didn't just use this class time to ditch." He smirked at a few select individuals.

The teacher turned to Ana as the students got up and stretched off their listlessness.

"I'm sorry Ana – did you bring a camera today?"

As though roused from anesthesia, Ana tried to find her voice. "Yes, sir, I brought it."

Mr. Frisk nodded in response, waved at the door and wandered back to his desk to slump down.

The last of the students filtered out of the classroom. Oh, well, she would rather work alone anyway.

"Guess we're the last two."

Ana's cheeks flushed as she heard a deep voice near her. She exhaled slowly and turned around. Hazel eyes made her insides turn like taffy on a taffy pull, whirling and twisting into a sticky mess. She let out a shaky breath. "Oh, I thought I was alone."

"Hey – I'm Chance." He grasped the strap of his bag and looked down.

"I'm Ana."

"And, you're new here."

"Um, yeah – just moved from Colorado."

Ana reached into her bag for her camera to give her cheeks time to recover. Her silver pendant slipped from the folds of her shirt. She looked up in time to see Chance's eyes trace over it. His brow furrowed and he abruptly turned away to retrieve his camera from his bag and started for the door.

They left the room together but Ana didn't know her way around yet and wasn't sure where to go. Kids were already on the basketball courts busy with the assignment, and she didn't want to be a copycat.

"Do you know any good places to go?" she asked.

"We could check out the garden. Follow me." Chance thrust his hands into his pockets.

He led her around the building past a grassy area to a small fenced garden. As they walked through the entrance and across some dried vegetation, Ana noticed how soundlessly her companion moved. For a moment she closed her eyes and heard her feet scratch across the earth. She would have guessed she was alone, but when she let her lids slide open, Chance was moving silently beside her. She stopped at the center of the garden.

"Perfect. I can work with this." Ana said in enthusiasm and wandered around the small lush enclosure.

Chance squatted in front of a tiny daisy. A bee was busy collecting pollen at its center. Ana left him there to take a couple of shots while she looked for a suitable subject.

Sure that his eyes remained on her, she kept her back to him because she didn't want to reveal the color that had risen to her cheeks.

A group of tiny white butterflies flicked around the garden as though attached by strings, tugged up and down by the air currents. Fascinated with their paper-thin wings, she turned to Chance. "I have an idea for a picture. Do you mind helping me?" she asked.

"Sure," he said.

"Would you get up on the bench and jump down with your arms out? The butterflies gave me an idea."

She pictured it in her mind, then set her camera on a birdbath that was flipped upside down and prepared for the shot.

She looked up at Chance. "On three. One, two...three."

He jumped off the bench arms outstretched, landed and paused before the camera. She pressed her finger down on the shutter release, and paused.

They huddled together and reviewed the image. Chance looked like he was flying with wing-like arms arched out. The delayed shudder speed and the movement created a motion trail that give the illusion of wide wings.

Ana met Chance's eyes as he said, "Wow...you're good."

Her heart stuttered, gave a squeeze, and she snapped her attention to her pale fingers curled around the camera. She shoved the camera back into its case and stuffed her hands into her fleece jacket.

The bell rang out across the school grounds.

"Thanks for helping me out," Ana said, staring at the ground., She turned to walk away. What was wrong with her? Why was her heart behaving this way? She was in a daze, woozy. It would be better to gain some distance from him so she could clear her mind. Boys were trouble, and she didn't need any more trouble.

As she wandered toward the large brick building lost in thought, she glanced sideways and discovered Chance in stride beside her. They passed a cluster of students who whispered and stared at them as they walked by. Ana noticed Chance's jaw tighten and his expression harden.

"So...what class you have now?"

Ana was surprised to hear his voice break the silence. "Um, English with Penroke, I think."

"Follow me," Chance said in a wooden voice. She was confused. He seemed angry with her. If he didn't like her, he didn't have to speak to her. Was he obligated to show her around? He didn't seem like the welcome committee type. In fact, she really couldn't figure out why he was focused on her at all.

As they approached a flight of stairs, he flew up them effortlessly, and Ana was left behind. Out of breath and tired, she wished he hadn't offered to lead the way. She was too thin to appear out of shape. It was too soon to tip her hand. Was a fresh start too much to ask for? She yearned to know what it was like to fit in without sympathy wherever she went. Eyes to the floor, she reached the top stair and followed beside him down a hallway until they stopped.

He opened the classroom door for her, followed her in and strode to his desk. The teacher signed Ana's form and pointed her to an empty seat at the corner of the room. She set her bag down beside her chair and breathed a sigh of relief. Now she could take a moment to collect herself.

"Miss Hughes, I'm sorry but we don't have enough textbooks in the class – cutbacks. You'll need to share with someone until we can get another," Ms. Penroke said. "Is someone willing to share their textbook with Ana?"

A couple of unenthusiastic hands rose around the room, but Ms. Penroke called the first one to rise. "Yes, Mr. Morgan. It's nice to see you participating in class for once. Go ahead and sit next to Miss. Hughes."

The teacher paused while Chance grabbed his belongings and settled into the chair beside Ana. An array of faces watched him shuffle across the room, then turned to snicker and whisper to each other.

"We'll continue reading *To Kill a Mockingbird*, and then you'll have some assigned reading tonight. Please open your books."

Ana was relieved to discover she was ahead in at least one of her classes. She remembered it well, one of her favorite books from last year. She turned to Chance. Something about him made her nervous, and it bothered her. No one caught her off guard like this. There was a certain convenience in staying emotionally distant from everyone.

Chance lifted his desk as if it didn't weigh a thing and brought it closer to hers.

"Um...thanks for sharing," Ana said and stared at her hands.

"No problem."

The class was just past chapter two. She read the pages held steadily before her and became unnerved when Chance finished the page well ahead of her. Prideful when it came to reading, she ate literature like a starved animal. When he stared at her while he waited, she became flustered and disoriented. After she finished a paragraph and realized she just reread the section twice, beads of perspiration dewed at her temple. Finally at the page's conclusion, Ana smiled at Chance to indicate she was done. *Finally*.

Dejected, she slumped in her seat and assumed he thought she wasn't very smart from her tortoise-like reading speed. Resolved to get her own copy soon, she glared at the book in agitation. Anyway, since when did she care about what a guy thought about her? As her mind wandered, she stalled out on the page and closed her eyes to collect her thoughts, which scattered and broke like spider webs in a fierce wind.

"Alright class, I want everyone to read through chapter three tonight. Within chapter two, one of our main characters says that you never really understand a person until you climb into *his or her* skin and walk around in it. I'd like us to explore this topic together. I want all of you to create a poem about this subject matter. Feel free to get creative. It's due Friday."

The bell rang and everyone grabbed their belongings, and left so fast Ana questioned if it had been a fire alarm.

She rested her head on her hand and said to her reading partner, "I'm sorry I was so slow – I threw you off pace."

"I'm *very* fast," he said and his face softened. "Good eyesight runs in the family. Sorry I made you self conscious. You can use the book tonight. I've already read it – I don't need it." As he held it out and placed it in her empty hands, his skin brushed against hers.

"I read it last year, but I guess I should skim through it tonight if there's a poem due at the end of the week. It isn't a bad read." She turned to slip the book into her bag so she wouldn't have to meet his eyes and falter in a lapse of stupidity – again.

She stood and walked out of the room into the sunlight. He followed at the same pace. It was like she just woke up from a trance.

He appeared to wait for her to lead on as though any direction she picked was fine. Why did he seem so interested in her? She didn't consider herself pretty and was disappointed she hadn't exhibited a great intellect in his presence, which she thought was her strongest attribute.

Ana broke the awkward silence and said, "I need to go pick up my little sister now. She's waiting for me."

"I'll walk you to your car...if you want," he said, and grasped onto the strap of his bag, as though it were the only thing that kept him from floating away.

"Sure," she said breathlessly.

"So, why'd you move *here*?"

"Oh, well, my mother got laid off, and her sister lives here and was able to get her old job at the bank – my mom grew up here. We needed a change anyway. It's a really small town...smaller than I'm used to. I lived just outside of Denver." Not wanting to ramble on, Ana stopped, and cleared her throat. "What about you?"

"I've lived here forever. It's a *really* small town- not much to say about it, like you said, it's small." He paused. "How do *you* like it?"

"It's beautiful. I didn't think I'd be happy here, but...I might have been wrong." Ana thought better of continuing, apprehensive to expose too much about herself.

"What?"

A pulse of heat flushed through her palms. She focused on the far end of the parking lot as she answered. "The night sky's so impressive – it's perfect."

Chance's eyes swept the sky, and he thrust his hands into his pockets.

As they approached Ana's bright yellow camper van, she grew uncomfortable. Chance chuckled as she walked up to it.

An explanation was necessary, so she said, "Um, my Uncle Jace gave it to me. It's not exactly inconspicuous, and it'll probably deafen me for life, but it works, sooo..." Her eyes flicked around to the trees that shaded her car, unsure where to rest her gaze.

"It seems to fit you." He said, and appraised her in silence, which made Ana's heart jump again.

Unsure how to take his remark, she paused in thought.

Was it a compliment or something else? Did he think she was odd, loud and ornate or someone who didn't fit in?

He seemed to sense her confusion, and said, "You're hard to ignore too."

Ana wasn't used to compliments from boys. She laughed nervously, completely baffled.

"If it needs any work – let me know. I work at an auto shop. I'm not a mechanic, but I know enough to be dangerous."

Dangerous, that's for sure, Ana thought.

"Thanks, my Uncle said it checked out – but I've learned not to trust his word about mechanical things." Ana unlocked her car and threw her backpack in between the front seats.

"Well, this is me, here." Chance indicated the black truck parked beside hers. Its shiny paint job and fastidiousness was the antithesis of Ana's camper. "It was my pet project when I turned sixteen."

"Nice. At least *it* isn't yellow." Ana gave a sideways glance to her van.

"Nothing a little paint can't fix." Chance walked around to his truck.

Ana caught him eyeing her surreptitiously as he leaned against the frame.

"So, I guess I'll see you tomorrow?"

"As appealing as it is being the new girl...I wouldn't miss it," Ana said and jumped into her van to cover her rosy cheeks. Without another look, she sped out of the lot to pick up Eva.

CHAPTER 7

The next day was easier.

Familiar with her new surroundings, Ana was more confident around school because she knew what to expect. Settled into her new schedule, she threw herself into classes and tried her best to catch up.

At lunchtime, Ana sat with Laura and learned her new friends' names. While they talked about a couple of teachers, Ana casually slipped in an unrelated question. "So, do you know Chance Morgan? What's his story?"

Laura gave her a suggestive grin, leaned in, and said, "Chance has lived here forever. He's super athletic, really smart and very good-looking, but not very sociable. He doesn't have a girlfriend and doesn't seem interested in dating. Jen Baker tried getting him to go with her to the Sadie Hawkins dance, but he refused. He's usually busy over at Kenny's auto shop. And I think I heard he's turning into a weirdo, wandering around the forest with some old dude. His dad has a jewelry store out near the Hope Marina, and I think his mom's a nurse over at the Sandpoint Hospital. Why... you interested?"

Ana tried to answer indifferently and combed her fingers through her hair. "Oh, I just wondered. I sit next to him in English and we were talking yesterday."

"He *talked* with you? That's promising..."

Satisfied with the new information, she diverted Laura with questions about the hiking trip she wanted to organize. Laura chattered on about the best places and who she thought about to invite.

"We should probably avoid the north side of the mountain though – I've heard of lots of cougar sightings. I don't want to become a statistic." Laura smiled.

Ana would have to think up an excuse for not joining in on the fun. Hiking was out of the question. She could barely climb the ten stairs in her house without getting out of breath. And she wasn't ready to let anyone know why.

After they confirmed their plans after school, they parted ways. Before her next class, she prepared herself so she wouldn't be caught off guard by those hazel eyes. W*e're friends*, she thought. *Just think of him as a friend*.

As she reached for the classroom door, someone beat her to it and it opened wide. Chance stood and waited for her to enter. A nervous smile broached her lips, and she walked into the class. She set her bag down beside her seat and noticed him take the chair beside hers as he watched her subtly.

"I see you came back for more. How'd you survive yesterday?" he asked with a sly grin.

Ana said, "Okay – I've recovered. I narrowly avoided being eaten by a pack of wolves."

"Oh, yeah?" Chance lifted an eyebrow.

"Yeah. Or, maybe I was just thinking about the hours of *agonizing* homework I did," she said and shook her head. "Afterwards, I gave myself permission to relax a little."

"Relax? How?" Chance asked.

Ana blushed and hesitated. "I like looking at the stars. There's this rock ledge near my house that was just made for lying on." She cleared her throat and shook her head. "How about you?"

"I had to work for a while after school – then I met up with my grandfather for a walk. I go outside to relax, too." Chance turned and met her gaze.

That must be the old man Laura mentioned, but she wondered why he hung out with his grandfather instead of his friends.

Mr. Frisk spoke up from behind his desk. "I'm interested in what you came up with yesterday. Take turns at the computer stations printing out your favorite images. I'd like them turned in by the end of class." He gave a creased smile and dropped back into his seat.

Eight computer workstations sat at the back of the room. Ana's tired body rose and approached the nearest one.

Chance followed her movement with his eyes before he joined her, and said, "You mind sharing?"

"Of course not." Ana pulled out a chair and invited him to join her.

While they worked together, Chance selected the photo of a bee in movement, hovering above a daisy in the garden. Ana chose the image of Chance as he jumped down from the bench. They congratulated one another on their hard work and turned the prints in to Mr. Frisk, who was splayed out at his desk again.

An awkward silence fell and Ana pulled her hair back, trying to find something to do with her restless hands.

Chance glanced at the neckline of her shirt. "Do you mind...can I see your necklace?"

Ana hooked her finger around the thin chain and pulled out the pendant from the folds of her shirt. "Sure."

He fumbled with the tiny silver shape in his fingertips, and his breathing quickened. "Where'd you get it? Was it given to you... or did *you* pick it out?"

Chance spoke so low she barely heard what he said, although it could have been the closeness of his hand to her skin that distracted her.

"At one of the stops from Colorado my mom bought this for me. I, um...I dream about flying sometimes. I like birds — and the card that came with it said it's supposed to be a good omen. Why–?" she asked and tilted her head.

"Know anything *else* about it?" he said with a strained look.

Ana saw his mood change and answered carefully. "No...that's all it said."

"It's a Thunderbird."

He handled the silver pendant delicately and touched the bird's wings. Curious about his fascination with her necklace,

Ana leaned forward and said, "Anything else?"

He snapped out of his concentration and said, "Nope."

Then he set the pendant back on Ana's chest.

She tensed. His hand grazed her hidden scar. The enjoyment of him near her was cut short. Having him so close to her imperfection rattled her, and she sat up straight. Clearly troubled by her reaction, Chance withdrew his hand and leaned back into his seat.

Mr. Frisk stumbled to his feet and cleared his voice for an announcement. "I look forward to reviewing your work. Now, I have a team project for you this week. It will be due on Friday, and it requires a partner. Your subject matter will be nature images. Let's see how creative you can be." He grinned toothily, and bounced on the balls of his feet. "I want two images," he said and held up two fingers. "One from each team member. They need to be related in some way. That's it – I'll see you all tomorrow."

As if on cue, the bell rang, which triggered a flurry of movement towards the door. Ana and Chance rose in unison and exited in stride with each other. Ana was puzzled. Why did Chance react that way to her pendant? She peered out of the corner of her eye and saw his face in deep contemplation, quiet. Did she do something wrong? Or offend him in some way? She was distressed to think he could be upset with her. Her own feelings surprised her, exposed her, like a jolt from an electrical shock. She glanced at the sky to clear her mind.

Chance muttered in distraction. "Sorry – ready for English?"

"Of course. I'll try to keep up with you today." Ana said

They entered the classroom and settled to await instruction. Again, they were required to read until the end of class while their teacher graded papers. Ana's attention improved today, and to keep up with Chance's fast pace, she created a private competition her opponent wasn't aware of.

***

Chance's thoughts kept him silent as they walked outside together. He was confused. What was the significance of the pendant? *It couldn't be a coincidence,* he thought. *Grandfather always says signs are everywhere – you just have to observe them.*

A sound beside him brought him back to the moment, and he glanced at Ana, who cleared her throat softly.

"So...want to be my partner for photography?" she asked, while staring off to a grove of pines that swayed in the breeze.

Chance noticed how aloof she looked, as if she would rather be somewhere else. His fears coalesced. *She must not be interested in me.* He kicked himself for getting so caught up. He shook his head; it had only been a day since he met her. It didn't matter, somehow. It didn't change anything.

But the sign. It *had* to mean something.

"I'm sorry – I was distracted. Photography? Sure...how about a hike tomorrow after school? I know some hard to find places you'd enjoy. I'll be your personal tour guide." He said, as he regarded her delicate features, searching for any signs he had been mistaken about her interest in him.

Ana froze.

Chance noticed the deer in headlights look spread across her face and wondered about its cause. After a moment, her face softened and she said, "Actually, out where I stargaze there's some areas I want to check out. It's so pretty around my house. I haven't gotten to explore yet. If you want...you could follow me home tomorrow?"

"Sounds good."

"See you tomorrow then."

***

As Ana walked to her van, she snapped out of her torment. How much longer could she keep up this charade? Exhausted just doing normal activities, she doubted she could explore the woods behind her house without wheezing and sweating. Chance would notice for sure. A wave of frustration hit, and her eyes stung. For a moment she wanted to run away, and not deal with any of it. Then she reminded herself – *Now, focus on right now, Ana.*

Her eyelids slid shut as she turned the key in the ignition and thought about picking up her sister and her calculus homework. *Just keep going. Things will work out,* she comforted herself. But a nagging thought kept curling through her mind, *But what if they don't?*

CHAPTER 8

After the last bell rang, Chance walked with Ana out of English class to the parking lot. Ana's yellow van sat lazily next to his black truck, one in perfect contrast to the other. He walked around to the driver's side as she called over to him. "Remember, I have to pick up my sister before we head to my house. She's just around the corner at the middle school."

"I remember it well," Chance said, feeling shy all of a sudden.

After they rumbled into the driveway, Ana's sister jumped out and rocked around on the balls of her feet as if impatient for an introduction. Her eyes widened when Chance stepped out of his truck and towered above her. She gave a sidelong glance at her big sister.

"Eva, this is Chance. Chance, my little sister, Eva."

Chance stepped forward with his hand out to the open-mouthed girl. Eva had to crane her head back to look up into his eyes.

"He's cute," Eva said to Ana from the corner of her mouth as they shook hands.

Chance glanced aside to see Ana's reaction and caught her blush. His stomach dropped.

Ana turned her back to her sister and welcomed him to their home. "Let's go inside – I should get my sister settled before we get started."

Eva followed close behind as they entered the house, her green eyes squinted as if measuring him up.

"Make yourself at home. I'll just get something for Eva real quick – it's my turn to make snacks today. You want anything? A drink or something to eat?" Ana asked, as she paused in the kitchen doorway.

"Don't worry about me – I had something on the drive over." Chance dropped down at the end of the couch and let his bag fall to the floor. He scanned the room and spotted old school pictures of the girls that hung around the fireplace. A hesitant movement caught his attention, and he turned to face Eva, who stood near the doorway with her backpack in her hands.

She sidled over to Chance, sat down and positioned herself perpendicular to him, placing her hands gingerly in her lap. Her expression was serious and Chance pictured a detective from a police show. The only thing she was missing was the badge and a five o'clock shadow.

She began her interrogation. "So, Chance...where do you live?"

"I live out on Howe Mountain, it's above the lake."

"And how old are you?"

"Eighteen." Chance caught her tone and kept eye contact when he responded.

"You like my sister?"

A metallic clank came from the kitchen as something fell to the floor. Ana's high anxious voice followed the sound. "Eva! Chance, you can go out back to wait for me, if you'd like."

Chance ignored the invitation and faced his interrogator. "Yes, I like your sister. She's a great photographer."

"Have any hobbies?" she asked as she stared intently into his eyes.

"Well, I like fixing up cars – I work over at Kenny's Auto Shop. I prefer being outside and take lots of nature walks. But there's not much else to do around here." Chance said unabashed.

Eva leveled in for her last question and narrowed her eyes. "What's your favorite color?"

Ana's green eyes flashed in his mind, and he stumbled over the word. "Green." He cleared his throat and returned his gaze to his resolute inquisitor with a grin.

Eva took a long hard look at Chance, then broke into a

sweet giggle that melted his heart and said, "I like you, Chance." Then she leaned in and added. "Don't hurt my sister."

"I would *never*." Chance spoke honestly after he saw how concerned Eva was. *Why is she so protective of her older sister?* It surprised him.

Ana walked into the living room with a bewildered expression, set a plate of apples and peanut butter on the coffee table and stared at her sister.

"Umm...ready Chance?" Ana stuttered and turned her wide eyes to her sister. "Here's your snack, D. I can help you with your homework later, if you need it. Oh, and remember Mom wants you to go through that box in your room."

Ana wasn't angry, and she seemed to keep a kind and patient tone with her sister. Eva groaned and made a production of her answer. "Fine."

Chance stood and shot a crooked grin at Eva. Ana clearly cared a lot for her sister, after she overlooked the embarrassment Eva caused a moment earlier. *They must be a close family*, he reasoned.

As they walked outside together, Ana said, "I'm sorry about that – I don't know what got into her."

 "No worries. Didn't mind."

Ana held up her camera and asked, "Ready? If you want...I could show you a kind of special spot I found... it's my favorite place, actually."

Intrigued, he coaxed her. "Lead on."

Her mouth pulled up into a gentle smile, and she wandered down the trail with Chance close behind, gripping his camera tightly. When he was near her he got pulled in. It was like gravity. Something he couldn't resist.

He couldn't understand the intensity of his feelings. After just a couple of days, he was anxious when they were apart, like a high voltage switch had flipped and he couldn't fight the current. No matter how much he told himself he didn't want or need a girlfriend. It made no difference. He was changed.

***

Ana searched his face before she walked on. She wanted him to see it, as though it would help unmask her. This seemed the most natural way to expose who she was without saying anything. She needed to show him the place that meant so much to her. He would be the first person to see her private observatory.

She broke through the copse and stood in the sunlight on her rock. Chance walked through and joined her on the stone slab.

"This is where you stargaze," he said matter-of-factly.

Ana nodded, and tilted her face upward. "Yeah – I love it out here. I see lots of animals – squirrels, birds and bats."

"Oh yeah? You like animals? You're not afraid of running into a bear out here?" He peered curiously at her.

"Well...it would be pretty cool to see a bear. But I don't want to become a rug. I just like animals – they don't require conversation." She shrugged.

Chance smirked, amused. "Well, you're right about that. Want to sit a while before we head out?"

She lowered herself to the granite ledge, sat cross-legged and faced the grassy fields below. Her hand dropped to her side, picked up some dried pine needles and snapped off pieces onto the rock.

"It's so relaxing – I feel like I can really breathe when I'm here."

Chance joined her on the rock and pointed at the dark river line in the distance. "You've got a nice view of the Clark Bend River over there."

He picked up a stone and threw it out so far Ana saw it arch, then disappear among the distant evergreens.

Chance leaned back and stared at the horizon. "So, you like being alone – don't you?"

Ana took a deep breath and said, "Sometimes, I'd rather be alone...it's simpler that way. I prefer being here than at school...or anywhere else really."

She began to feel the same way around Chance as she did out under the stars – comfortable and relaxed.

He said, "I thought so. You don't seem comfortable at school. You look... different when we're outside."

Was she that transparent to everyone? Or was he that observant? Chance seemed to understand her well for someone she just met. She liked being understood.

As though an invisible band that compressed her chest had burst, air rushed into her lungs and her heart beat like a mustang running free. Joy trickled through her willowy body.

Ana decided to ask about something that had stayed on her mind. "I wondered how you know so much about my necklace? The Thunderbird?"

Chance turned to her, and she met his clouded eyes. After a deep breath, he said, "From my grandfather, really. He's taught me a lot. He's from a direct line of Navajo shamans or medicine men and lived on a reservation until he was a teenager. He's taught me a lot about his life and the old traditions."

"That's pretty cool – I bet he has plenty of stories. Can you tell me more about the Thunderbird? What's its story?" She prompted him, fascinated.

"He told me the Thunderbird is a revered bird to the Navajo. And other cultures. It's supposed to be a large magical bird that protects the tribe from evil. It's said it rides on the wings of a storm. And when it cries out, lightning's heard." Chance's steadfast eyes were clouded with unreadable emotions. However, she *could* see he was holding something back. There was more to the story. But what?

Ana pulled out the small silver pendant from under her

shirt. An arrow sat beneath the symbol of the bird.

"Do you know what the arrow means?"

Chance gazed again at the silver shape, and his brow wrinkled. "The arrow…it symbolizes protection. The Thunderbird and arrow are seen as good luck and a good omen – happiness."

I could use a little of that – happiness and good luck. She held it within her fingertips, the metal warmed at her touch, and she imagined some of its fortune pass into her.

Chance stared at the horizon. Dark hair moved over his head in short waves, and she fought the urge to run her fingers through it, to feel how soft it was. Bronze skin framed the canvas of his face, his vivid eyes a brilliant umber in the light. She followed his strong jaw line down his throat and noticed a thin leather band.

"What are *you* wearing?" she asked, as she moved her hand toward his neck and stopped short, unsure about touching his skin.

He pulled out a small silver pendant attached to the worn leather strip that was in the shape of a bear. An arrow ran along the center of its body, down through the heart. "It's something Grandfather gave me. It was his. He said it's called the bear heart-line. The arrow down the middle shows what you allow into your heart from the outside world will affect you. Moving you toward good or evil. A kind of protector." He shrugged. "Known for its power, strength and healing abilities. A leader."

"It's nice." Ana smiled at him thoughtfully.

"You know, you're the first person I've taken here," she said, changing the subject. It had been a battle to remember why she had avoided boys for so long. Life was so much better with him, than alone. Like a stone dropping into a well, the realization sank down into the pool of her soul.

Ana took a deep breath and acknowledged the time. "Well, we still need to take some photographs. Do you want to go explore a little?"

Chance jumped to his feet like a cat and held his hand out to help her.

"I heard there are cougars around here. We should probably be careful."

Chance laughed. "I've only seen one my whole life...we're safe, don't worry."

"Okay then. Where do you think we should go? The field?" Ana asked and faced the firs.

"If you'd like, I can lead us. I think it could be good this way," he said and pointed at a window between two fir trees. "Maybe we can explore down in the field next time."

Ana flushed. *There would be a next time*. She followed his lithe body through a thicket and tried to pursue her guide. Chance seemed to sense her pace and slackened his stride to allow her to catch up.

They stopped often to take pictures. Ana used the excuse to take a photograph when she grew tired or got out of breath. She wasn't sure if he noticed her fatigue, but at the very least he hadn't said anything. For that she was thankful.

The light started to fade and Chance recommended they turn back. By the time they reached Ana's rock, the sun had just descended behind the Kaniksu Forest mountain range.

A click nearby made her turn. Surprised by the camera directed at her, she met his eyes as he lowered it and grinned sheepishly. "The light —"

Ana felt her cheeks burn and returned her attention to the sun as it melted into the landscape. She asked shyly, "Do you want to join us for dinner tonight? If you can..."

"Sure, I'll give my mom a call."

They walked back down the darkened path to the blue house, emerged onto the yard, and entered the back door. The smell of pizza engulfed them as they entered the warm kitchen.

"Ana? Is that you?" Melissa's voice called from the living

room.

Her mother sorted through papers while Eva sat on the couch with a book. When Melissa saw them together, her face lit up and she got up to shake Chance's hand.

Ana shot her mom a warning glare before she said, "Mom, this is Chance. Chance, this is my mother, Melissa Hughes."

Eva watched the introductions, and then her eyes turned to the pizza that sat on the dining table.

"You can call me Mel – everyone else does. I brought pizza home – it's Eva's favorite. Are you joining us for dinner tonight, Chance?" Melissa asked.

"Yeah, sounds great – Would you give me just a minute? I need to call my house."

"Of course, go ahead."

Chance pulled his phone out and walked into the kitchen.

Ana's mother touched her arm. "He's so handsome! And he has such a friendly smile – I like him."

"Shh! Mom, don't embarrass me!" Ana's cheeks heated at her mother's comments. She had often thought Melissa would be happy if she brought the frog prince home or any yahoo for that matter, but it secretly pleased her to see her mother share in her excitement. Ana knew her mom worried because she never encouraged attention from boys or anyone, really.

To find someone who would look beyond the medical problems and uncertainty could be a challenge, but Ana had no interest in the trouble. It was cruel to bring someone into her world. But here she was, skirting along the fringe of friendship with a boy she just met.

Doubts about her upcoming doctor's appointment were pushed to the side for the moment.

Chance wandered back into the room while he flipped his phone shut. Eva jumped up from the couch and resettled at the table before her empty plate. Her saucer eyes grew wide seemingly in an effort to will everyone to the table.

"Mom says thanks and wants to invite Ana to our house...to return the favor. Could you come for dinner on Friday, maybe?" Chance said, looking down at the floor.

They joined Eva at the table as Ana sought her mother's face to see if she had any objection. Without a word, Melissa gave her a grin and wink of encouragement.

"That'd be great. I'd love to come over," Ana said.

When everyone appeared full, Chance stood up and collected the dishes and took them to the kitchen. Ana joined him at the sink and they washed dishes together like it was common place.

Ana took a plate from Chance, placed it into the dishwasher, and asked, "There's one more picture I'd really like to take. You don't have to if you need to head home but it's perfect out right now."

Ana imagined herself under the night stars with Chance. It filled her with so much joy, it leaked out into a smile. New found happiness pulled her in like a drug. She wanted, or maybe *needed* more. Ana decided she would face the real world later.

"Great – no bear could keep me away." Chance splashed water at Ana who laughed and splashed him back.

***

After they finished up, they dried their hands and searched for their cameras for the last images of the night.

Outside, with cameras around their necks, Chance took the lead again, confident he had better night vision. The thought made him chuckle.

The waxing moon provided plenty of pale light along with a multitude of glimmering stars.

After dozens of photos of the night sky, Ana seemed satisfied. She turned to Chance, and grinned. "Well, we should have enough to work with. Out of all of those images there has to be a *few* that'll work." She paused before she continued. "Thanks for coming over today – I enjoyed myself."

"Me too," he said in an undertone.

He took the lead again and walked Ana through the concealed pathway around the brightly lit house to his truck parked discretely on the driveway.

Ana moved toward him uncertainly and gave him a sudden hug goodbye.

Chance was surprised by it and then by the mysterious heartbeat against him. It was unusual. The syncopated beat joined with his and made a unique musical rhythm. Their own song.

***

They parted and said goodbye. Chance darted to his truck and backed out of the driveway. The red glow of his taillights disappeared into the darkness, and the dust trail rose and dispelled. Ana stood still until the night was calm and unstirred once again.

After she finished her homework, Ana grabbed a sweatshirt and returned to the forested observatory alone.

Quiet and still, she lay and stared at the stars, except for the occasional bat that flitted by her line of sight. She remembered the poem assigned in English was to write about not truly understanding a person until you walked in their shoes. Different possibilities tumbled in her head until a shadow much larger than the bats flew above her. Its movement was oddly disjointed and unlike any bird she could think of. After she considered the time of night, she figured it was probably just an injured owl. A *large* owl.

A poem began to fill her head, and it formed like a song. Hazel eyes flashed through her memory as she hummed a soft melody.

The evergreens that encircled her observatory held her close. A statuesque fir offered a perch for a black form with pale yellow eyes. There was such a large array of wild life there. She didn't mind being a minority in the forest. Animals were simple, she mused. They lived their lives in such a basic way.

A nearby fir snapped and rustled, which drew her attention back to where the yellow eyes had been. She could sense movement on an upper branch. She laughed inside. *What a clumsy owl.*

She sang her poem to the night sky and to the watchful visitor in the trees until her eyes closed at the sound of the crickets. Then she stumbled back to the house.

When Ana settled in bed, she gazed out her window while tendrils of sleep crept into the dark recesses of her mind. An elated owl's cry cut through the darkness and met her ears. She fell asleep with a tender grin on her face.

CHAPTER 9

Wind combed through the firs, which inspired a family of birds to abandon their homes and ride the swelling currents. The sun caressed the tips of the needles and delivered one last kiss of warmth before it relinquished the sky to the moon and stars.

Trees swayed outside Ana's second story window. The forest calmed her while she waited for Chance to arrive. She smoothed the creases in her jeans, then closed her eyes. Friday had finally come.

She had changed out of her wrinkled shirt from school and into a thick woven green sweater with a thin white cotton tank underneath to cover her opaque scar. She hoped they would wind up outside after they ate dinner, and knew it would be cold.

Eva's voice burst through Ana's solitude. "Ana, Chance is here!"

Ana stood up slowly – an ingrained habit. Her jittery fingers combed through her dark hair as she glanced in the mirror. She turned off the lights and went downstairs.

Chance waited near the front door, still in the clothes he wore to school, jeans and a black t-shirt. He could wear anything, really, and he would be handsome. The black t-shirt hugged his chest, accentuating his strong physique.

Melissa and Eva sat on the couch together. Sounds from the television echoed as they shared a secretive smile.

When Ana entered the room, an extra burst of oxygen filled her lungs as she breathed in Chance's spicy scent. A grin lingered on his lips.

Melissa spoke and interrupted their moment. "You two have a nice time tonight, and Chance – please thank your mother for the dinner invitation."

"I will. Thanks, Mel. Don't have *too* much fun tonight!" He winked at Eva as he opened the door for Ana.

Outside, the wind picked up strength, bursting through the yard, and tossing Ana's hair into a flurry around her face. Chance pulled aside the stray hairs behind her ear and grinned at her surprise.

He opened the passenger side of the truck, waited until she was in before he closed the door and darted around to the driver's side.

Buckled up and settled in for the drive, Chance turned to face Ana before he started the engine. "You look nice in green – it brings out your eyes...not that they need any more help."

"Thanks," she said, self-conscious. Compliments were out of place in her world. Like sunshine warming her from the inside out, it wasn't an entirely unpleasant feeling.

"So, how was your first week in Clark Bend?" he asked, as he slid his arm behind her headrest.

"Oh, besides this obnoxious guy I have to sit next to in English and photography, it was okay." Ana glanced slyly at Chance. "I guess as first weeks go – with all of my experience – it went pretty well. Better than expected. I think I've caught up with all of my classes."

"And, how about your house?"

"Besides the fact it reminds me of Grandma and smells like menthols, I love it. There are so many stars here. Colorado had too much light pollution... couldn't see the stars as well as I do here. You don't have any nice views from your house, do you?" Ana asked hopefully.

A crooked grin slid across his face. "I have something in store for you. I *think* you'll be happy."

"Hmm, mysterious."

Chance arched his eyebrow and chuckled. "Heh, heh, heh."

She laughed with him. "You don't scare me. Nice try. So, tell me about your parents. What are they like?"

He cleared his throat and said, "Well, my mom's a nurse at

Sandpoint Hospital and my dad's a jeweler. He owns a shop down around Hope Marina. My grandfather lives with us, too. After Grandmother died, he was lonely. He hired his old friend to manage his ranch and came to live with us about two years ago."

"So, your grandfather lives with you? How's that?" Ana frowned at the thought of her grandma sitting on their couch, chain smoking.

"I'm pretty close with him. We go hiking a lot... when I'm not working."

"That's nice – I wasn't really close to my grandparents. Didn't know them too well." She gazed at darkened shapes flitting by her window and wondered if he had any friends.

After a moment of silence, Ana asked, "So, your mother's a nurse? She's following your family's tradition for healing?"

Chance frowned. "Uh...how so?"

"You said your grandfather came from a long line of Navajo Shamans, right?"

"Riiight. I guess you could say that. She's a very compassionate person and loves her job. Ever since she was a little girl she wanted to help people."

"And, what about you? Do you want to heal people, too?"

An enigmatic expression crossed his face, and he shrugged. "That would be cool, but I don't know if that runs in *my* genes. I'm not sure...if that's possible. What I *really* want to do is travel. Although, that isn't *exactly* a profession." He laughed and returned the question. "What about you – what do *you* want to do?"

Unprepared to give an honest answer, she grappled at a quick reply that was true but unrealistic. "Well, I'd love to see the world, too. The drive from Colorado is the most I've ever done. I'd like to make it further...see things I've only seen in magazines." Ana ran her fingers along the contours of the door, her excitement fading into sorrow.

Just past town they drove along a large lake, then turned

north and wound up in the mountains. Ana knew they were close when he turned off on a gravel road and reduced his speed to a crawl. Evergreens filled her view until they passed a curve in the drive. Nestled in the trees, his home seemed to belong in the verdant growth. Tiny lights lined a rock pathway that led to the front door. The interior of the house glowed and poured soft yellow light from the windows, illuminating elongated rectangles on the ground.

Chance parked at the end of the drive next to a sedan and got out. He circled the truck, opened the passenger door and led Ana along the walkway down to a porch that wrapped around the length of the home. It was unlit, except for what emanated from two long windows that paralleled the large carved front door.

"Nice place," Ana said, her eyes wide. Her house would look like a guest house compared to Chance's.

His cheeks reddened as he opened the door and ushered her past a stairway and into a brightly lit living room. She lifted her eyes and stared at the vaulted ceiling and skylights.

"Niiice," she whispered.

A large tapestry hung on the inner-most wall. An angular bird with wings outstretched was displayed at the center, and intricate designs framed it. Ana recognized the emblem immediately and peered down to her necklace. A Thunderbird.

Just past the living room was a dining table, set for five. An archway appeared to lead into the kitchen, based on the noises and smells that were issued from that direction.

"Mom...Dad?" Chance called out.

A moment later, two figures emerged, one holding a dishtowel, the other a spatula.

"You're here. Welcome – you must be Ana. We've been looking forward to meeting you. I'm Aiyana." Chance's mother gave her a reserved smile. Ana could see where he got his good looks. She was a graceful woman with long dark hair and chestnut skin. Soft hazel eyes crinkled when she spoke, and her melodic voice instantly captivated Ana.

Chance's father stepped forward. "Hi Ana, I'm Ben. I hope you're hungry – we've been cooking a feast for you. We're just so happy he finally brought a friend home." He gave a stiff grin and grasped the back of a chair tightly. Deep blue eyes squinted behind his glasses and sandy brown hair frolicked in waves around his head.

Chance shot Ben a glare and Ana quickly spoke up to relieve the tension. "Thanks for inviting me."

"Ana, let me introduce my father to you." Aiyana said, and fixed her gaze behind Ana. Ana turned, surprised. She didn't notice anyone there when she entered the room.

An old man sat almost camouflaged in the padded chair near Aiyana. His eyes shone like reflective pools. Deep creases lined his leathery face, and long gray hair was pulled back into a tight ponytail. Sober eyes appraised her silently. Ana felt hollow, like he could see right through her.

"Father?" Aiyana touched her father's shoulder. "Father, this is Chance's new friend, Ana Hughes. Ana, this is my father, Niyol."

His still face watched her. Ana turned her eyes down, and said, "It is a pleasure to meet you."

Chance was fortunate to have such a close relationship with his grandfather, she thought. Chance's hand rested on her shoulder, and she met his face.

"Grandfather takes me on hikes a lot. He's taught me all about the animals here, and he enjoys stargazing, like you."

Niyol turned his face to his grandson and nodded steadily. His eyes drifted past Ana's necklace and widened. He searched his grandson's face, questioningly. Chance didn't react.

Aiyana looked at her father, patted him on the arm and spoke before she returned to the kitchen. "Ready to eat, Father? We'll go get everything ready. I hope you're hungry tonight, Ana. Please, make yourself at home."

Niyol turned to Ana and asked, "Do you like Clark Bend, Ana?"

"I really like it here. The view of the sky is fantastic."

"Indeed." He nodded without taking his eyes off of her.

Everyone moved to sit around a large, hand-crafted wooden table. The food placed before Ana looked like it was straight from a cookbook. She couldn't remember the last time she smelled anything so rich. Compared to this meal, pizza was boring. Neither she nor her mother were very imaginative cooks, so she relished the flavors and the time put into this savory food.

"The soup is so good, what is it?" She stared at the bright orange residue in her bowl.

"Oh, that's butternut squash soup. And the beans have been stewing all day. The pulled beef is Chance's favorite." Aiyana said with a proud smile.

Niyol sat across from her, his gaze tracing between her eyes and necklace throughout dinner. Ana, likewise, felt Aiyana survey her closely. Uncomfortable with the attention, she focused on Chance, who seemed aware of his families lingering stares.

"Well, I guess it's time for you two to get going," Ben said and pushed away from the table.

Full and satisfied, warmth spread through Ana's body. She stood up and helped clear the table and began to do the dishes.

Chance rushed into the kitchen and startled her as he whispered in her ear. "Give me ten minutes and then we'll head out."

The hairs on the nape of her neck rose from his warm breath. Chance left the kitchen with a backward glance and left her holding a dripping plate at the sink with Aiyana.

Aiyana studied her closely, and said, "Chance tells me your family just moved here. Do you like your new home?"

"Yes, I do. I was hesitant about moving, but I'm glad we came. It feels more like home than my old home did, strangely. I think I'm happier."

"You weren't happy before?" Aiyana asked, clearly curious.

Tangled in a web she didn't want to be in, Ana paused. It was hard not to speak about the major force in her life, but the purpose of the move was to have a second chance, and she was enjoying her try at normalcy too much.

"Things haven't always been easy. My dad left when I was ten. It's always just been Mom, Eva and me. This is a second chance for us, starting fresh." The question hadn't been directly answered, but she spoke the truth. She hoped Aiyana would be satisfied.

"You must be close to your mother and sister then?"

"Yes, very. I spend all my time with my little sister when my mother's at work. I prefer being with my family...but I've enjoyed my time here with your family, too." She stumbled. "And I like spending time with Chance. I'm...comfortable around him...and that's a first." Her voice trailed off, and she hoped she hadn't insulted her host.

Aiyana's expression was hard to read. Ana got the feeling she was being assessed. Her host wasn't being rude, or mean even, but something was bothering her. That much was clear.

"Well, I'm glad you've found friendship with Chance. He's such a special person, like no other – he always finds a way to surprise me. I'm happy you two are so comfortable with each other." Aiyana's eyes darted to the door, as though to confirm her son wasn't near. "When my mother died my father came to live with us. Chance took her death real hard – he hasn't been the same since. He spends most of his time with father now. I would hate to see him hurt again..."

Aiyana handed Ana a plate to dry and held her gaze.

"I understand. I wouldn't want to see him hurt either." A lump formed in her throat. *You should stop now, Ana, before you get in too deep. Someone will get hurt. You can't promise you won't hurt him.* She stared at the water running from the faucet and swallowed.

Aiyana grinned the first time that night. "I'm sure you don't. Sorry to get so serious. Anyway, you said this feels more like home here — what's different? Why do you think this feels like home just after a week?"

"Well, since I got here, everything feels like it's fallen into place so perfectly. It's never been like that before. Now I'm afraid it will fall apart." She couldn't help but speak from the heart. Her cheek gave an involuntary twinge, and she tried to let her worries go. A warm hand settled on her back, and she met Aiyana's sympathetic eyes.

"Life has rhythm, Ana. It's like the ocean's tides. Water comes in and pulls back, repeating infinitely. There will always be good and bad. But I believe we are never given more than we can handle. I can see in your eyes that you have *much* strength." She paused to face Ana and continued. "You deserve the good in your life. It belongs there — I think I can see why Chance is so comfortable with you. You're a sweet girl."

Ana was confused. She wished *she* knew why he was interested in her because she couldn't figure it out. Aiyana seemed to understand more than she had intended.

Ana turned when Chance and his dad walked back into the kitchen. Chance held out his hand to Ana.

Aiyana stepped forward and embraced her. "It was a pleasure meeting you, Ana. I look forward to seeing you again, real soon. You're welcome any time."

"Thank you, Aiyana. It was really great meeting you, too. And thanks for the wonderful dinner." Ana waved before leaving the kitchen. Chance stopped in the living room where Niyol sat in his comfy chair. He met his grandson's gaze as he addressed him. "Goodnight, Grandfather — rest well. I'll see you in the morning."

Niyol gave Chance a warm smile, but his gaze turned almost cold as it lingered on Ana's pendant. "You two have a nice evening."

Chance patted Niyol's shoulder before he guided Ana out of the house.

CHAPTER 10

"Okay – where are you taking me?" Ana turned towards Chance and smiled.

He led her to his truck which looked different in the darkness, engorged and distorted. She looked closely and realized a dark green boat was strapped lengthwise across the bed of the truck. Ana was confused. *Boating at night?*

"Just wait and see. Trust me. I think you'll be happily surprised."

They got in and he quickly fired up the engine and backed out of the driveway. Soon they moved down the incandescent mountainside. The full moon cast a brilliance over the landscape, which spilled its magic onto everything below. The wind disappeared and left the night and lake still, except for the occasional ripple from lurking fish.

Chance drove along the water then pulled off to park on a gravel shoulder. He reached for his door handle and said, "Stay here a minute."

He leapt from the cab. The truck rocked back and forth as he untied and removed the boat.

Suddenly, her door opened and Chance's flushed face met her surprised gaze. She slipped down from the cab, and let her eyes adjust in the moonlight. A short slope dropped down to a tiny peninsula where the boat waited for them.

Ana was excited and curious, eager for an adventure with Chance. As long as *she* didn't have to paddle, this would be great.

At the boat, Chance gestured for her to get in at one end. A soft cushion sat on the seat and she settled in, thankful for his thoughtfulness. He pushed the boat onto the dark glassy water and jumped in at the opposite end, grabbed the oars and began to row fluidly. He paddled out for a couple of minutes then paused, and they glided in silence.

"Look up, Ana," he said.

A stretch of skyline spanning above was so large her eyes widened just to absorb it all. A brilliant band encircled the moon in a silvery glow, like a halo. The stars seemed to attempt to out-glimmer the moon in jealousy and twinkled so bright she almost had to squint as she gazed at them. The heavens had found an empty canvas to rest upon and the dark glassy water below appeared twice as grand. Blood coursed through her animated body.

Ana lowered her gaze and met his face. He waited while she grappled to string some words together, or anything remotely intelligent.

"It's...it's the nicest thing...anyone's ever done for me," she whispered. No one outside her family had ever been so thoughtful. And true enough, she normally didn't allow anyone to get close enough to give her anything. Until now.

Ana saw Chance stare at her as he rowed the boat forward. He paddled with ease, like a knife cutting through soft butter. It was a calm rhythm and it made a peaceful sound as the oars dipped into the lake and dripped as they were lifted up. Chance appeared deep in thought, his jaw clenched and his brows furrowed.

"What are you thinking about?" Ana asked.

Chance's tension seemed to ease as he looked up and said, "I was wondering if...if you had a boyfriend...back in Colorado?"

"Oh." Ana wished she had a different answer, but shared her lack of history anyway. "I've never really dated." Chance seemed surprised, and her embarrassment deepened. "No, really. The last person I went out with was in my freshman year. We just went to the movies a couple of times – that was it."

She thought back to the year she needed surgery. It had proven to be a bit more than the boy could handle, and that had effectively cured Ana of the urge to date again. The sore subject sat heavy on her shoulders, and she looked up at

Chance and fired back. "How about you? I hear you don't date?"

"Me? My life's been...well, I hadn't found anyone I wanted to spend time with."

Ana blushed and studied the dark mirrored water beside her and wondered what was hidden beneath.

Chance raised an eyebrow. "Wait a minute – you asked about me?"

Ana flushed again, and hoped he couldn't see in the darkness. "Caught me – I asked Laura about you."

"What'd she say?" His voice came out gruff.

"Why? Do you have a shady past?" Ana teased. "Don't worry, she didn't have much to say, just that you didn't seem interested in dating anyone around town."

"Sorry. You never know what people will say about you in a small town. Everyone's so bored with their own lives, they start talking about everyone else's – making things up to make it interesting."

"Oh, I'm sorry. I'm really not a gossiper but – I was curious. I know what you mean anyway, about people talking about you – it's not just in small towns." Ana remembered people gossiped about her behind her back. They said she was going to die, or that she had some rare made up disease. Maybe some things were true, but that only made the sting of it all burn worse.

"Speaking of gossip, your mom told me about your grandmother – I'm so sorry."

Chance shrugged. "Yeah, it was a bummer. It completely devastated grandfather. But now he's around, I get to spend more time with him."

"Oh." Ana was confused. Aiyana made it sound like he was really close to her.

"Why? What did she tell you exactly?" Chance's voice turned cold and agitated.

"She said you took the death of your grandmother real

hard – that you hadn't been the same since?"

Chance snorted. "She's happy thinking that – but she doesn't understand me. She doesn't know who I am, not really. All she wants is for me to hang out with the guys and go on dates and be normal."

Ana couldn't relate. Not exactly. No one knew her better than her mother. His comment only added a mysterious layer to Chance. One she was determined to learn more about.

Quietly adrift in the boat, they lingered without a word, each within their own thoughts. Ana couldn't work out what she felt when she was with Chance. Until now she had been content without anyone in her life. Without her permission, the picture she had painted for herself changed and melted into an entirely different vision. In unfamiliar territory, she tested the waters carefully, cautiously.

"So, what are you doing tomorrow?" Chance said and stared at the inky black water.

"I actually promised my sister I'd help paint her room. But you could come over after." She flushed again.

"Great. Call me when you finish and let me know."

He pointed the boat back toward the tiny peninsula. "It's getting late."

The rowboat scraped onto the shore, which forced Ana to grab the edge for support. Chance jumped out and offered his hand to help her out. When Ana stood up, she became unsteady as blood pounded in her ears. *Oh no! Not now! Please don't pass out!* Chance's arm wrapped around her waist and secured her. Focused on her breathing, the head rush passed slowly.

"Thanks. I can get a little – unsteady sometimes," she said, relieved she composed herself in time.

"I don't mind," Chance said, and his cheeks lifted into a grin. He let go when she was stable but remained close on their walk back to the truck. After he started the engine and turned on the heater, he went to load up the boat, which gave her time to scold herself in private for coming so close to fainting.

The ride home went too quickly. The lights were on in the living room when they pulled up.

"Thanks, Chance. This was an unforgettable night." Ana blinked back her emotions. All the pent-up exhaustion from her long week swelled, ready to spill out. She let her hair tumble down around her face to shield her.

***

Chance was speechless, unsure what to say. He wanted to reach out and touch her soft face or trace her pale, delicate fingers, but instead, said, "Sleep well. Talk to you tomorrow."

He watched her movement while she walked up the path to the front door. As she entered the house, she gave him a small wave goodbye and disappeared inside.

On his drive, time slowed as he moved further away from his source of solace. Like a hermit crab without his shell, he scurried home to bide time until he could find his way back to her.

CHAPTER 11

"Cactus Flower." Eva read off the paint can that sat on her desk, clearly excited at the chance to paint her room.

The girls had taped off the entire bedroom and with Melissa's help had moved the furniture into the center of the room.

"I can't wait to see it on the walls – it'll be like living in a flower!" Eva's eyes twinkled. Part of the bribe to move was the promise of decorating her room the way she wanted.

Ana poured the paint into the trays, careful not to drip. She wore a pair of ratty old black sweats and a holey white t-shirt. Her hair was pulled into a ponytail to protect it, but she expected to get pink spotty hair despite the effort.

With a roller in each hand, she gave one to her sister and snickered. Eva's saucer eyes were filled with enthusiasm as she clutched her roller and jumped in place. Ana looked over to her sister and nodded. "Go ahead."

"Yay!"

They rolled 'Cactus Flower' paint onto the sterile white walls. The color was reminiscent of Pepto-Bismol, and Ana's stomach growled as it acknowledged the resemblance.

After two long hours, the girls went downstairs to get lunch. Sunlight slanted in through the kitchen windows while Melissa wiped them vigorously with a cloth. "Well? How's it look?"

"Good, we're done with the first coat – now for lunch." Ana opened the fridge and pulled out the ingredients for turkey and cheese sandwiches.

Melissa pointed to a pile of mail on the kitchen table. "Hey, Ana – a brochure came from North Idaho College."

Ana shrugged and ignored her mother's statement while she finished up the sandwiches. Melissa sighed and continued to clean the window.

"I think I'm going to go eat my lunch at the rock," she said as she placed Eva's food on the kitchen table. Eva raised her eyebrows at Ana. "Oh, relax. The paint needs to dry before we add another coat. I'll be back after a little break."

In a snap decision, she grabbed her camera and threw it around her neck. If she saw some wildlife while she ate her lunch, she wanted to be prepared.

It was cool outdoors. The sun slipped behind some clouds, and a gentle breeze tousled Ana's hair. She walked through the bower of vegetation, approached her large stone and sat down.

Ana's stomach gurgled, and she picked up her sandwich while she gazed at the grassy fields below her and the distant snow capped peaks. Butterflies trembled among the flowers in the long grasses, and small sparrows darted between trees.

Achy from rolling paint, her sore arms resisted every time she lifted her sandwich to take a bite, and her drooping eyes blurred from fatigue. The night before, she lay awake and thought about her time with Chance. His face seemed imprinted under her lids. Every time she turned over and struggled with sleep, his handsome face greeted her. She didn't mind it, but at a certain point, sometime close to one o'clock, her mind filled with visions of stars, and the sensation of being rocked lulled her to sleep.

After Ana finished lunch, she picked up her camera and used the zoom lens like a pair of binoculars. As she swept it across the grassy valley. A blur of red fur caught her attention. She centered and adjusted the focus. A beautiful red fox settled in a sunny patch at the side of the field. Without hesitation, she snapped a picture, paused and then took a few more.

She lowered the camera to see if she could spot it without the aid of the lens and saw a puff of fur in the field. It seemed to turn its gaze on her. Still, they stared at each other until Eva called. Ana was surprised to see the fox remain still as she stood up to return to the house. It seemed to keep its eyes on her as she stepped onto the forest trail.

Inside the kitchen, Eva stood at the bottom of the stairs and tapped her foot. "It's time for a second coat – c'mon."

"Okay, hold on a minute. I need to call Chance first."

Ana forgot Aunt Tera and Uncle Jace were supposed to come for dinner, but Melissa had suggested they include Chance. Uncle Jace planned a fishing trip for that day and promised some fresh trout to grill, and Aunt Tera was going to make her delicious potato salad the girls loved so much.

Ana called Chance and left a message after his voice mail picked up, wondering what he was up to.

She joined her sister upstairs. They painted until she could barely lift her speckled fuchsia arms and Eva's walls were thoroughly coated in Pepto Pink, Ana's private name for the color.

She began the cleanup process while her sister mysteriously disappeared. Her cell phone rang and she answered it, careful not to get paint on it.

"Hello?"

"It's me. Sorry I missed your call – I was out on a walk. So...what's up tonight?"

It was good to hear his voice again. *You miss him only after a few hours?*

"Well, if you don't mind meeting my aunt and uncle, eating trout and getting assaulted with never-ending fishing stories...then you're welcome to come over. I forgot they were going to be here tonight."

"Um, sounds great – when do you want me?"

"The sooner the better. I'm headed to the shower now so I don't look like cotton candy when you get here." Ana pulled her hair out of the ponytail and picked at pink spots that looked like girly lice.

"Hmmm, hold on...let me picture it. Nope,...wait ten minutes so I can see for myself." Chance laughed into the phone. "Don't like pink?"

"Ha, ha. I have enough paint for you too." Ana threatened.

"Okay – be right there."

"Bye." Ana shut her phone and dropped it back into her pocket.

After she sealed the paint can, Ana grabbed the rollers, brushes, and trays, and carried them all downstairs. On her way outside, she passed her mom. She called to her. "Chance is on his way – he'll be here soon."

Melissa ran to open the front door, held it open and said, "Great! Can I put him to work? That light bulb needs changing on the back porch..." Melissa winked at her.

Ana snorted in response and hurried with the paint supplies to the shed at the end of the driveway. She cleaned the brushes, tossed the used rollers into the trash and walked back to the house. As she approached the house, she saw a dust trail rise behind the glint of black paint.

Chance pulled up and got out of his truck and appraised Ana with a grin. He stood back and made a show of checking her out from head to toe. Ana curtsied and flipped her hair as she played along.

"Okay, you caught me in my shining glory." She held her arms wide open to display her ratty clothes, oddly comfortable in front of him even at her worst.

He walked up to her, scrutinized her hair and said, "May not be your favorite color, but hey, you'd look good in anything." He reached up and rubbed a smear of paint off her neck and laughed.

Ana closed her eyes at his sudden touch. Electricity coursed under her skin. Her cheeks burned and the heat drifted down her throat.

Chance seemed to notice how tired she seemed. His eyes stopped at the edge of her old droopy t-shirt. Ana tugged at the back of her shirt, pulled the v-neck upward, and quickly covered the light line on her chest that rose to the top of her sternum.

His eyes drifted to the door while he said, "You deserve your shower now."

***

After Ana showered, washed her hair and cleaned the paint from beneath her fingernails she felt human again, albeit a tired human. She passed her sister's room, hairbrush in hand and discovered Eva red-faced, as she pushed her bed back into place.

"Don't hurt yourself, Eva. You coming downstairs? Have you said hi to Chance yet?"

"Chance is here?! Oh, okay, I'll be right down." Eva went to her closet.

In the kitchen, Ana found Chance and Melissa talking as they prepared a dish for dinner.

"Putting him to work, already?"

"Hey now, he volunteered. Tera and Jace are on their way – think you can go start the barbecue for me?"

Ana withdrew a long lighter and went out to the back deck. The sun created a soft sepia light that illuminated everything around her in an apricot veil. She sucked in the crisp air and tasted the fir trees on her tongue. Just past the evergreens, her favorite interchange had begun – the sun saluted its compliment, the moon, in a slow embrace.

Ana thought she heard the sound of tires on the driveway and lit the barbecue, then went back inside to tell her mother.

Melissa was busy doing something with carrots that didn't resemble anything Ana was familiar with. She looked up at Ana, a knife held midair. "Baby – can you get the door for me? My hands are a mess. Welcome them in, please?"

Chance stopped chopping his pile of vegetables and joined Ana who beckoned him to the living room to greet her family.

With Chance behind her, she opened the door just as Aunt Tera's hand was mid-air in motion to knock.

"Hi, Sweetheart! Oh, the house looks *so* cute! I can see your mother's touch – and it smells like it's been airing out nicely. Where's Mel?" Aunt Tera stepped inside with a flowery bowl filled with potato salad. She stopped in front of Chance. "Oh! Now, who are you?!"

Uncle Jace wiped his shoes off on the mat and popped inside after the exclamation from Tera. He wore the same hat as last time. It seemed fastened to his head by sweat, his damp hair curled beneath the darkened band.

"Aunt Tera, Uncle Jace – this is Chance."

Jace hooted. "Finally! One more for the team! Please tell me you fish?!" His brightened eyes were ready for an audience, and he held a large zipper bag with four dead trout packed in ice.

Chance shifted his weight to his back foot. "Yeah. I go out with my dad sometimes." Chance's eyes darted to Ana, who gave him a thumb's up sign and a guilty smile.

Uncle Jace seemed to taste victory. For once in a long time, he wasn't alone in a sea of estrogen. His eyes sparkled. Ana thought he could hear angel's singing – or maybe fish splashing.

"Now, calm down Hun. It doesn't mean you can unbutton your pants after dinner or go leaving the toilet seat up. Us girls still outnumber you!" Aunt Tera patted his shoulder, and winked at Ana before she went to the kitchen. "It's a *pleasure* to meet you, Chance."

After Jace's zealous welcome, Chance appeared to take everything in stride. He did, however, adopt an amused expression like he was watching a really bad "B" movie he couldn't help but enjoy. Uncle Jace's unabridged fishing stories streamed one after another, and Chance remained in rapt attention. Ana wondered if he was truly interested, or if he was counting ceiling beams, or if he was bored beyond belief and a convincing actor. The only danger he appeared to be in was falling into a coma induced by boredom, so Ana gave him a sympathetic glance and disappeared into the kitchen.

Aunt Tera was deep in conversation with her sister when Ana entered. "...It's so great she's finally reached out to someone, but why hasn't she told him..."

After they saw Ana, their discussion grew quiet and Aunt Tera started up about the kitchen décor. "I think a creamy buttercup yellow would lighten it up considerably. If you put a nice white valance above the window – it would look *so* cute." She pointed at the bare casement.

"Don't let me interrupt your conversion." Ana muttered and walked up to a cupboard just to shut it with a bang.

Melissa and Tera exchanged a glance. Then Melissa said with a nervous laugh, "I guess we can't fool her like we used to."

Aunt Tera nodded in agreement, and said, "Caught." Then after a moment of silence she smiled. "So... Chance seems like a nice boy?"

"Yes, we seem to have a lot in common."

"He's quite good looking." Aunt Tera grinned and gave her a wink.

Ana blushed. She was just about to leave when Aunt Tera wrapped her arms around her.

"You deserve all the best, Sweetie. I'm so happy to see you with a new friend." Tera whispered in her ear. Ana reluctantly turned and hugged her back.

"Thanks, Aunt Tera," she sighed.

"So, now, tell me a little about him?"

"Well, I met him in photography class. He likes being outdoors, like me. I guess he works at an auto body shop. And his family's really nice. His mom's a nurse, and his dad has a jewelry shop near some marina."

"That's great, Ana – it sounds like you have some things in

common."

Just when Ana thought she had escaped without too much humiliation, her aunt continued. "I was wondering though – why you haven't told him?"

"Nice, Mom. Thanks for talking about me behind my back." Ana glared at her mother, upset. Ana told Melissa in confidence that she hadn't told him about her health yet. Her mother was concerned about her choice and counseled her to be honest. "It will only be harder the longer you take."

Melissa flinched and she looked guilty. "I'm just concerned, baby. I know you like him – and understand why you don't want to. I just worry that holding onto your secret will hurt you more in the end."

"It always ruins *everything*!" Ana said with a hiss. "I'm enjoying being normal. Everything will fall apart anyway. So, I might as well enjoy a piece of cake before it goes *bad*." Ana kept her voice low, not wanting to alert anyone in the other room about their discussion.

"Ana," Aunt Tera said with a bewildered look.

She didn't want pity, so Ana walked out the back door to get a breath of fresh air. Overwhelmed and with eyes stinging, she ran through the path to her sanctuary.

Perched cross-legged on the rock, her vision blurred as she let the tears flow. The warm drops found a pathway down her cheeks, and a soft groan broke from her lips. She picked up a piece of shale from the rock below her and threw it as far as she could, tracking its arc into the dark wilderness.

A branch snapped behind her, and she turned to see Melissa emerge from the trail. Ana spun back and folded her arms across her chest.

"I'm sorry to intrude, but I need to apologize. I'm sorry I talked to Aunt Tera about everything. You know I'll support you in all of your decisions and try not to question you. You're old enough to make your own choices. After all...you *are* an adult now."

Ana grimaced at the horizon and released her tension. She opened her palms upward. "I know you just worry about me, Mom. I know you mean the best. It's just that...it's been bothering me too."

The tears started to flow again.

"I don't want to lie to Chance. Maybe it isn't really lying, but it feels like it. I *don't* want him to know. I'm afraid he's just going to leave when he finds out." Ana threw her head into her hands in defeat, her shoulders slumped. As her mind spiraled into a tornado, her mother's hand anchored lightly on her shoulder.

"Baby, it was never your fault. Your dad didn't leave because of you. I don't want you carrying around this pain inside. Dad and I just weren't meant to be. He would have left even if you weren't born...different. He was never mature enough to have a wife and kids. Don't let your dad ruin what you have with Chance. I can see how you feel about him, and I want you to be happy. You're a caring, unique person who *deserves* to be loved – broken heart and all."

Ana saw her mother's worried eyes and the love within. Her mother was right. But she couldn't help feeling like a bug repellant for people – extra strength formula.

"Thanks, Mom. I love you."

After inspecting her hands, she noted the slight purple tinge near the tips and said, "I know you're right, I just want a little more *time*."

In so many ways.

"If he hangs around for another two weeks, I'll tell him after my doctor appointment – no later. I *will* tell him."

Melissa said, "I can't remember where I heard it, but it clicked for me – 'The truth will set you free, but first, it'll piss you off.'"

An involuntary laugh ripped from Ana's painful lungs as she wiped the tears from her face, worried it was splotchy. It was like she had a neon sign above her head that said, *I've been crying*. She hated to draw attention to herself which is why she never got so upset.

"By the way, baby... this is really nice. No wonder you spend so much time out here. I'll see you inside – take your time. I won't let anyone know. I love you." Melissa walked back to the house.

Ana sat for a few more minutes and hoped her inflamed eyes would fade so she wouldn't need to explain.

As she walked back, she smelled the smoke from the grill. When she walked inside she spotted Chance and her anxiety ebbed.

***

He was happy to see Ana again and noticed how bright her eyes were. She must have been crying. He wanted to comfort her, but had seen how sensitive and proud she was. He moved near and allowed the warmth from her closeness to satisfy his need to soothe her. It would be enough.

Ana swayed on her feet and leaned against him for support. Chance squeezed her hand. When she met his eyes, he looked at her with concern.

Jace appeared with a platter of fish and boisterously exclaimed, "Prepare yourselves for the best thing on earth." He set the platter at the center of the table with an extra flourish.

Ana seemed to struggle to keep her eyes open while she ate. Chance kept his eye on her throughout dinner. He grew unsettled while he observed her and noticed her lavender fingers and lips. Unsure what was wrong, he sensed he should protect her, but from what, he didn't know. All he wanted to do was keep her safe and happy. He wondered how easy that would be.

After dinner, Tera and Jace gathered their things to go. Melissa attempted to send the fish leftovers home with her sister, who laughed at her when she tried. "Are you kidding, Mel? I have enough fish in my freezer to repopulate the Great Lakes."

Everyone hugged before they left. Uncle Jace waved and led Aunt Tera outside as she continued to chat with her sister until Jace shut her car door with a satisfied grin.

"Well...you look tired. I think I should leave too." Chance said and eyed the door.

"It's only eight o'clock though," Ana said discouraged. "How about watching a movie on the couch?"

Without an answer she grabbed his hand and led him to the sofa. She put on a comedy and settled in beside him.

Eva joined them, while Melissa went upstairs to gather a load of laundry. Ten minutes later, she came into the living room with a basket of clean clothes.

"Make yourself useful, Eva. Can you fold these for me?" Melissa had dark bags under her eyes but a spring in her step. She disappeared into the kitchen, and soon he heard the familiar sound of dishes being washed.

"Fine." Eva dragged herself off the couch to fold the mish-mash of white laundry that stuck out of the battered blue basket.

Something heavy weighed against him. Ana's head rest on his shoulder, and he realized she had fallen asleep. Rather than being amused, he frowned apprehensively. He turned to Eva, who hummed as she busily balled up socks. She broke off after she looked at her sister with solemn eyes.

"Maybe I should carry her to bed?" he asked Eva.

She nodded, averted her sad eyes and continued to fold the laundry in silence.

Chance scooped Ana up in his arms and walked to the kitchen. Ana didn't stir. As he carried her into the kitchen, Melissa turned. Silently, she led the way. Upstairs, she pointed to the end of the hallway. Chance pushed through the door into a darkened room. Melissa flipped the switch and pulled down the sheets to Ana's bed.

With a deep breath, Chance filled his lungs with Ana's scent, lay her down on the bed and brushed his lips past her forehead. Melissa turned away quickly, but Chance saw her reflection in the window. Her cheek quivered, and he heard her deep raspy breath. When she returned to her daughter's side composed and in control, she removed Ana's shoes and without a sound, he left the room. As he descended the stairs, the sound of sheets rustled and a soft whisper met his ears. "Good night, baby."

Melissa rubbed her eyes when she joined Chance in the kitchen, she seemed sad, but she wore the emotion like an old pair of jeans. It made him uneasy.

"Thanks for taking her up," Melissa said and touched his arm. She stared at the floor for a long moment before she looked up and held his gaze. "It's nice having you around. It's good knowing there's someone else looking out for her." Melissa seemed to stop short as though she had said too much.

"Anything else I can help you with tonight?" Chance asked. He needed to feel useful.

Melissa's eyes softened. "You're sweet, Chance."

Frustrated and powerless, he knew something was wrong. It was as clear as day, but he just didn't know what. Everyone was skirting around the subject, but it was obvious as a smoking caterpillar on a toadstool.

Melissa stepped forward and gave him a hug, as though she hoped to smooth his concerns

"We're fine, really, thanks for offering. Don't worry, Chance. She'll be okay after a good night's sleep. You'll see," she said.

Chance nodded and reluctantly wandered into the living room as Melissa trailed behind. He gave Eva a high five before he pulled out his keys.

Outside by his truck, he stood and listened to the trees

sway around him. The sounds from other animals were absent, but he knew they were there. He could *feel* them.

CHAPTER 12

Sunday morning came early, but not for Ana. She remained asleep until she heard cupboards bang. Wings flapped outside her window earlier, but it wasn't enough to wake her. She plunged her head deeper under the pillow.

When she finally got up, she saw how late it was. She couldn't remember how she got to bed or when Chance had left. Clothes stuck to her moist skin, and she realized she was still wearing what she had on yesterday. Nice.

With a shake of her head, she peeled off her sweaty, wrinkled garments, threw them in the hamper and grabbed a fresh set. Maybe I was abducted by aliens, she laughed to herself. She gazed at her tangled reflection in a small mirror on the wall and combed out the bird's nest.

"Good morning, sunshine," Melissa said as Ana walked groggily downstairs. The sound of cartoons drifted in from the living room.

As she rubbed the sleep from her eyes and stretched, an unwelcome head rush returned, and she grabbed a chair for support. Melissa eyed her cautiously and then forced her daughter into the kitchen chair that she held, her knuckles white.

"What can I get you for breakfast?"

"I'm not hungry, Mom," Ana said defensively, while she pushed at the ridges in the tablecloth.

"Wrong answer. How about some yogurt – or at least a banana?" Melissa said, holding out the yellow fruit.

"Fine." Ana grabbed the banana. As she took a bite she asked, "What happened last night, I don't remember going to bed."

"You fell asleep after Tera and Jace left, then Chance carried you up to your room. He seemed really concerned about you." Melissa faced out the kitchen window and avoided her daughter's eyes. Ana appreciated that her mother maintained her promise to keep her thoughts private.

"I'll call him. Let him know I'm fine."

Ana took another bite of banana while she walked out the back door. She dropped onto a patio chair, closed her eyes, and tilted her head back to let the sun warm her skin. She slipped out her phone to call Chance, and watched three red squirrels race across the lawn, scavenging for food.

"Ana?" Chance answered.

"Hey, I wanted to call you and let you know I'm feeling *fine* this morning." She emphasized the word *fine* and continued. "I just needed a little rest. It was a long week. Mom tells me you helped me get to bed – um…thanks."

"Yeah, I was worried. I'm glad you're feeling better now."

A bird screeched near her house, and she thought it echoed in her ear from the phone.

"Where are you?" she asked, suspicious.

There was a pause before Chance answered. "Taking a walk in the forest. I need to head back though. Grandfather's expecting me." He seemed impatient.

"Okay. You want to call me back later then?" she said.

"Yeah. Thanks for everything last night – your family's certainly…entertaining." Ana heard his deep chuckle and joined in.

"Aren't they? Well, I'll talk to you later. Bye, Chance."

"Bye, Ana."

She snapped her phone shut and went back into the house, and her thoughts turned to the pile of homework that was due. It was time to come back to reality, to face her responsibilities. After she tossed the banana peel into the trash, she lumbered upstairs to her desk covered with books.

CHAPTER 13

Cool blades of grass tickled Ana's exposed skin as she lay in the warm sunlight during lunch period. She heard muffled voices around her in the courtyard as though she were behind sheet glass.

Suddenly the heat from the sun dissolved into cool shade. She opened her eyes and blinked at the form that blocked her light.

Chance stood with an amused grin as Ana attempted to focus on him. She smiled and patted the grass next to her. He sat down beside her.

Five sets of eyes turned to face Chance, while Laura threw a suggestive grin at Ana. Ana looked away and fixed her gaze on the grass. A moment passed and the girls resumed their conversations.

"I've been waiting for you," Ana said as she closed her eyes.

Chance propped himself back on his elbow and asked, "Want to go on a nature walk tomorrow?"

Ravens squawked and pecked at some scattered chips strewn on the ground. Chance threw a pebble at them, and they scattered.

Ana saw Chance's hands ball up. His face darkened. Then she heard the guffaws from across the lawn near the chain link fence and noticed some boys glancing over at them.

"What's wrong?"

"I don't like what they're saying."

Ana frowned. "But, they're too far away to hear. Ignore them."

Chance stared back over at the ravens, which had resettled around the spilled chips. With each breath, his face dropped, relaxed. "So, I thought I'd show you what *I* do to unwind. I've tracked the area really well. There are some pretty sweet places I'd like to show you," he said. The crows stopped their chatter and glanced at him.

"I'll have to check with Aunt Tera – see if I can drop Eva off with her after school." Then she added. "I'm not much of a hiker. Is the trail flat or rocky?"

"No worries. I'll take care of you." Chance's serious face met hers, and Ana nodded. She wanted to believe him but didn't feel much relief from his assurance.

***

While they stood in the parking lot after school, Chance pressed her to call him as soon as she spoke to her aunt.

When Ana got home with her sister, she called as she had promised.

"Aunt Tera, is it okay if I drop Eva off at your house after school tomorrow? Chance wants to take me on a walk."

Ana could just imagine the suggestive grin her aunt displayed at that moment and heard the smile in her voice. "Sure, Sweetie. I can just pick her up from school if that makes it easier for you. Mel can swing by after work and get her before going home."

Eva stared at her suspiciously, questioning what was happening on the phone. She began to tap her foot and narrowed her eyes, clearly annoyed.

"Thanks, Aunt Tera, I appreciate it."

Before she hung up the phone her aunt said, "You have fun and say hi to Chance for me."

Ana pleaded with her sister as she flipped her phone shut. "Please? I bet Aunt Tera will make you those awesome chewy chocolate cookies if you ask."

The thought of their Aunt's cookies made Eva grin, and she nodded. Getting stuck at Aunt Tera and Uncle Jace's house ensured, at the very least, that you'd be fed well. This was probably the reason for Uncle Jace's pot belly.

Ana phoned Chance. He seemed to have anticipated her

call, because he picked up before the first ring had finished.

"Alright, we're set for tomorrow. Aunt Tera's gonna pick Eva up after school. So, I'll be ready when the bell rings."

"Excellent," he said.

"Remember – take it easy on me," Ana warned him.

"Scout's honor." He laughed into the phone.

"Are you even a boy scout? Anyway, are you taking me somewhere special, or is it a secret?" she said, thinking about their nighttime trip to the lake.

"You'll like it...and I promise, no hiking." Chance seemed to enjoy Ana's curiosity. It was obvious he was excited to share his knowledge about the local wildlife.

"Well then...I can't wait."

An awkward silence came when it was time to say goodbye. He cleared his throat and said, "I'll see you tomorrow, Ana." His voice sounded glum.

"Bye." Ana said and rested the phone against her cool lips.

CHAPTER 14

After school Chance grabbed her hand and led her to the parking lot.

"Where's the fire," Ana said, glancing from side to side in mock horror. She enjoyed the contact with his hand. Her skin tingled at his touch.

"Let's get out of here. I want as much time possible outdoors before sundown."

She slid into the familiar cab and Chance joined her within moments. Their travels began in the same direction as Ana's house, but then he exited along an unfamiliar stretch of highway. They drove along the river for ten minutes before he turned onto a road, taking them closer to the water. Eventually they came to a dead end and parked.

"Where are we?"

"This is the Clark Bend River. If you go south as the bird flies, your home isn't far."

"You go fishing here?" Ana remembered his reference to fishing with his dad when he spoke to Uncle Jace.

"This is a place I go...to observe animals." One brow arched and his mind seemed engaged elsewhere.

They got out of the truck. The grassy plain stretched before her, bright spring grass interspersed with purple flowers. Distant mountains shone bright with white capped peaks.

Chance held his hand out and Ana took it, as he led her through the calf deep growth. Both of them avoided looking at the other, nervous with physical contact. Ana's palms prickled from the electricity shared between them.

Chance tilted his head and stopped. Ana peered in the same direction, unsure of his focus and discovered a small herd of elk. Still a distance away, they were grazing. One lifted its head and seemed to catch Chance's gaze.

"Elk," he said in an undertone. "They eat just like cows do

and have two stomachs. They need a huge amount of food every day. They chew it, regurgitate and chew it again before it goes to their second stomach. This is a herd of females and that one, over there-" He pointed toward a round bellied female who was watching them. "Is pregnant. Her calf should be born soon. In the next couple of weeks," Chance said to Ana, who listened intently, amazed at his expertise.

"How do you know so much about them?"

"I'm outside a lot. Grandfather's my guide. He knows everything about the plants and animals in the area." He answered briefly, leading her forward.

They wandered along a faint trail with Chance pointing out plants and animals along the way. Ana marveled at his knowledge and became enthralled with his hazel eyes as they flashed in the soft light.

"Here...this is for you." He picked a yellow flower. The leaves formed a perfect heart shape and the flower itself reminded her of a yellow daisy.

"Heartleaf Arnica," he said, his eyes staring straight into hers.

"I think I've heard of Arnica." Ana thought out loud.

"It's used on the skin to prevent infections. It's put in salves."

"You could fill an encyclopedia with all of your knowledge." Ana laughed and pushed against his solid chest. Distracted by his sinewy build, she dropped her hand slowly.

Chance's breath caught. Her physical contact had clearly broken his concentration. He seemed lost in thought, unable to find words for a moment.

Her stomach flipped, and she decided to start a new conversation to distract herself. "Umm...maybe you can tell me something about foxes. You know, I saw one out at my house the other day. It was the first time I've ever seen one – it was so cute. And it didn't seem frightened of me at all."

Chance's breathing quickened, and he began to fidget with his hands. Ana assumed he was distracted by her touch and blushed.

"Red foxes. Well, red foxes are omnivores. They eat just about anything and have excellent hearing. They hunt alone and are at the top of their food chain. I mean, as long as coyotes don't come around." Chance shuddered slightly and continued. "When they shriek, it sounds weird, like a human screaming. They're cunning and wise. Native tribes consider them a noble messenger."

"Hmm, a messenger? Wonder what message it was delivering? Hey, aren't they nocturnal?"

Chance answered slowly, "Yes, they're known to be nocturnal...but *can* be active in the daytime."

"Hmm, well, the one I saw was during the middle of the day. I wonder if I'll see it again...maybe its den's nearby."

Ana also remembered the yellow eyes that tracked her at night while she stargazed. She saw them every evening in a fir tree above her rock.

"What about owls?" she asked Chance. He coughed and shoved his hands into his pockets and rolled a pebble around with his foot.

His brow wrinkled. "Hmm?"

"What types of owls are around here? I saw a pretty big one the other night. My star rock must be near an owl's territory 'cause I keep seeing eyes watching me at night when I'm stargazing. It must be injured though, it's not very graceful. It doesn't fly very well."

Chance chuckled.

Had she said something funny?

Chance's smile disappeared, and he answered, "It could have been a horned owl. They can get pretty big." His voice trailed off.

Ana's body drooped with fatigue from their walk. They hadn't gone very far. She could still see his truck from her vantage point, but simply standing on her feet was too much for her.

"Do you mind if we find a place to sit? I'm feeling a bit tired," she said.

Chance nodded and led her down to the river's edge. A granite boulder served as a perfect seat. They sat beside each other as the water swirled past, moving like billowing smoke as it caught in eddies and flowed past submerged bedrock. Occasionally, Chance would point out the form of a fish moving below them. Ana wondered at his ability to see and hear the elements around them.

Ana's stomach growled, and she realized how late it was. "I need to get home. I still have homework to do," she said as she threw a smooth flat stone, skipping it across the water.

Chance stood and helped her up. "Me, too."

***

Because they hadn't gone far, it took only a few minutes to walk back to the truck. Hours had elapsed since the start of their walk, but they had made many stops along the abundant wildlife trail.

Chance drove Ana to her car in the empty parking lot at school. He looked over at her wilted silhouette and was suddenly anxious about leaving her.

Ana rubbed her arms after goose bumps rose from a cool breeze. She reached in her pocket for her car keys as Chance pulled off his thin jacket and draped it around her shoulders. He caught the fragrance of her hair as he brushed by her, a fresh smell like the forest after a rainstorm. He drank it in. How could she smell so good?

She pulled her arms into the sleeves. "Thanks...I'll return it tomorrow."

"No problem."

Chance held her gaze then walked to his truck and waved

before he got in. He marveled at the physical pain it caused for him to separate from her.

He waited for Ana to get into her van and leave before he leaned his head against the wheel. His feelings were intense and expanded into every cell of his body. Helpless, he started his truck and wondered about the outcome.

CHAPTER 15

The rest of the week went smoothly.

Happiness began to take hold of Ana where secret loneliness had once reigned.

She came home after school on Friday excited about her plans that night with Chance. Dropping her bag to the floor, she filled her mother in. "Tonight we're going out on the lake again. Then Chance wants to take me on another nature walk on Sunday!" Her voice exuded the hopefulness she felt inside.

Melissa said, "That's great, baby. Maybe you should take a light jacket tonight. It looks like it's getting a little windy."

"Are you going to stay for dinner?"

"Nope, Chance is bringing something for us to eat."

Ana ran up to her room, changed into warmer clothes and waited for the clock to read the right time. Finally, she heard tires on the driveway and ran downstairs. Her mother was in the kitchen with an unwrapped frozen lasagna dinner and a stack of bills beside her on the counter.

"Chance is here, Mom. I'm gonna go now – I love you." Ana leaned in and kissed her mother on the cheek.

Eva walked into the kitchen with a disappointed look. "You're going out, *again*? Leaving me with Mom alone? I wanted to hang out with you," she said, her shoulders slumped.

Ana rubbed her back. "I'm sorry D. We'll hang out in the morning. I bet Mom would love doing something with you tonight."

Melissa nodded and flashed her a dazzling smile.

Eva shrugged and walked glumly back to the living room. She plopped herself down on the couch and tilted to the side.

The doorbell rang. Ana rushed to the front door to meet Chance and said, "Can you give me just a minute? I need to talk to my sister before we go."

"Sure – I'll be in the truck." Chance touched her shoulder

before he turned back.

Ana shut the door and returned to the couch to sit beside her sister. She wrapped an arm around her. "What's wrong?"

Eva clutched her folded arms against her body. Her brow pulled down as though she was determined not to answer. Ana continued to hold her, waiting patiently.

"You're gone so much now. You don't spend *any* time with me anymore." Eva's lower lip trembled.

Ana took a deep breath. "I know...I'm sorry. You're used to me being around all the time. Say, maybe I can check with Chance and see if you can come on our nature walk this Sunday. Would you like that?"

Eva peeked up at her sister, and the corners of her mouth pulled up in response. She shrugged and answered. "Sure."

"Alright. I'll talk to Chance tonight and let you know tomorrow. Have a good time with Mom, and I'll see you in the morning."

Ana gave her one last squeeze, got up and gave a thankful grin to their mom who stood in the doorway, monitoring the discussion. Melissa gave a small wave and took her daughter's place at the couch.

Ana left the house with a heavy heart. She hadn't considered how her sister felt. Eva had grown used to being with her older sister all the time. Ana had always been there for her. And now, it was like she was abandoning her.

When Ana joined Chance in the cab, he saw her sad eyes.

"What's wrong?" He adjusted his body to face her, resting his fingers on her shoulder.

"It's my sister. I haven't been thinking about her much lately. She misses me. I used to be around all the time, but now..." Ana looked out the window toward the house and pulled some loose strands of hair behind her ear.

"I see. We can take her along on Sunday? You think she'd like that?" he asked.

"That'd be great Chance, thanks." Ana hugged him,

relieved that he understood. They pulled away awkwardly from each other, still unsure of the foreignness of physical closeness.

"Alright, are we ready?" he asked. She turned around and peeked out the cab's rear window to inspect the boat strapped to the truck.

"Yeah, let's go."

As they drove along the lake, Ana recognized the previous spot Chance had brought her to, but they passed right by it.

"Are we going somewhere new?"

Chance flashed his bright teeth at her, which caused her heart to flicker. "There are too many beautiful places here for me to take you to the same place twice."

They continued to drive for another five minutes before Chance parked at a turnout and jumped from the cab. Safely inside the cab, Ana observed him carry the boat over his head down to the water's edge. She couldn't help but notice his biceps bulge.

When Chance returned, he grabbed the oars and a basket from the back of the truck. Ana followed him down to the shore and helped load their things into the boat. She climbed in. Chance threw in the paddles first and pushed the boat out before he jumped in.

"So, I hope you like burritos. Something easy to eat, I figured." Chance glanced at the basket that lay between them at the bottom of the boat.

"Sure, sounds great...better than frozen lasagna." Ana chuckled, then thought about her mom and sister at the table without her. A pang of guilt stabbed at her heart.

"There are a couple of islands in the middle of the lake. We could eat on one of them."

"That sounds nice," Ana said. "It's so pretty here. I thought it was beautiful in Colorado, but now that I'm here...I love it even more."

"Yeah. There's a ton of wildlife, and it's secluded. But I

can't wait to travel and see more – learn more. Though I'm not as excited to leave Clark Bend anymore," he said.

Their eyes locked in the darkness.

CHAPTER 16

Chance stared at Ana's silhouette as he rowed toward a contour of land appearing over the dark water. The fuzzy profile grew clear as they approached the island. Evergreens flourished and towered up into the deep blue sky.

After they arrived ashore, they climbed out in search of a place to picnic. Chance carried a large blanket as he walked up the pebbly beach. In one sweeping motion, he laid it on the ground. Ana set a camping lantern in the middle as he began to unpack their meal. Two silver aluminum wrapped burritos emerged along with a couple of drinks and napkins.

He beckoned for her to join him. When she settled on the blanket, a bunch of bright yellow flowers materialized before her eyes.

"Heartleaf Arnica." Ana smiled and accepted the flowers from his outstretched hand. "Thank you."

They ate beside each other and watched the indigo horizon darken, as it set the stage for the radiant stars. Neither pressed to make conversation, and they were perfectly content to sit in solitude.

After the last bite was eaten, they placed the remains of the picnic back into the basket and lay down to gaze at the night sky.

"So, have you ever moved before, or is this your first time?"

"This is the first time I've moved out of state. We moved a couple of times before, but I've never had to change schools," Ana said.

"Did you have many friends?" Chance asked with a serious demeanor.

"No, not many close friends. *That* isn't the hard part. Uncertainty – *that's* what's hard..."

"Yeah, I agree. Uncertainty *is* hard." He looked at her thoughtfully. "But...some things aren't," he said and his hand brushed against her fingers. Ana's breath stuttered, and Chance turned to search her eyes.

After a moment, she asked softly. "You know the night I came over for dinner? I noticed your grandfather react when he saw my necklace...do you know what's up?"

Chance was surprised by the question and frowned while he considered his answer. "Well...my grandfather is very superstitious. The Thunderbird is sort of our family totem. He thought it meant something...I wouldn't worry about it. It's nothing."

Ana frowned and grew quiet. He could tell his answer didn't satisfy her, so he asked his own question. "It's cool if you don't want to talk about it, but I was wondering about your father...where's he at?" Chance asked. With no trace of any pictures in her house he wondered where her father was. He guessed it was a painful subject.

Ana paused then said, "Well, Mom and Dad met when they were really young – just a little older than we are. My mom got pregnant with me, and then they got married. They were never madly in love – they weren't exactly made for each other and only stayed together for me. When things started getting rough, my mom got pregnant with my sister. Dad hung in for a while and when the fighting got too bad, he left. Mom says he was never mature enough to have a wife and kids. Anyway...we haven't heard from him since. We're happy together and don't need him." She winced bitterly.

Chance sat while she narrated the story and grabbed her hand, squeezing gently. Now he understood why her father's picture wasn't around and was thankful she wasn't upset at him. The visible pain in her eyes made him regret his question.

"I'm sorry," he said.

"Yeah."

Ana dropped back onto the blanket, and stared at the stars as they flickered in the night sky. Anger swelled as

Chance thought about her father's abandonment. *How could he walk away from her? And leave her alone, unprotected? What kind of man was he?* He squeezed her hand without realizing it.

Ana asked, "What's wrong?"

"It's nothing," he said.

"No, c'mon tell me?"

"I can't imagine leaving someone I love."

Ana lay in silence, and they listened to the lake lap at the shore. Chance tightened his warm hand around her cold fingers and she sighed. "No, me either."

He wanted to lighten her mood and started a conversation that would give her peace. "Say – you know any constellations? I can tell you a few Navajo constellations Grandfather taught me."

Clearly happy to focus on something else, she pointed up above their heads and identified a cluster of stars. "That one, of course, is the Big Dipper."

"To the Navajo, that's known as the Northern Male. He represents the father and protector of the home."

"Really? Do you know more about it?" she asked enthusiastically.

Chance shook his head. "No, that's all Grandfather told me about it."

"I can tell you more about The Big Dipper...if you want..."

"Sure, lay it on me." Chance stretched back and folded his hands beneath his head.

"So, um, did you know The Big Dipper's also known as The Great Bear? The Greek myth says that Zeus fell in love with a beautiful maiden, Callisto and had a son with her. She was one of his wife's virgin hand-maidens, which naturally peeved off Hera. Trying to spare Callisto from Hera's wrath, Zeus turned her into a bear to hide her. Callisto's son was turned into a bear as well and is by her side- the Little Dipper." She pointed up to the constellation. "Protected for all time..." She shook her head and as an afterthought, added, "But that's really the PG version. It's funny- Greek myths about the gods always seem to involve them misusing their powers. And with all that power, they were so obsessed with keeping it." She rushed on, her eyes glittering, passionate about her story, "There was a prophesy that said Zeus's dad would lose his power to one of his kids...so he destroyed them. Too afraid of losing his control. But Zeus escaped his father and grew up to save his brothers and sisters...and the prophesy came true." Ana trailed off, appearing self conscious after she realized how much she had been talking.

Chance had been totally absorbed with Ana, who glowed with excitement, completely in her element. He blinked. "Okay, I'm impressed. How'd you know all of that?"

Ana blushed in the darkness. "Well, my interest in constellations led me to Greek mythology. It's way better than a soap opera."

"So, what else? Tell me more."

"Well..." Ana said, embarrassed. "Do you know how to find Polaris?"

"Polaris?"

"Yeah, the North Star. See the Big Dipper? The two outer stars of the spoon guide you..." Ana pointed up, and drew her finger along an invisible line. "Then you can find the North Star just there. The point of the Little Dipper. Polaris is true north. No matter where you are in the world it always points north." Ana shrugged. "So, how do you know the Navajo constellations?"

"Oh, my grandfather only showed me a few. I just lucked out – you happened to pick one I know," he said sheepishly.

Ana grinned over at him, but he was already staring at her.

Chance stood up, disquieted. A hunger grew deep within him, and it took everything in him to suppress it. He held his hand out and pulled her upright gingerly. Something about Ana made her seem fragile, breakable. Reluctantly, he let her fingers fall from his hands.

***

She was almost light on her feet. It was a like a dream. Was this what it was like to be normal? On a date, and falling in love?

"How about a friendly competition?" Chance asked with his eyebrow arched. "Know how to skip stones? Let's say the first person to one hundred wins." He proposed as he reached down, grabbed a round flat stone and handed it to her.

"Oh yeah? Wins what?" Ana asked laughing.

"Hmm...to be determined at a later date." Chance leaned over and picked up a handful of smooth stones and dropped them into his pocket. He held his open hand out to the water. "Ladies first."

Ana arched her eyebrow, then squatted down with her arm held parallel to the water and skipped her stone across the inky mirrored surface.

"Ten, not bad," Chance said and followed her lead, sending his stone out across the water.

They continued to skip stones, counting along the way.

"Um, I get the feeling I just got played."

"I'm what you could say, experienced. I used to take trips down to the lake near my old house, and I'd practice. It was something I did when I was angry or frustrated. I'm *very* good at it," Ana said with a smirk.

"One hundred to eighty-two. Better luck next time," Ana said, and stepped towards him to shake hands. As she placed her foot down it slipped sideways across the surface of a slick rock, which caused her to tip forward precariously.

Chance caught her within his ready arms. He lifted her upright and gazed deeply into her eyes. Ana's mind went blank, except for one thing.

The scent of fir trees blew past and imprinted the moment in her senses. A breeze wafted by and moved her hair, but not her focus. It remained on Chance, who held her so close it felt like they were the same living, breathing organism.

His hazel eyes held Ana captive and made her heart race. She knew what came next. Chance's face seemed to reflect her anxiety.

In slow motion, he slid his trembling hands from their resting place at her waist, up her back and to her pale face. Simultaneously they took a deep breath, as their faces drew closer, and held each others' gaze. In a moment of shared surprise their lips met in a tender dance, each cautious and tentative in unfamiliar territory.

As Ana delighted in the moment, a lack of oxygen made her faint and her legs weakened. Chance dropped his arms to hold her around the waist. A concerned expression crossed his face, and Ana groaned.

"Are you okay?" he said, breathless.

"How embarrassing." Ana whimpered in exasperation. She almost fainted in front of him. Her fragile hands found a place to rest on his chest, and she noticed his rapid heartbeat, which reflected her own. White spots filled her vision as she blinked repeatedly, trying to see clearly. "I forgot to breathe."

Chance lifted his hand to run his fingers through her hair and shook his head in bewilderment.

"Please breathe next time so I don't have to row you all the way to the hospital," Chance said in gentle vexation.

She buried herself into his shirt, and held on tight, for fear this was the last good moment in her life. Chance held her affectionately, as if unaware of the turmoil that erupted in Ana's head from his innocent comment.

They moved away from each other. Both seemed surprised and withdrawn after their kiss.

Ana hadn't planned on taking things to this point. Guilt

ridden, she thought she had led him on. In just a week's time, she'd share her news with him. He'd either be mad at her for not telling him sooner or would leave, like her dad. *Having a sick girlfriend isn't what every guy wishes for*. She was just so content and normal with him, she couldn't stop herself.

"Are you ready to head back?"

Chance seemed to misinterpret the sad expression on Ana's face, and said, "We can take our time...and you can stargaze the whole way. I don't want your mom worrying about you."

Chance loaded the basket into the boat, wrapped Ana in the wool blanket and helped her onto her seat. As promised, he took them slowly across the lake toward their launch site.

***

As Chance paddled them back he couldn't shake the sense that things wouldn't stay the same for much longer.

CHAPTER 17

The next morning Ana came downstairs lighthearted and smiling. Melissa walked up to her tired daughter to give her a big hug. Ana leaned back questioningly.

"What...I can't hug my daughter?"

"No – sure you can," Ana said, confused.

The look on her mother's face worried her. She seemed so melancholy. It forced her to think about her doctor's appointment. It was only six days away.

Ana sniffed and asked, "Pancakes?"

Eager for a diversion, Ana walked to the dining table where Eva was already perched, glued to her morning cartoons. Eva crammed dripping pieces of pancake into her engorged mouth and looked like a rabid chipmunk gone mad on Bisquick. Eva gave her sister a nod when she joined her at the table.

"So... Chance wants you to come along tomorrow on our walk," Ana said as she touched her sister's free hand.

Eva glanced over with a trickle of syrup on her chin. "Weawy?"

Melissa smiled at her girls across the table and tossed a napkin to Eva. "Really Eva, you could at least try to eat like a lady."

In response, she stuck her tongue out, grabbed the napkin and stuck it to her chin. Ana laughed out loud, which became contagious. Soon all three were laughing themselves into tears.

CHAPTER 18

Monday moved too quickly for Ana. She wanted to savor everything, but it seemed like someone had hit the fast forward button. Her days began to move faster than she wanted.

Chance seemed to notice her change in attitude and grew more troubled. Ana could see he was extremely observant. She could sense him monitor her, far more closely than she would have previously guessed.

When Ana grew faint, he turned to her as though he could hear the blood pound through her veins, as if he knew something was wrong. She saw him gaze at her purple tinged lips with his brows knitted together, and suspected he wasn't just thinking about kissing her.

Nostalgic and a little sad, she switched on her computer after school and decided to examine the photographs she took since they arrived in Clark Bend.

The black screen of her computer flickered to life. She clicked through the slides, taking a moment to appreciate each photograph.

When she got to the series of images taken at the school garden, she stopped. There was Chance with his arms outstretched in movement. She touched the screen, focused on his face and sighed.

Ana rubbed her watery eyes and decided to get a drink while she checked on Eva and her school friend. She could hear snickers coming from the living room.

"Hey D, how you doing?" she asked, leaning over the back of the sofa into her sister's surprised face. Eva and her friend were at opposite ends of the couch with crumpled up pieces of paper between them.

"Good," Eva said as her cheeks turned fuchsia. Both girls giggled and slid off the sofa.

"You guys need anything to eat? I'm getting myself a

drink." After a long period of laughing snorts, Ana shrugged her shoulders, retreated to the kitchen and pulled a bottle of water from the fridge. Then she headed back upstairs.

She placed a pillow on her desk chair and settled back in front of the computer to continue her slideshow.

The next pictures were of the forest behind her house, the twilight she shared with Chance, and then the friendly red fox. As she flicked through the series of pictures, something caught her eye. Something shiny.

Ana tapped the zoom button and increased the image size for closer inspection. A puzzled look crossed her face.

She immediately flipped back in the series of images, opened the one of Chance in motion, and zoomed in again.

"What the...?"

Ana focused on Chance's necklace. The silver bear heartline hung from a simple, worn leather band.

Baffled, she clicked back to the fox and noticed a silver bear hung on a leather strap around the animal's neck.

Ana's mind went blank.

She didn't know how to process this. Sure, it was weird, but all it could be was a coincidence. What else could it be? Was she seeing things?

A bird darted through the gloom outside and disappeared in the forest. An odd sensation, like she had swallowed a brick, sank into the pit of her stomach and settled. Nonsensical ideas swirled in her mind, only to confuse her more. Then without further thought, she shut off her internal noise, saved the photographs to her desktop, and decided to review them again after her doctor's appointment.

If it mattered anymore.

The rest of the night Ana was quiet.

"So... I double checked with my boss today, and it's fine if I take Friday off... to take you to Spokane," Melissa said while she brushed out Eva's hair.

Eva peered over to her taciturn sister her head jerking

around from her mother's overzealous efforts. "What about me? I wanna to go, too!"

Melissa grimaced. "I know – I know you want to be there. I think it may be best you go to school though. It might be hard for you to focus, but I think it's the best place for you. I've already spoken to Tera, and she's going to pick you up after school."

Eva's shoulders slumped, and she whined, "But, I want to go with Ana. It's not fair!"

Silence.

Calmly, their mother whispered. "No...none of it is."

Eva looked up to her sister with tears in her eyes. "Oh, Ana."

CHAPTER 19

Tuesday left Ana topsy-turvy.

Her resolve had been torn apart when her sister cried in her lap the previous night. She was still shaken.

Ana tried to keep her mind off of the image of the fox and Chance's necklace. Any more absurdity was just too much to process. With her doctor's appointment, she didn't need the added weight from worrying about bizarre things she couldn't understand.

Chance sat close to her through photography and English class while Ana kept an attentive eye on him. She stared at his bear pendant perplexed. How could the fox have the *same* pendant? And why? Was it a pet? It didn't make any sense. There was probably a simple explanation —she just didn't know what it was.

Ana asked, "Chance? Umm...do you have a pet?"

He leaned back, his eyebrows raised. "No. Why?"

"Oh, never mind...it's nothing."

***

Something had changed. And he wasn't sure what. He saw her fixation with his necklace and couldn't understand it. She was quiet and contemplative, and it unnerved him.

As they walked to the parking lot after school, he asked, "Want to go on a walk tomorrow after school?"

"Yes, definitely. Let me check with Aunt Tera and see if she can pick up Eva. I'm pretty sure she'll be willing to help out."

In the shadow of her van, she pulled him in for a hug goodbye. She seemed desperate to hold on and not let go. Her unique heartbeat fluttered against his chest, until she drew away, and said, "I need to get Eva. She's waiting."

She stared into his eyes as though she were searching for

an answer to some unknown question. "I'll call you later," she said and stepped back to reach for her door.

Chance was left perplexed after she pulled out of the school lot. He was anxious. His muscles were pulled tight, like rubber bands ready to snap.

A sudden breeze blew past. He wouldn't have been surprised if he had been blown away, feeling so ungrounded.

The time was coming. Either they would part ways, or the truth would come out, somehow. A chill tore through his body, and he slunk off to his truck, eager to leave his worries in the parking lot.

CHAPTER 20

The next day Chance noticed a more haggard appearance in Ana. He was confident she wasn't quite this affected when he first met her. Her skin, lips and fingers had a continuous pale mauve tinge. It may not have been so out of place in the cold of winter, but it was spring.

Did she seem so sick when he first saw her? He didn't think so, but when he first held her eyes, she glowed, radiant. She was the most beautiful person he could imagine. He hadn't dwelled on the obvious signs, which were so blatant now – her lack of energy, her coloration alarming his instincts whenever she was near. But still, no explanation. He didn't want to press her unless she wanted to tell him, but he wasn't sure he could go much longer without asking.

It didn't matter.

Whatever the problem was, he would accept it and take her as she was. If he couldn't accept her, then he was a hypocrite.

Chance focused on the road, attempting to shed his torment. He could see for himself she couldn't make it far, so he thought of a place with a short easy walk.

Ana's hair moved in the breeze from the cracked window. Chance studied the individual fibers as they flitted around her beautiful face. Her green eyes stared back at him through a tangle of hair.

***

Ana studied Chance's handsome face. His jaw was clenched in deep introspection. He seemed as engulfed in thought just as she was. Inner peace grew inside her, because she knew the secret would be out soon. Its weight was so immense it pressed on her so she could barely breathe.

"So, where are you taking me today?" she asked.

"Don't worry. There won't be much of a walk and it has a great view. We're almost there." He smiled at her and reached out for her cool hand.

Chance pulled onto a dirt road and parked at a turnout with a trail marker. Ana let her head drop back against the seat while she waited for him to open her door. She breathed out as she slid off the seat and allowed Chance to lead her toward the path.

Tall lanky firs surrounded them and a dirt trail wound delicately through their long bracken covered trunks. Ana sensed the cool earth below her feet and heard the serenade from the birds high above in the canopy. They meandered down a slope toward a granite ledge which formed a rocky bench. It offered a perfect view of the grassy valley below them. Ana sat down on the stone as she allowed her body to relax. She spotted the winding dark river in the distance.

Chance pulled out a set of binoculars from his bag and held them out to her.

"Thanks."

"Look to the west and you'll see the edge of the lake."

Ana held the binoculars in her hands and stared at him with a blank expression.

He smiled and pointed in the proper direction.

After she gazed at the lake, Chance took the binoculars back and identified animals for her. She marveled at his proficiency. He pointed the binoculars in a direction and handed them immediately to her after he spotted something. Without hesitation, he knew where the herd of elk grazed and where the falcon circled the mountain range to the south.

An hour passed, and Chance turned to speak. "I don't have to work on Friday. We can come here again after school – or, I know more places that would be easy for you."

There it was.

Ana took in a deep breath and answered. "I won't be

around for most of the day on Friday. I won't be at school either – I have to be somewhere. But when I get back-" She paused. "I need to talk to you. I'm not sure what time it'll be, probably afternoon sometime." Ana fidgeted with her shirt and continued. "I've been avoiding telling you something – but it's time. I need to get it off my chest."

Chance looked at her with apprehension.

"Now?" Chance encouraged.

"No – Friday. I'll know more after I get back." Ana's eyes burned, and she blinked furiously, in an effort to hold back the tears. Her lungs threatened to deflate as she thought about saying goodbye to him. She must be heartless to lead him along only to drop this terrible bomb. How could he forgive her? Or want to go through an uncertain future with her?

"It's time for the truth."

***

On Thursday, as soon as Chance saw Ana he grew concerned. Light chit-chat was not in her personality description, but she seemed to make an effort to distract herself with empty conversations.

When lunch period came, he sat loyally by her side while she talked with Laura's friends. She appeared determined to avoid any serious subject with anyone. The dread that had started as a tiny seed grew into tree and found root. He worried how bad the news really was. Not knowing tore him up inside. But to protect her, he remained placid to help her through the day.

Soon.

He could wait. For her.

They walked to photography class together in silence. He held her against his side as they moved to the door. The instinct to protect Ana absorbed all of his attention and sharpened his senses.

***

As they sat beside each other in English class, Ana was unable to focus on the book opened before her.

She allowed herself to fall victim to worst case scenarios. *I just know I'll need another surgery*. Even with the weight of her health that hung over her, she was thankful for the three blissful weeks with Chance. As though she was loaned a priceless Tiffany diamond, she knew it had to be returned. The time would come. The end was near. But she was thankful for the gift.

That's what Chance was. Priceless.

After school, Ana and Chance held each other in the parking lot. This was it. Goodbye.

Finally she pulled away. She was about to lift onto her tiptoes, but Chance leaned down to meet her lips in a passionate kiss. But it wasn't like the last kiss, which had been tender and unsure. This was the type of kiss reserved for a final farewell.

A slow tear ran down Ana's cheek.

She withdrew and said, "I'll call you tomorrow when I get back in town."

"I'll be waiting."

***

That night Ana picked at her dinner while her mother and sister watched with unease. Neither felt hungry but ate for the action of it and for the appearance of normalcy.

"Baby? Are you nervous?" Melissa asked while they did the dishes together.

"No, I don't think I'm nervous. It's just that I think I know what the doctor will say. I'm sad though." Ana handed the dish to her mother who set it back into the sink and gave her daughter a hug.

"We can do this. We've done it before. Ana…I love you so much."

The words were spoken with such strength and determination she allowed them to soak in to add to her own dwindling supply.

"Thanks, Mom. I know you're right – we *can* do this."

After the dishes were done, Ana went outside to her rock. In desperate need of tranquility and inner strength, she drank in the blackened starlit expanse.

The sky was clear, a perfect stage for the stars. They seemed eager to perform for her and to cheer her spirits. Ana counted three shooting stars. Their tails spanned the sky like silver moonlit rainbows.

She made a wish on each one.

The yellow eyes that often shared her observatory were there again and kept her company. The owl's presence calmed Ana. Although she wasn't up for a conversation with her mother about the fears that writhed inside her, she also didn't want to be alone. Thankful to have her nighttime companion nearby she smiled, and a tear fell on the granite below.

The owl's eyes never left her face. It continued to serenade her until her head lay upon her cool pillow and she fell into a deep slumber.

CHAPTER 21

Ana woke to a silent house. A bright red card caught her attention. She opened it, and an explosion of hearts with the words *I love you Ana – Love Eva*, were written inside. She set it down and walked out to the landing and called. "Mom?"

She realized Melissa must have taken her sister to school, so Ana decided to take a long shower to relax. The hot water did the trick and left her body warm and soothed. Her room welcomed her back like an old friend, and she sat on the bed to brush out her wet hair.

The bleak view out her window made her choose a soft sweatshirt and jeans. Melancholic firs hid in the sunless gloom outside. The birds must have all gone in search of an illusive sunny spot, or had tucked themselves deeper into their nests. The stillness pierced her.

At the kitchen table, she waited for her empty stomach to get hungry enough to eat the bowl of cereal she had poured. Just then, her mother returned from dropping Eva at school.

"You almost ready?" she asked while Ana poked at the flakes that floated in her milk.

"Yeah, I guess so."

Ana stood up, dumped the contents of the bowl into the sink and walked upstairs to grab the book, *To Kill A Mockingbird.* Better to read than leave her mind free to think.

***

Melissa and Ana trudged into the white sterile building over two hours later and inspected the facility's directory. They took the elevator up to the third floor, stood in silence, and stared numbly ahead. Ana was empty except for the hollow echo in her chest.

She went through a series of routine tests before waiting for the doctor. The room was like all the others she had visited in the past, stark white and so well sterilized it gleamed. Ana perched on the padded blue exam table, secured her hands under her legs, and studied the boring pattern on the wallpaper border that ran along the edge of the ceiling.

A woman with a cart came in to take an EKG of her heart. Ana smelled coffee on her breath. The sour smell turned her stomach. Electrodes were clamped to familiar jelly stickers dispersed across her chest. She held her breath and waited for the technician to finish. After she was done, the cart was wheeled back out and her mother came into the room to wait with her. Melissa gave a smile of encouragement as she sat on a beige seat across the room from her daughter.

After fifteen minutes, another technician came in and led her to a dark room lit only by a television in the corner. A long cushioned table lay next to an ultrasound machine. For what seemed like an eternity, Ana lay still while the tech took images of her chest for the doctor to review. Pure silence filled her ears, and then clicks from the dials on the machine and her swishing heartbeat. The black and gray movements on the monitor made her recall the same images throughout the years when her mom held her hand, encouraging her to be patient. She didn't require a cartoon to lie stationary any longer or her mother's presence. Instead, she counted the swishy beats in boredom.

Finally, the technician handed Ana a towel to clean the ultrasound jelly off her chest and said, "We're all done here. You can go back to your room after you clean yourself up."

Melissa was in the waiting room when she returned. The florescent lights made the bags under her eyes more obvious, which posed the question – had her mother been getting any sleep? Ana flashed her eyes past the window and realized it had begun to rain since she left the waiting room.

"It's raining," she said.

"It started after you left – gotta love Washington."

Melissa gave a weak smile. Perched woodenly in her chair, the wear began to show from the long wait in anticipation of the doctor's arrival.

After Ana stared out the window at the dreary scenery for another twenty minutes, there was a soft knock on the door and the doctor entered. She had black curly hair and a slight build. She wore a maroon blouse with a long flowing black skirt. A stethoscope hung around her neck. She smiled warmly at them as she stretched out her hand first to Melissa, then to Ana.

"Hello, I'm Dr. Tilgan. I hear you just moved from Colorado. Dr. Schelling was your doctor there?"

Ana gave a nod of confirmation, not ready to speak yet. Unsure she even had a voice.

"Well, it's a pleasure to meet you Ana – and this must be your mom?" Dr. Tilgan looked at Melissa with a questioning expression.

"Yes. I'm Melissa Hughes," Melissa answered quickly, clearly ready to move the conversation past introductions.

"Well, I've spoken to Dr. Schelling, and we reviewed your history. I've also taken a look at the tests we ran on you today. I understand you were told that your Cardiomyopathy was getting worse, right?" She waited for a response, and Ana was only able to whisper in affirmation.

Dr. Tilgan continued. "Your heart muscle is thickening at an increased rate and has been for the last year. It's enlarging and hardening your heart, making your medication less effective. Your move to a lower elevation may have initially given you a boost, but it appears your condition hasn't stabilized and is continuing to degrade." She softened her gaze and said, "I know Dr. Schelling spoke to you about transplants as well..." The doctor slowed in her progression, and adapted her face to match the mood, cautious and serious. "If you deteriorate to a certain point...we should consider placing you on the transplant list. We may not be there yet, but I want you to be prepared for that possibility."

Melissa cleared her throat and adjusted in her seat.

Dr. Tilgan smiled, and soft lines creased around her eyes. "Because you were born with heart defects, they were tracking your heart function anyway. I understand this is how they discovered the Cardiomyopathy? You're lucky – many people don't know they have it until it's too late. Any vigorous activity can cause the heart to stop. You're fortunate to be aware of it. You avoid strenuous activity, of course?"

Ana nodded in response.

"Well, I see Dr. Schelling has tried a variety of different medications..." she said, as she flipped through the thick folder of papers. "You know...I'd like to try bumping up your dosages and see if it makes any difference." She scribbled on her prescription notepad and handed Ana a couple sheets. "I can see you've had your share of heart cath's and don't hate me, but I'd like to personally take a closer look at your heart before we discuss any other treatments. I want to rule out any other disorders, just to be sure." She faced Melissa and gave a gentle grin. "So, if it works for you, I'd like to schedule you for a heart catheterization soon because of your deteriorating condition. I don't want us to get to the point of transplant. I'd prefer exhausting all avenues before getting to that point. At least you aren't currently on the brink of failure, and your liver and lungs haven't begun to show too much wear and tear – which is good. Do either of you have any questions for me?"

Ana and Melissa stared at each other. Melissa was the one who spoke up. "At what point *would* you recommend a transplant?" She stumbled over the word transplant, as it got stuck in her mouth.

"Well...if Ana begins to have trouble with lung congestion and liver enlargement, or if the heart begins destabilizing and we are worried about failure but we don't want it to get to that point. We need to be aggressive, that's why I want to take a look inside soon. Do you have any questions about the cath?"

Ana shook her head. She had been through countless heart catheterizations. The process was usually just a day procedure. They would go in through the artery in her neck or thigh to feed the tiny camera into her heart and observe the heart's function. She would only need to stay for a couple of hours afterwards to make sure the entry points wouldn't re-open and cause bleeding.

Dr. Tilgan shook hands with Melissa and faced Ana. "Well, it was nice meeting the two of you. And Ana, keep up on your medicine and avoid *any* activity that raises your blood pressure. Otherwise, we'll see you back here in the next couple of weeks. I'll let the scheduler know up front."

There it was. What Ana had been waiting for.

"This sucks," Ana said. Numbness spread through her body. Time suspended in the room as she gazed at the cars driving through the stormy weather and the people running out of the rain to the dry safety of their cars or offices.

"I know, baby." Her mom reached out and held her hand. Melissa took a deep breath and continued. "You can do this. You're the strongest person I know. I knew it the moment the doctor handed you to me, all swaddled in your baby blanket. I saw your tenacity and courage. You've had to go through surgeries, and you even started taking medicine before you could eat solid food.

"I'll be there for you, and so will Eva. I'll do whatever I need to for you. Let's just wait and see what the cath results are. Let's not jump to conclusions yet."

"Right...thanks, Mom." Ana pushed the frantic emotions away and welcomed the calm that her mother had inspired. She knew she could do this. The thought of tubes sticking out of her chest again and the staples down her sternum like she was a Frankenstein freak made her cringe. She had been on the bypass machine before; she could do it again.

If she had to.

What other choice was there? Her fighting spirit rose. Maybe she wouldn't need a transplant after all. *Maybe this doctor will be different... maybe she'll fix me*, she thought halfheartedly.

Then again, maybe not.

They stood up and left the room, escaping the sterile environment only to enter the rain that pelted the parking lot. Ana preferred the rain to the white walled numbness. At least she could feel her skin out in the rain. It was wet and cold.

CHAPTER 22

Chance arrived at school late.

He didn't really want to be there, but figured it would help keep his mind engaged until the afternoon.

He gave up trying to stay focused on his studies and lumbered through each period with a callous scowl frozen on his face. The teachers and other students sensed his mood and stayed clear of him, giving him a wide berth as they passed him in the hallway.

When the final bell rang, he trudged to his truck and got in. He sat, glaring at the trees until most of the parking lot emptied. The roar of the engine tore into his ears and filled his head with a resonant thunder. The thoughts that tormented him throughout the day fell silent. *Ahh*.

Work was slow at Kenny's shop. For once. Chance had already stocked the auto parts earlier that week when the shipment came in. Kenny was busy at work on the only car there.

"Why don't you take off? I don't have much for you today. Go see that girlfriend of yours," Kenny said from under the hood of a sedan.

"Right."

Of all days.

Patience wasn't one of his strong suits. He needed to keep his mind distracted. In a snap decision, he jumped into his glossy black truck and rumbled down the road.

He wanted to be close by whenever Ana called, unable to wait longer than he had to. Her street was just up ahead.

Dust billowed behind him as he tore down the road and rumbled past her driveway. The dark sedan was gone and the house was lifeless.

He continued down the gravel drive a short distance, then pulled over and got out. The obscured sky reflected the turmoil inside him. The only thing missing was thunder.

Chance walked through a field of tall grasses and approached a grove of firs as the branches called to him.

CHAPTER 23

Melissa dropped Ana off at home before she went to pick Eva up at her sister's house. Rain continued until they got to the western edge of the lake and cleared once they reached Clark Bend. Clouds remained in the sky in a threatening posture.

Ana walked into the house and went up to her room, turned on the light, and slumped over on her bed. She stared at the time. It was after four-thirty already.

It was time.

She pulled her phone out of her pocket and called Chance. After the first ring, he picked up. His voice was raspy and sounded relieved.

"Finally. I missed you today. It's good hearing your voice."

"I missed you, too." Ana's throat closed up and her voice came out strangled. Afraid to commit to speech, she was at a loss for words.

"Is it time? Can I come over?"

"Yes." *Let's get it over with,* Ana thought, as she picked at her finger nails.

"Be there in a minute."

The line went dead. She stood to pull a sweatshirt over her head and left the hood up. Her bleak silhouette slunk downstairs and lingered near the front door to wait. Trapped by her worst fears.

Ana heard tires on the driveway, and then a soft tap swiftly followed. Her hand paused on the door before she let him in.

When his face appeared, relief and sadness flushed through her.

Then Ana sank into him. She needed to feel his warmth against her. His spicy scent made her eyes snap shut, while she drank in each breath.

She reluctantly pulled away to look at him. "I thought we could go out to the rock to talk. Do you mind?" she said, frightened of what lay ahead of her. She was petrified to lose him; he had become necessary in her life, and it caused physical pain to think about life without him. Even though it was cold and dreary outside, she wanted to be at her gazing stone. The minerals that formed the rock had been in existence for millions of years, and that thought lent her inner strength.

"Sure." He slunk in and grabbed her hand, anchoring himself to her. The tight grip he held her with seemed desperate, protective.

The dank forest blocked the clouds overhead and left the wilderness a murky gray. It didn't seem to improve when they emerged out the other side of Ana's sanctuary.

Side by side, they faced the inky green vista. Chance waited, lifeless as a statue, for Ana to start.

As though she threw herself from a ledge, she started without any forethought. "I've been keeping something from you. It wasn't done to be hurtful. I just wanted to know what it felt like to be *normal* for once."

She concentrated on her lap a moment more before she continued. "I know you've noticed how tired I get. There's a reason." She exhaled sharply. "I was born with heart defects and a disease that hardens my heart. The condition is getting worse. My heart's enlarging and hardening." She forced her eyes to the trees and scratched her temple. "One of the reasons we moved here was because it's a lower altitude than Denver. It makes it easier for my heart to function. With my Aunt Tera here, it's convenient if we need help."

Chance brushed his thumb on Ana's hand. She studied their entwined fingers and continued on, unable to lift her gaze. "I was at my doctor's appointment today...in Spokane. My doctor scheduled me for a heart cath. She wants to take a closer look at my heart function, to see why I keep getting worse. Soon I may be..." *You're almost there, Ana – just say it.* "I may have to be put on the transplant list. But the good news is I'm not there – yet."

There. She said it.

Instantaneously her chest was light and free. But then the despair began to set in. She didn't want to wait for his almost certain awkward reaction. *How else do you respond to something like that?* She couldn't bear to see him squirm, and she continued before he could react. "So...I know it was terrible of me not to tell you. And I understand if this is too much to take. It's okay...it was too much for my dad also. I don't blame you for not wanting to get involved in...all of this. It isn't your battle. I'm sorry I dragged you into my crazy life. I hope you can forgive me." She stared at her hands.

***

Chance sat in stunned silence.

How could she ever think I would leave her? If this was how it had to be, so be it. He adored her. If he could only have her for a short time, then he would take what he could get.

This explained her doleful behavior over the last week. He sensed her grasp at their time together as though it were limited. Then he realized that their time *could* be limited. He just hadn't realized how sick she really was. Everything fell into place. The scar on her chest and her constant exhaustion, her anxiety about hiking, all flooded his memories. A tidal wave of compassion almost drowned him.

Ana fidgeted with her hands as Chance remained silent. Finally, he turned and fell under the spell of her green eyes. Chance absorbed her face into the palms of his hands and said in gentle exasperation. "Ana! Where'd you get the idea I was going anywhere? I could never leave you. Anyway, your life isn't any crazier than mine. Sorry to disappoint you."

"Whaat?" she stuttered.

Chance laughed in frustration.

"I can't believe you thought I'd leave."

Tears welled, and Ana began to cry. With her head buried in her hands, he was able to make out her smothered voice. "It's what happens though."

Chance gently removed her hands from her face to meet his gaze.

"You mean your dad?"

Her teary eyes met his. "Yeah. It was too much for him – I *know it*. Chance, you don't know how it's been tearing me up inside keeping this from you."

"I *do* know." Chance's expression grew dark.

Ana snuggled into his side while he wrapped his arms around her and closed his eyes in concentration. "So – have the doctor's done everything they can? Is there any medicine or treatment that could help you?" Fear gripped him. He never thought this might be how everything would work out – he was powerless, something he wasn't used to.

"They've tried different medications," she said. "I had a valve replacement surgery a couple of years ago. Anyway, I've been a dutiful guinea pig for the doctors." She shrugged. "This is where we've wound up."

"When is this thing? What's it called?"

"Two weeks from today. A heart catheterization. They'll feed a long wire with a camera up into my heart to watch the heart work. I'll only be there for the day but I'll be sedated while they do it. I've had it done lots of times."

***

Chance sat in silence and thought about what she said. How could he help her? What he really wanted to do was go home and talk to his mother and grandfather. He needed to understand everything better.

He sympathized with the reason she hadn't told him, which brought him closer to her. He understood her reason.

The need to feel normal.

It all became clear – why he was so protective of her. Why his instincts had warned him. He knew she was in danger, and now he knew from what.

Ana's true depth of character struck him. He admired her strength. They were so similar, and it frustrated him that he couldn't share it with her.

"So, tell me the rules. What are you allowed to do?" Chance wanted to make sure he never pushed her too far. He didn't want to hurt her. If the walks were too much, he would sit on the couch and play board games with her. As long as they were together, he would be satisfied.

"Well, I'm supposed to avoid exertion. If my heart becomes too agitated it *could* stop," she said and looked away. "I self regulate though. I don't do anything that tires me out. I think I can still go on walks with you as long as I go slowly and it isn't too elevated."

Chance thought about the times she almost fainted, like when they kissed on the island. He had sensed her heart race and wondered if he had inadvertently hurt her.

"What if your heart races *too* much? When we were at the lake…" He didn't know how to ask, a bit self conscious. Ana's brow wrinkled. Chance held her cheek in the palm of his hand and leaned closer. Both of their hearts raced in anticipation. Chance stopped and searched her eyes. "I don't want to hurt you. Let me know if this is too much." He withdrew a little to see comprehension flit across Ana's face, followed by a rosy blush. "Oh," she said.

She leaned in closer, rested her forehead against his and closed her eyes. He rested his hand gently on her neck and sensed her heartbeat go from a quick sporadic beat to a slower, controlled rhythm within a few minutes.

Ana leaned in until her lips brushed against his like a butterfly's wing gracing the tip of a flower. She pulled away with her eyes closed and said, "I think with practice. I can do it without causing my heart any trouble."

Chance smiled, as his own heart pounded away, and laughed. "At least *I* don't have to worry about *mine*."

Serious again, he touched her cheek. "Thanks for telling me. It must have been hard for you. It's better now that I know. I knew something was off." He combed down her stray hairs and suppressed the unease that left him vulnerable.

"How did you know?"

"Well, you got tired after our walks. Your fingers and lips are always purple." He reached up to touch the tip of his finger to her lower lip. He hesitated, wanting to ask one more thing.

Ana said, "What?"

"One day I noticed the faint scar on your chest."

Ana reached up and placed her hand over her scar. "Why didn't you ask me then? If you noticed so much, you must have known something was wrong. Why didn't you just ask?"

Chance held her gaze while he answered. "I thought if you didn't want to tell me, then I wasn't going to ask. I figured if you wanted me to know, you'd tell me – It didn't really matter *what* your secret was."

***

Ana breathed out her response in gratitude and said, "Thanks. I never realized. I knew you understood me – I just didn't know how well." She smiled at him.

She felt lucky. Something completely foreign to her. She reached down and held the Thunderbird talisman between her fingers while the anxiety in her stomach lifted away.

Eva's voice broke the quiet and lifted above the trees. "AAAANNNNNNAAAAA!" The loud call disturbed nearby birds, spurring them to take flight.

"She hasn't gotten to see me yet. We should go back."

Before Ana could raise herself from the ground, Chance

stood next to her with his hand extended. She accepted his help and was lifted upright slowly.

Chance held her for a moment and smiled. Bliss radiated from her as she identified his protectiveness. This was something she could adjust to.

Ana didn't need to be strong enough to endure in silence any longer. Finally, she had someone to lean on for support.

As they walked hand in hand into the house, Melissa and Eva watched them with silent, cautious eyes. Ana put their curiosity to rest. "It's okay – I told him."

The relief was obvious on Melissa's face as she sighed and rubbed her temples. Eva shrugged as though it never mattered much anyway, she embraced her sister so tight that Ana coughed in surprise.

Eva smiled and said, "I missed you today. Mom told me you have to go back in two weeks though. Can I go to *that* one?"

Ana and Eva turned to their mother. She seemed bothered and took a minute to respond. The pressure built in Eva's lanky body. Her tight hold around Ana's waist forced her to touch her sister's arm in reminder. Eva loosened her grip and looked back at her mother in disappointment.

"I'm not sure what to do about that. I just started this job, and my boss has been very understanding, but I'm just not sure if I can take another day off so soon. Tera said that she could take you Ana, but then Eva would be waiting around all day as well – and, now, don't get mad, but I just don't want you there, Eva." Melissa lifted her brows as a challenge to Eva's pouty lower lip. "I'd rather you stay in school. The clinic's no place for you – you should be with your friends, continuing your daily schedule."

Chance raised his hand. "*I* can take Ana. It's not a problem taking the day off. My parents wouldn't mind, and to be honest I'd prefer being there than waiting here. If it's okay with you." He asked politely, but Ana heard the determination laced in the offer.

Melissa embraced Chance, and choked out, "Thank you."

Chance flushed.

"I should probably leave you guys to relax after your long day. I have a couple things I need to do anyway."

"Okay, Chance. Thanks, again. We'll see you later." Melissa smiled and dabbed at her reddened eyes with a Kleenex.

He shuffled out of the house with Ana beside him.

They stopped at his truck, and he secured her against him and initiated their goodbye. Ana welcomed the intimacy, now that her protective barrier had been splintered into oblivion. There didn't seem to be any reason left to push him away except habit. A habit she was cautious to break.

Chance pulled back some stray hairs from her bewildered face and tenderly said, "I'll call you later. We can set something up for tomorrow – if you're up to it."

Ana nodded, speechless, and then backed away from the truck. She watched him drive off in silence, as the numbness crept in. The day had been overwhelming. There was so much for her to process. She had not been prepared for Chance's response.

She stumbled through the front door and into the welcome arms of her mother who waited in the living room. Ana cried so hard at first it was silent, but then it grew into a torrent of gasps and sobs. Melissa smoothed her hair and rubbed her back in large circles.

"I know, baby. it's been a long day."

CHAPTER 24

"What are you going to work on at Aunt Tera's today?" Ana asked.

"She's gonna show me how to make pot roast," Eva said, her eyes wide. She slipped a notebook into her backpack with bold block letters written on the top, *Recipes*.

"Mmm, can't wait to try it," Ana said enthusiastically and flung her bag over her shoulder.

Over the last two weeks, while Ana bathed in the refuge Chance offered, Eva had hung out at Aunt Tera's house every day after school and became her aunt's sidekick.

From the regular exposure to Aunt Tera's cooking prowess, Eva's knowledge expanded past hitting buttons on the microwave and boiling water. Now a budding chef, she discovered a whole new frontier she had never been exposed to before.

Melissa and Ana watched in awe as Eva flitted across the kitchen, grabbing pans and fresh ingredients, to create nutritious dinners that she planned with Aunt Tera's help. Most of them were even edible.

With Eva occupied, Ana was able to enjoy her time with Chance even more.

She looked forward to their walk that afternoon. It was their last opportunity to relax and unwind before the trip up to Spokane the next day. Ana tried not to think about the outcome of the procedure and was focused on how Chance was taking it. He soldered on in silence, which made her nervous.

With a vice grip on the steering wheel of her van, she drummed her fingers in rhythm with the radio music and glanced over at Eva who was content, doodling in her notebook.

Ana stared at the lines on the road and recalled the last couple of weeks. She and Chance savored their time together along hidden trails that entwined the mountainside behind his house, but never got very far before Ana required a rest. Chance waited, like a silent guardian by her side until she was able to continue, and offered his hand when needed.

She ambled beside his powerful body like the tortoise being escorted by the hare. An unlikely pair, though neither was interested in the finish line.

Nothing could match her blissful contentment right now, a strange new emotion which took some getting used to.

The middle school came into view, and Ana dropped Eva off at the curb.

"Bye, Ana. See you later – have fun today!"

"Bye, D. Love you!" She waved as she pulled away.

Throughout the day Ana noticed how quiet Chance seemed. Every time she faced him and smiled, he returned a grin, but his eyes were distant and gray.

Now, as she stared at familiar scenery fly past her window as he drove, Ana turned to study Chance's face. His features were tight and drawn, and she wondered what he was thinking about.

***

Chance glared at the cloudy gloom outside; the weather matched his mood. While he drove up the hill he recalled that earth shattering night Ana revealed her secret.

After he left her house, he sped home to tell his family. His mother was saddened and grilled Chance on Ana's condition so she could teach him more about it. But he sat with deaf ears, unable to hear anything.

Niyol remained silent and offered no response. That night he took Chance out for an evening hike so they could talk, although that did little to calm Chance's fears. Grandfather couldn't offer him what he wanted. Maybe he wanted too much.

He frowned and tightened his grip on the wheel, and his knuckles turned white.

Ana looked at him from the corner of her eyes, scooted closer to him and rested her head on his shoulder. He relaxed at her touch.

"So, did you let the school know you're going to be absent tomorrow?" Ana asked, her tone calm and light.

"Yeah. Turned in a note. Also printed out the directions and filled up the truck. Ready." But the tone of his voice said otherwise.

"So am I. I have everything I need packed in my bag." Ana touched his arm and said, "Don't forget I've done this plenty of times before – it's old hat." She sat up and played with her necklace between her fingers, regarding him from the corner of her eye.

"Right...I keep forgetting."

Ana caught the distressed twitch of his hands. His fingers grasped the wheel so tight they blanched from pressure.

The familiar sloped roof came into view and Chance visibly relaxed when he saw it, exhaling with a soft hiss.

After they popped into the house to greet his father and grandfather, they went outside to take one last walk before their road-trip the next day.

The habitual walk always satisfied. There was no need to ask any longer; it was assumed they wished to be outside together.

"Are you nervous?" Ana asked Chance and reached for his hand as they began along one of the trails that led south down the mountain through a dense grove of pine trees.

Chance grabbed Ana's fingers. His thumb brushed hers in a skittish movement as he said, "A little."

"I'll be fine. It's just a simple procedure – I've done it plenty of times." She rubbed his shoulder with her free hand.

"I know. I just *hate* thinking about you lying helpless. I just don't like it," he frowned.

"Thanks for caring." Ana kissed his cheek affectionately, trying to lighten the mood.

Chance slowed down. This was the point in the trail Ana usually required a rest. He turned with a softened expression, and caressed her cheek, which evoked a shiver down her spine like a feather drawn down her back.

"Of *course* I do." A half bewildered and crazed expression touched his eyes and shocked Ana. He pulled her near and stared at her lips.

She knew he was holding off, waiting to see if she was ready. Ana leaned in, let her lips brush against his, but kept it brief to retain control of her hysterical heart. His hands grasped her shoulders, and she saw a hunger reflected within his eyes. He withdrew slowly and his eyes focused on the trail. A slight frown crossed his face, and he dug his hands into his pockets.

"I want to take you someplace new. It's just up ahead. Take another minute to rest, and I'll lead you there."

His eyes traced the branches above as they sat on some mossy stones that lined the worn trail. Distracted by mountain jays flitting between trees, the forest eased Ana's mind. After her body calmed, she stood and found Chance at her side almost immediately. His quick movements were often hard to anticipate. It was something she admired but didn't understand.

"Ready?"

The words whispered in her ear brought featherlike chills to her skin again.

He led her to a rocky embankment that formed a high craggy peak.

"Hold on. Wait here a second – I see something I want to get you."

Chance climbed up the rocky ledge behind them. He scaled the embankment like an experienced mountaineer and quickly reached an upper precipice thirty feet above her.

He examined something at his feet, leaned down and picked it up. Then he turned to climb back down and descended the rocky face. Rocks tumbled free. Chance flung himself aside from the falling shale, as chunks just missed his head but hit his forearm and ricocheted off.

"Careful, Chance!" Ana alerted too late.

He continued his descent and made his way down to Ana within moments. She rushed over to him and grabbed his arm to inspect the injury.

"Are you hurt?" Ana grew anxious.

"Oh, don't worry – it's nothing." Chance tried to pull his arm from her grasp, but she wouldn't relinquish her hold. Her strength surprised her.

She straightened his arm to determine how bad the injury was. A long scrape ran along his forearm. The top layer of skin was razed off and blood covered the wound. The sight of blood made Ana weak.

"We should go back so we can dress your cut. Maybe your mom has something to put on it," Ana said and tried to pull him back up the trail.

Chance held his ground and grabbed her arm. "It's okay, Ana. Don't worry. It's really not that bad. I'll be fine. I heal fast. Plus, I have something for you." He held out his hand. In it was a long feather. "It's a golden eagle feather. The nest is up the mountain. Sometimes feathers drop down."

She accepted the gift and admired it. "Thank you."

Then she glanced back down at his arm and crinkled her brow. "Um – that looks like it hurts. Are you *sure* you're okay?"

"Yes, don't worry about me." Chance had a cool expression on his face and shrugged. Then he leaned in and kissed her sweetly on the nose before he rubbed her back and asked, "So, are you up for seeing one more thing? No more injuries, I promise."

CHAPTER 25

Early the next morning, Chance waited for Ana at the kitchen table with a full plate of toaster waffles, a banana, yogurt and a tall glass of orange juice.

Melissa provided him with a cornucopia of food. She pushed him down into the seat, smiled, and waited for him to begin. Chance was restless but decided it would be easier to placate Melissa rather than reject her kindness. He grabbed the banana and forced down a couple bites before Ana appeared.

"Want some breakfast? I have plenty," Chance asked, not wanting the responsibility to clear his plate to fall wholly on him.

"I can't," Ana said and cringed.

Chance cursed to himself. "Damn. That's right – I'm sorry. I forgot you can't eat anything." *What an insensitive jerk*. She couldn't eat before anesthesia. As punishment, he force-fed himself while Ana went over some paperwork with Melissa, checking to ensure nothing had been forgotten. Melissa handed Ana a credit card to use for gas and to cover the payment at the clinic. She somberly hugged them both and gave Chance a grateful smile. Melissa's eyes welled up, and she rushed upstairs.

Eva clomped down the stairs one at a time and emerged with a sullen look on her face.

"Don't worry Eva. Everything will be fine. I'll see you tonight. I promise. Have fun at school today, and say hi to Aunt Tera. I love you." Ana tugged her little sister to her and her gave a long embrace. Eva wound her long arms around Ana's waist and snuggled in for a moment and said, "I love you too, Ana." Eva released her and wandered to the stairwell with a despondent backwards glance.

Ana stared at Chance with a barren expression. Chance closed the gap between them and held her close while he caressed her back in little circles. He inhaled Ana's delicious fragrance and imagined himself in the forest with her. Away from there. Away from the reality that he could lose her.

***

Ana procrastinated while she gathered her bag. As she walked through the living room her eyes lingered on the painting over the mantle. She walked over and adjusted it, then touched the eagle soaring over snow-tipped mountains.

Ana closed the front door behind her and stepped outside to join Chance. Too early for the sunrise, the dark morning beckoned her silently. Chance's ebony truck shined in the dark; the lights flashed on, and the engine fired to life.

As they turned out onto the highway Ana said, "Hey, how about a game of I Spy?"

Chance nodded. "Yeah. I warn you though – I'm good."

After half an hour of playing, Ana lost severely, unable to spot anything Chance had.

"Ugh! You're impossible! I can't see anything that matches your description! You have *way* better eyesight than me. I think I need to get my eyes checked." She crossed her arms and then her eyes lit up. "Maybe it's time to play a spelling game." Ana lifted her eyebrows in a playful challenge.

While Ana thought about the next game she glanced at Chance's arm. "Hey...what happened to your scrape? It's gone..." She touched his arm in confusion.

Chance remained silent and grimaced at the highway ahead. "I told you it was nothing. Mom put something on it, and it cleared right up."

Chance continued to stare at the black asphalt that curled through the wilderness. Ana thought he tensed in response to her question.

She frowned at him. "Nothing heals that fast. I saw it – you had like a four-inch scrape on your arm. Where'd it go?

You don't have a mark of any kind on you."

"What can I tell you? I'm fine — obviously." Chance seemed irritated with her questions.

"Geez, if I healed as fast as you..." Ana cut herself short, unable to continue.

Chance closed his eyes and winced. He grasped for her hand.

"I wish you could, too." His strangled voice caught her up short.

For the remainder of the drive they sat in silence. Ana slid over so Chance could wrap his arm around her. The quiet spoke volumes.

At the heart clinic, they walked hand in hand to the admissions desk. Chance sat in silence beside Ana as she signed forms and completed the necessary paperwork. He watched people pass by with a blank expression.

As Ana rose, he joined her, clutched her cool limp hand, and walked with her into the elevator. An awkward hush fell in the cold iron vault. When the doors chimed and opened, they stepped out.

She approached another desk where a girl, who looked barely older than herself, sat. The girl smiled and appraised Chance with her eyes as she asked for Ana's name. "If you go sit down, someone will be out to get you soon."

Ana abruptly wandered over to the outdated seating area. She was pleased Chance seemed oblivious to the receptionist's attention. Then she noticed he seemed oblivious to everything. As though lost in a fog, his eyes seemed unfocused. She wanted to comfort him, but was too numb to try, and leaned against his chest. He wrapped her in his limp arms, and she took a deep breath.

"Ana Hughes?"

Ana's head snapped up and saw a woman dressed in blue scrubs with a clipboard. The nurse smiled at them, and Ana reluctantly withdrew from Chance's arms.

The nurse led them down a hallway illuminated by windows that blinded them with morning sun light. She pulled a badge out, paused at an indistinguishable door and swiped a security sensor to unlock it. She stopped Chance, and asked, "Are you a family member?"

His shoulders slumped as he stared down at the blue Berber carpeting and said, "No."

"I'm sorry, Honey. I can only allow family in now. I promise I'll come update you as soon as there's news. I wouldn't expect anything within the next two hours though. There's a TV down in the lounge and free coffee if you'd like. You can come see her in recovery once we're through." She touched his shoulder, then with sympathetic eyes, said, "Ana, I'll give you a minute to say goodbye. Come into room two – it's just there on the left after you enter. I'll be waiting for you. 'Kay, Honey?"

Ana nodded and held the door open as the nurse disappeared down the hallway. She lifted her face to peer into Chance's deadened eyes.

"Oh, that's right." She dropped her head and unclasped her necklace. "Would you hold onto this for me...until I wake up?" She lowered the chain and pendant into his palm, and he closed his fingers around it.

He moved into Ana, caught her up within his tight embrace, and lifted her off the ground.

Incapable of repressing a giggle, she laughed, thankful Chance was with her. The part of her heart that had never been reached before felt alive, even if it was clumsy and irregular. No doctor could heal her the way he had.

She gazed into his deep hazel eyes and let her cool lips brush against his. Chance seemed to wake from his distant exile and returned the attention she initiated. Ana's chest squeezed tight, caught up with excitement and she gave in. The heart clinic was the best place for a kiss like this. She grew lightheaded and faltered. Chance pulled back suddenly, the fire still present in his eyes.

"I'm sorry," he breathed. "I got carried away." He stared at his feet and his jaw tightened.

A shadow crossed his features, and Ana drifted her fingers along his temple, and shrugged carelessly. "You can carry me away any time. Don't worry. I'll be fine." With a mischievous smile she added, "I'll beg the nurses to let you in as soon as I wake up." She looked down at the ground. "I really appreciate you being here. See you soon. And, thanks – for everything." She lifted up on her toes and kissed his eyelids.

***

When his eyes opened, she was already gone, the door swung shut with a loud and final *thud*.

CHAPTER 26

Blurry shapes phased into view as Ana blinked. She moved her head to see where she was. Her limbs were heavy and sluggish, and an unpleasant metallic taste filled her mouth. Consciousness returned like the sun creeping above the horizon, slow but intense. As the anesthesia wore off, her eyes cleared, and she remembered where she was.

"Welcome back," a cheerful voice echoed in her ears.

She tilted her head on the table and focused on a bright face above her.

"Hi, I'm Jenny. You've been out for a while. Everything went well. They didn't have any problems going in through the femoral artery. I was just checking the entry point on your leg now. How's it feel?"

Cool air touched Ana's legs, and she realized she was uncovered as the nurse carefully lifted the edge of her gown to peek underneath.

"Ouuch, ewww, that hurts." Ana winced.

"Well, it looks good. I'll get you something for the pain." Jenny patted her arm and said, "I think Sue just went to go bring in your – boyfriend? Brother?"

Ana cleared the bitter gravel from her throat and weakly answered. "Boyfriend." That was a first. The first time she used the title. That's what he was, right?

Suddenly apprehensive, she touched her face with her deadened hand. How did she look? Ill probably. How would Chance react to her pale skin and gaunt eyes? She normally didn't care how she looked, but now she worried this could be the final straw. He may not have realized what it would really be like, to see her go through...all of this. Hospitals made even the strongest people quake in fear.

"You don't...have a mirror I can use...do you?" Ana stammered as she noticed Nurse Jenny's strong penchant for cosmetics.

The nurse disappeared then scurried back with a black compact. "You'd better hurry up. He's on his way in."

Ana grabbed the mirror and opened it to assess the damage. She readjusted her gown and combed through her hair with her fingers to flatten the strays against the bed. She rubbed her puffy eyes and pinched her cheeks to brighten her color. Well, there wasn't much she could do except hope her appearance wouldn't rattle Chance. She tossed the compact back to the nurse and said, "Thanks."

***

Chance followed a plump nurse through the long recovery ward, past curtained cubicles and heard the low murmur of voices and intermittent beeps. Disinfectant tangled with a metallic smell made him queasy. The bleak and unnatural surroundings left a hollow feeling inside of him. He wasn't sure how his mother could stay so positive working in a place like this.

As Ana came into view, sickness and elation rushed to his stomach. Immobilized and very pale, she smiled up at him and held her hand out. It had been the longest three hours of Chance's life. His anxious pacing in the waiting room provoked equal parts of understanding smiles and annoyed glances.

He approached her swiftly and stopped beside the bed. His hand found hers, and like two magnets, they snapped together.

***

Ana tried to adopt a peaceful expression on her face. She took a deep breath and visualized her body sinking into the bed beneath her. Punch-drunk with drooping eyes, she opened them wide to appear alert. Her heavy body felt like it was submerging into the mattress, and she noticed the nurse inject something into her IV. She fought to keep her eyes open but found the back of her eyelids particularly soothing.

Soon she floated through the clouds with Chance by her side. Everything slowed and grew heavy, and her consciousness fell into darkness.

When Ana woke again, Chance sat beside her with his hand resting on her arm. The pulse of her blood pounded just below the weight of his fingertips.

Chance squeezed her wrist. "Hey, there. Just when I was beginning to miss those green eyes."

Ana turned her head and regarded his calm face; his amber eyes glimmered in the florescent lights. All traces of worry and fear that were visible earlier had been replaced with a serenity that surprised her.

She cleared what felt like rough debris from her achy throat and winced as her groin flared up in pain. "What'd I miss? Has the doctor come by?"

"No, not yet, but your nurse says it should be soon."

He glanced down the table toward the source of her discomfort, and she followed his gaze suspiciously.

"What *else* happened?" she said, unsure of what he saw.

Darkness visited his face and then disappeared as quickly as it came. He shrugged, but his eyes grew serious. "You started bleeding. They had to put pressure on it for a while." He frowned and stared at his hand.

"Are you okay?" she said, her voice barely cleared her throat.

He sat stone still. "I don't want you to worry about me, Ana. I'm fine. What about you? You seem sore."

Just then, she realized she was clutching the bed, her body taut. She tried releasing the tension in her limbs and smoothed a smile across her face. "No. I'm good." The soreness at the entry point radiated down her leg. She boxed it up and kept it away from her thoughts. It took all her effort.

***

As convincing as she was, Chance didn't believe her. *Does she really think I can't see through her?* Although, if he were the one on the table, he'd probably say the same thing. But the only difference was, he'd never wind up on the table.

Chance adjusted in his seat and pulled out Ana's necklace from his back pocket. He fumbled as he reached around her neck to fasten the clasp, and it took him a couple of tries.

"Much better. I missed seeing it on you."

She lifted her hand to touch the metal shape. "Thanks...I missed it too." Then she curled her cool fingers around his. "So, how about Mom? Have you...talked to her?"

Chance chuckled, and said, "Oh, every hour since we got here!" His eyes traced her face. "It's hard for her not being here." He thought about the day he was left to himself and his anxieties. If it were him, he'd be up a tree already. By the strain in Melissa's voice, Chance could tell she was holding on by a thread.

"How much more time do we have to wait? What time is it anyway?" Ana glanced at the clock on the wall.

"You came out from the procedure at quarter after one, and it's five o'clock now." As he spoke, Chance noticed a woman walk toward them. "Is that your doctor?"

Ana lifted her head off the bed and nodded.

The curly haired woman approached with a kind, creased smile. It looked like she hadn't slept in days, each sleepless hour added a dark circle to her tired eyes. As she stopped at the bed, she unwound the stethoscope from her shoulders and cupped the metal end in her hand.

"Hi Ana, how are you feeling?" Dr. Tilgan said, with a softened grin. "I understand your entry point opened up a while ago? Let me take a peek." Chance focused on Ana's face as the doctor lifted her gown.

"I feel fine. I'm ready to go!" She delivered a bright grin, which turned into a grimace. Ana with a forced smile was unfamiliar to Chance. It was unnatural.

"Well, the entry point looks good. If you can keep some liquids down, then we could have you out of here within the hour." The doctor patted Ana's leg and covered her up with a folded blanket. She called over to a nurse for some water and ice chips before she refocused on Ana. Dr. Tilgan's expression grew serious. A jolt of fear pierced his chest.

"So, Ana. We got some very clear images of your heart. We were able to confirm the thickening and hardening to an extent I'm not happy with. How have you been feeling with the increased dosage of medication?"

Ana frowned. "Well, I haven't really noticed a difference..."

Dr. Tilgan nodded and paused. "Hmm, okay. I plan on presenting your case to the board, and we'll see if we can come up with another approach. At least your lungs aren't congested. I want to keep a close eye on you, Ana. I don't want you getting to the point of transplant." She frowned, and looked between Ana's and Chance's faces.

"Do you have any questions for me?"

Chance sat numbly and tried to register what the doctor said.

"No, no questions," Ana said. "When do you want me back?"

"Come back in one month – no more. I want to continue monitoring you closely. Keep up on your medication. And it's *very important* you don't overexert yourself. Don't push yourself; your heart can't take it."

The doctor distractedly glanced to the other end of the recovery ward where loud voices were raised above the beeping machinery, and added. "I'm sorry, but I need to check in with another patient – I'll get your paperwork going so you guys can take off quickly."

Chance listened to the doctor's footfalls until they faded away.

***

Ana was afraid to look at Chance. Although she had grown to need him, like air to breathe, she would rather not see him suffer through the heartache ahead. If this dose of reality was too much, she would understand.

His fingers entwined hers, and she closed her eyes as a wet stream began to flow down her cheeks.

He wiped away her tears and kissed her eyes.

When he met her gaze, she was alarmed. What she saw reflected in Chance's normally benevolent features made her think of a wild animal.

CHAPTER 27

On the drive home Ana sipped a clear soda the nurses gave her. She observed that Chance's fierceness had faded. He was once again the kindhearted, tender person she knew.

For part of the drive, she fell asleep. It had been a rough day.

While Ana's eyes remained closed, Chance held her hand and traced his thumb rhythmically along hers.

She awoke as they approached her home. Ana was relieved she didn't have to face her family when she told them the news. She had called her mom from the clinic before they left to tell her what the doctor had said. Melissa appeared to take it in stride over the phone, but something in her voice left her daughter questioning how well she had really taken the news.

When they drove up to the familiar blue house, Ana was eager to see her family. If she could only make it through the evening without all the doting and fussing, it would be painless.

The front door of the house burst open in a flurry of movement.

Melissa wrenched open the door on Ana's side and hugged her before she could get out.

"Mom! You could at least let me out first!" She laughed weakly and attempted to free her legs.

As she climbed out of the truck, hands reached past her and retrieved her bag. Another set of hands touched her shoulders, and she was pulled into another hug. Lilac filled her senses; Aunt Tera's favorite perfume.

"Oh, Sweetie. We love you." Her aunt's tough-as-nails demeanor broke as her voice cracked with emotion.

Ana was led inside by Melissa and Eva, who sandwiched her between them. Aunt Tera and Uncle Jace positioned themselves alongside Chance as they escorted him through the doorway. Tera gave him a kiss on the cheek.

A feast was laid out on the table and filled the room with smells that roused Ana's deadened appetite. She was mildly hungry for the first time that day. Although only moderately interested in food, she sat down and allowed her loved ones to shower her with attention, while Chance stuck to her side.

"I made the Focaccia bread with Aunt Tera today, and I helped make the soup." Eva said, pointing at the food she contributed.

"It looks delicious, Eva." Ana congratulated her and noted how much she had grown since the move.

"We don't want to tire you out, baby, but we wanted to show you how much you mean to us. Plus, you should really try the soup – it'll be mild on your stomach after anesthesia." Melissa eyed Ana with a troubled look, and added. "Eva and Tera worked on it all afternoon."

Melissa's face seemed flushed.

Thankfully, no one mentioned the results of her procedure and she let her worries ease.

Chance sat like a silent mute throughout dinner and quietly accepted the gratitude and food that was offered. His mind seemed elsewhere; his distraction evident only to her.

Around her, the family kept the evening chatty and light, so she leaned in to Chance and asked, "Are you okay?" She grasped his hot hand within hers and noticed faint creases on his forehead marking his otherwise smooth skin.

"Sure. I'm just tired. I'm fine." He patted her hand and offered a canned smile which threw Ana into immediate suspicion. He was clearly concerned, but there was something more. It seemed like something had been awakened in him that startled her, a new, ragged edge that had never been exposed before.

All too familiar with painful secrets, she sensed he was withholding information, and it began to bite at her.

CHAPTER 28

At nearly eleven o'clock, Ana emerged from behind the door at the end of the hallway. She wandered slowly, reminiscent of a zombie, to the bathroom. The sterile odor from the clinic lingered on her skin. She stumbled into a hot shower to rinse the aroma from her body, satisfied only when the shampoo's fragrance remained.

Ana came downstairs refreshed and heard Melissa announce as soon as her foot touched the bottom stair. "Chance called checking up on you – maybe you should let him know you're okay."

She walked through the kitchen and gave her mother a peck on the cheek. Melissa wore yellow rubber gloves and was busy cleaning the cupboards. All the dishes and glasses were piled along the counters while they awaited their spotless resting places.

Ana arched her eyebrow, shocked at her mother's cleaning madness.

"Well, I haven't given them a good scrub since we moved in. I don't want all those years of dust on our things." Melissa wiped her forehead with the back of one glove.

Ana knew her mom hated cleaning. And she only scrubbed cabinets when she was stressed. Ana gave her mother a smile before she went out onto the back deck to call Chance.

He picked up after the first ring and answered with a casual tone Ana thought sounded a little put on.

"Hey. Mom said you called. I'm fine – just sleeping off the anesthesia from yesterday." She paused to yawn and asked, "What've you been doing?"

She extended her arms above her, careful to avoid a head rush.

"Oh, uh...I'm just out taking a walk with my grandfather."

"That sounds nice. Well, I heard you called earlier checking up on me and wanted to let you know I feel fine

146

today. Much better than yesterday."

"Good. Wanted to check that everything was okay. Say, why don't I call you later when Grandfather and I wrap things up. You rest, maybe hang out with Eva a little, and I'll see you later today."

Ana had the distinct feeling she was being told to sit down and stay put. She didn't mind it coming from Chance, although he was the exception. She didn't like anyone telling her to rest; she resented it.

"Alright. I should hang with Eva anyway, it's been a while. Have fun and I'll talk to you later."

Ana closed her eyes as the sunlight warmed her face. She took a deep inhalation of the brisk fir scent before returning inside to sit beside her sister. The two snuggled on the couch beneath a blanket and watched their favorite animated movie while they ate popcorn.

Afterwards, Ana decided to go upstairs when Melissa pulled out the broom and began to dust the ceiling.

She sat at her computer and remembered the images she had saved to her desktop weeks ago. With the drama of her doctor's appointments, she had entirely forgotten about the photographs. Maybe she had purposefully forgotten them.

She inspected them again and assumed her memory had been off. After all, at the time she had a lot on her mind and probably mistook what she *thought* she saw. The silver glint at the fox's white chest hadn't changed. The bear pendant still dangled from the animal's neck.

The fox's eyes pierced through her. She frowned and began to pick at her desk with her fingernail.

Why would an animal outside her back door have Chance's necklace on? Albeit elaborate, this had to be some kind of silly prank he had played on her. That was the only logical reason she could think of.

Chance must have played tricks on her all along, ever since he spoke of his shaman ancestors, to frighten her or give her a thrill.

Chills ran through her body. Anger welled up, and her cheeks burned. He allowed her to think he healed inhumanly fast, his prowess outdoors – all of it used to demonstrate some kind of weird magical story.

Ana was NOT amused. It was at her expense, and while she was in poor health too. What kind of person was Chance? Obviously not the person she *thought* he was.

She had allowed him into her heart. *I'm a fool.*

Ana bolted downstairs faster than she should have and grabbed her keys.

"I'm running over to Chance's real quick. Be back soon!" Ana called out, flung herself out the front door, and jogged in determination to her van.

She peeled out of the driveway and sped towards Chance's house. Along the way, she considered the fact she could have jumped to conclusions. Maybe he hadn't intended to be cruel. Just the same, he had some answering to do.

When Ana arrived at his driveway, she slowed to a crawl up the gravel road. She sat and stared at a meticulous wood pile at the end of the drive before she got out, revisiting all the unanswered questions in her mind.

She stumbled down the rocky pathway to the front porch, stepped up to the door, and knocked. After a few moments, the door swung open to reveal a surprised Aiyana.

"Hi Ana, how are *you doing* today?" Aiyana said and stared as Ana leaned against the door frame for support.

Ana was so upset when she left her house, she had forgotten about the procedure the day before. It dawned on her why Aiyana was concerned. Foolish and embarrassed, Ana looked down and said, "I'm fine. I just needed to sleep off the anesthesia."

"You sure? Why don't you come in and sit?" Aiyana opened the door wide as she welcomed her inside.

Ana remained where she stood, recalling why she was

there. "Actually, I needed to talk to Chance. Is he here?"

"No. He's still out with his grandfather. I'm not expecting them back for another couple hours. They like finding new paths. When we bought the property, we didn't realize how many trails there were. If you want, I can have him call you when they get back." Aiyana frowned.

Ana faltered and remembered he had said he wouldn't be around until later that afternoon. She shook her head and faced Aiyana. Her shoulders slumped as she said, "That's right. Thanks, Aiyana. As soon as he gets back — it's important."

"Is everything okay?" Aiyana tilted her head.

"I just need to talk to him." Ana backed up. She waved as she departed the porch and walked back down the gravel walkway. Ana heard the door close as she reached the driveway.

Great. She drove all the way out to Chance's house, and he wasn't even home. Anger bubbled up again, and she kicked at the gravel, which sent a piece ricocheting out into the shrubs that lined the drive.

She rested her hand on the van's door handle, about to wrench it open just as a noise tore through the peaceful forest.

Her head whipped around in surprise, and she squinted in the direction it came from in the woods. It sounded like a large mountain cat screeching. A path cut through the forest in the same place as the growl.

"Chance!" Ana yelped, and her stomach writhed.

The cry sounded again, and without any thought, Ana ran up the path. She stumbled past berry bushes, the brambles scratching her arms as she propelled herself forward.

She knew Chance was out hiking with his grandfather on one of these trails. *What if they're in danger?*

Familiar markers moved past her as she continued to a place on the trail that wasn't familiar to her. She dropped her head down and grabbed her knees to catch her breath as it tore through her throat like fire. Ana's heart pounded from exertion and fear. Willpower kept her upright.

Suddenly, the screech called out again, but this time much closer. A quick intake of breath sent a shooting pain down her throat. Ana imagined a pair of menacing eyes watching her from the bushes, and she gave a whimper. With urgency she moved sideways up the mountainside and forced herself forward, but her body cried for rest. Her run through the forest had become a dangerous and regrettable choice. She didn't know where Chance was, and now she was lost. And more significantly, in danger.

If she could just find her voice, she would call out to Chance. But if she *did* call out, it could lead the mountain lion right to her. Ana's heart hammered in a perilous and irregular rhythm, which caused her to stumble on the rugged earthen path.

She stopped at the top of a ridge to view the grassy valley below that was encircled with pine trees. Her feet tripped over themselves as she followed the trail to the basin. She searched the terrain from the shaded scrub brush to the tree trunks, fearful of the wild beast lurking. Her whole body ripped in pain, but she forged ahead.

She toppled into a tree near the bottom and allowed the trunk to hold her upright. All she could hear was her blood pounding in her ears.

Then she heard voices.

Chance's voice.

"I held it better that time. I think I'm getting it now. How did I look?"

Her eyesight played games with her. Two forms stood in the clearing, but they were blurry and doubled.

She rubbed her eyes and was able to identify Chance. He was only wearing a pair of jeans, which he was in the process of buttoning up. His broad chest was uncovered. If she wasn't terrified for his safety, she would have appreciated his muscular form. He held a gray shirt, ready to pull it on and his feet were bare. *That's an odd way to go hiking.*

Niyol stood before Chance and spoke so low Ana could barely hear his voice over the blood pounding in her ears. "You held form. It seemed easier for you this time."

Ana remembered why she ran into the woods and stumbled forward. As she passed the last trees to enter the grassy valley, Chance and his grandfather spun around, clearly surprised at her presence.

"Ana! What are you *doing* here?!" Chance asked and dropped his shirt to the ground.

Ana's head grew cloudy, and she sank into a darkening abyss. "Look out...for the...cougar."

"Ana!"

***

Chance closed the distance between them in a flash and caught her before she hit the ground. He held her in his shaking arms and brushed the hair from her face. Her lips turned a deep plum. Her breathing slowed and became sporadic and scratchy.

"Grandfather! What should I do?! Her heart!"

"You can save her, but you must hurry."

"But, I haven't been able to take that form yet!" He argued, and his voice cracked in distress.

"Chance, you must hurry! She needs you! *Believe* in yourself."

***

Ana continued to fade in and out of awareness. Relinquishing to the nothingness that engulfed her, she had the impression of movement. She heard heavy breathing, which she determined wasn't coming from her, which sounded more like snorts. She felt like a towel draped over a rack, her body limp and unwilling to forfeit control back to her numb mind. As though she was lost at the end of a darkened hallway, she was pulled back into a hollow chasm. Inky fingers entwined her mind until there was nothing left.

***

Ana reappeared from the empty vacuum and sensed hard ground beneath her. She was no longer in motion. Was she hallucinating? Her blurry vision revealed a form move away from her faster than was humanly possible.

It was like watching a movie where she was an observer not directly involved in the drama. The sound of elevated voices and shouts met her ears. Someone called for mom.

Whose mom?

Her eyes flickered shut, and she dropped her back into the calming depths of her mind.

CHAPTER 29

A tickle inside Ana's nose woke her. She wrinkled her face and raised her hand to rub the itch. Something dropped into her lap after her fingers brushed against it. Confused, she tried to open her heavy lids.

A bright haze met her eyes. She squinted at her lap where the mysterious item fell. An oxygen tube lay across a fuzzy blue blanket.

"Ana." A deep velvet voice found its way to her ears.

She tracked down the origin of the sweet sound and found him. He sat beside her bed and leaned in so close she could smell his spicy scent. It made her feel safe and calm.

Another familiar smell unlocked many memories, which forced her to survey her surroundings. A hospital. She knew that smell anywhere. It was so ingrained in her she could never forget it. Even if she tried.

Chance cupped her face in his hands.

"You're okay. Didn't know for a while." He grimaced. "I've never been so scared in my life...I thought I was going to lose you."

Ana frowned, befuddled. "Chance, what happened?"

Chance shook his head and took a shuddering breath as he spoke, ignoring her question. "Seeing you lying there – lifeless." He paused and steadied his voice. "I could have lost you and I never got to tell you...Ana, I *love* you. I went crazy on the drive to the hospital not knowing if you were going to live. I just kept thinking about how much I cared for you and that you'd never know and I *want* you to know."

Did he just say I love you? Involuntarily, Ana's heart gave a squeeze as his hazel eyes disoriented her. Happiness filled her every pore. "You love me?"

Chance was so anguished she wanted to hug him, to reassure him, but the IVs and cords restrained her. Instead, she laid her hand on his arm and then noticed the dark bags under his eyes. How long had she been unconscious anyway?

She began to remember bits and pieces of her darkened memories. *What had happened?* The odd fragments just didn't make sense.

"Wait a minute." She choked out. "I went to your house for a reason." She frowned at Chance. "I'm supposed to be mad at you right now...about something..."

He groaned and sat back, his shoulders sagged as though he knew what was coming.

"Why...have you been playing games with me?" She blurted out, as tears welled in her eyes. "A month ago I took some pictures of a fox and it had on *your* necklace." She bit her lip and pushed on. "You must think it's fun pulling pranks but *I* don't find it amusing. Oh – and then your arm *miraculously* heals? Have you been having fun at my expense? What's going on?" Ana lifted her wet angry eyes to the ceiling unable to face Chance. The beeping from the machine beside her bed increased as she grew agitated.

Thoughts tumbled around her head, but the words wouldn't come. She didn't know what else to say.

As Ana stared fuming at the ceiling panels, she wiped away tears, and fresh memories rushed into the dark spaces of her mind. She grimaced. "Wait – was there a cougar? I heard a mountain lion cry out and you were out hiking – I was so scared. Hold on..."

Chance paled as he watched her with wide eyes and appeared to wait to see what would happen next.

"You were with your grandfather and you were standing there, half naked. What were you *doing* out there?" She shook her head. "Nothing you said made any sense."

A memory hidden within her body surfaced, such an odd sensation of blood rushing to her head as she hung from her waist. Was there snorting sounds, too? She frowned and gasped, utterly bewildered. "Was I carried...on an *animal*? Chance! What's going *on*? Am I crazy? What are you keeping from me?!"

Chance dropped his head into his hands and clutched his hair. The only audible sound came from the heart monitor beeping while Chance took his time to answer her.

When he spoke, his voice came out in a groan. "Ana...I've wanted to tell you for *so* long. You *know* what it's like having a secret you're afraid to tell." He looked up, and his hair twisted in every direction. "Ugh! Where do I start?" He fell silent again as he stared out the window. "Just – wait until I finish before making your judgment. I'm afraid my secret will disgust you. I have to be careful who knows. My *parents* don't even know. You have to *swear* not to tell *anyone*. Please Ana?!" His frantic eyes searched hers until she nodded guardedly.

He walked away from the hospital bed and shut the door, sealing them off from the noisy hallway. Quick on his feet, he paced to the opposite corner of the room and began to speak but kept his eyes on the ground. "Back to the beginning. It'll make more sense that way...hopefully. Remember your promise – just wait for me to finish."

He waited for confirmation from her, so Ana gave a brief nod, and he continued to pace. "You know how I told you my grandfather came from a long line of Navajo medicine men? Well, that's not *exactly* right. A long time ago, Grandfather isn't sure how far back, my ancestors turned up. And through them the legend of the Thunderbird began – a powerful creature that protected the tribe. Like an enormous eagle with a body the size of a man's and a *huge* wingspan with the power to direct lightning. The Thunderbird was my *ancestor*, Ana."

Ana waited for his story to start making sense. *What is he talking about?* Had she hit her head? She shook her head and frowned.

"I know you've noticed how observant I am of wildlife." He cleared his throat. "I'm not sure how to tell you – maybe with the first time. When I turned sixteen. I was sitting out behind my house one day watching squirrels scavenge around the trees. I was staring at one and then my skin started tingling, and I saw this trippy blue light shining from it."

Ana's mouth dropped open, and he continued without stopping. "Think of a squirrel and imagine it wrapped in bright blue glowing threads. Minutes later, I found myself, well...standing inches off the ground and covered in fur. It was an interesting time. I had a bushy tail, and I was sniffing for nuts – no lie." Chance laughed as though he were sharing a private joke. "I kept it to myself, not knowing *what* was happening to me. Being able to change into animals was cool...but I felt like a freak- weird, ya know? That was around the time Grandfather moved in. When he discovered my secret, he helped me work through it. He knew about everything that was happening to me and told me about our ancestors – and how I was – *special*. He became my teacher. Even though *he* doesn't have the power, he knows a lot about it. His father was a *shapeshifter* too so he knew all about the legends. I guess only males inherit the gene and not every male gets it.

"So, that's my story, weird as it sounds. You can see why I haven't told you. Or anyone. Like you, I was enjoying feeling normal, too. But I'm obviously far from it and don't blame you if...if you don't believe in...monsters. Or want to be around one." Chance took a raspy breath and glanced over at her, waiting for a response.

***

Ana's face was frozen. The sound of her heart monitor was the only thing that exposed what she felt inside. Rapid beeps triggered the machine to alarm. Just then, a tear formed at the edge of her eye and rolled down her cheek.

Chance touched the wet salty drop as it reached her lips.

He pulled away, and the tear fell to the floor.

Ana sat in the midst of the repetitive beeping, listening raptly the entire time, but then she realized he had stopped talking. Her wet cheeks and lips surprised her, and she stared at the noisy machine. Her mind spun like a salad spinner. Was Chance lying to her? How could she believe such a fantastic story?

She turned to look at his tormented face. Pinched in anguish, he was staring at the pale cracked floor tiles. She considered the fact he seemed so miserable. He didn't appear to be making it all up, so she allowed herself to consider his story. Her thoughts fell to the fox that wore Chance's pendant, his animal-like senses, fast movements, uncanny hearing and his miraculous healing ability.

It was not what she had expected to hear, and it caught her off guard. Although, she wasn't sure what explanation wouldn't be out of the ordinary at this point.

Movement brought her back to the present. Chance stood up and turned to leave.

"Wait, where are you going?" Ana croaked and reached out to him. She didn't want him to go; it hurt to see him turn away from her. She needed him by her side. It was where he belonged.

He paused and closed his eyes. "It's okay. I understand. Just a little too weird."

"Chance, you *swear* you're not messing with me?" Ana whispered.

He turned and stared into her teary eyes.

He shook his head fervently. "No. How could I lie to you and make up stories while you're recovering in the hospital? "

"So, it'll take me a while to work this out, but…" Ana said confused and tried to decide if she was still angry or hurt.

Then she met his cheerless hazel eyes and found what she needed. Relief flooded her. He was still the same person she had grown to love. Maybe a bit more *dynamic* than she originally thought. And definitely other-worldly.

She paused with all of her doubts and knew he was telling the truth. The desperation in his face made it clear. But it would take time to sort out, and she wasn't just going to take his word for it; she required proof. She shook her head and shrugged.

"You accepted me with all of my problems when I thought you wouldn't – I could never walk away from you. Sooo, you may have a deeper animal side than, well, *anyone*...but it just hurts too much thinking about being without you." Another tear rolled down her cheek and dropped to the blanket below. "Maybe I didn't know you could turn into a *squirrel*. But I *do* know your heart. I don't want to give you up; you mean too much to me."

The stunned look on his face made Ana uneasy, and she continued with a shaky voice. "I'm sorry I jumped to conclusions...about you playing tricks on me, but..." He darted across the room, silencing her, his swift movement too quick for her to see. Chance's face hovered inches away, and he stared intently at her. He seemed to be holding his breath, like he was afraid the moment would end.

She guided his hand to her heart. They gazed at each other until the sound of a car horn blew in through the window. Ana pulled back with a frown.

"Now, assuming you're *not* kidding, can I see you, um, shapeshift?"

Chance blushed. "I promise I'll show you but – this isn't the place. When I phase I leave my clothes behind."

"Okay. But soon – *right*?" she said a little more harshly than she meant it.

Chance smiled and nodded.

Ana glanced down at his arm and remembered something. "What was up with you healing so fast? You didn't explain that."

"Well, when I shapeshift and phase back to my human

form, I return to how I'm *meant* to be. Any injuries I have before are gone when I turn back. I don't know – it's just the way it works. I've never had a broken leg or anything, nothing serious to test it with, but it works for minor stuff."

Ana traced the inside of his forearm where his scrape had once bled, and she felt him shiver at her touch.

Her mind continued to whirl. "So, you're the *fox* I took pictures of the other week?"

He nodded and blushed. "Yeah."

Ana touched the pendant around his neck. "Have there been *other* times you've visited me as an animal?"

He traced the contour of her face. "I hope you don't get mad, but I visit you almost every night." He seemed embarrassed or ashamed; she couldn't tell which.

Ana racked her brain trying to think of anything that stuck out in her memory. Then, chuckling she said, "*You're* the clumsy owl!"

"Hey, it isn't easy learning to fly when you've been walking on two legs your whole life! I'm a beginner. I prefer to be in the form of a mammal. They're closest to our own chemistry. Walking on four legs is easier than flying. I only used the owl so I could fly here and home more quickly. After I met you, I wanted to learn more about you. I almost fell out of the tree when you started singing to me." He reached up to scratch his head. "Anyway, it's easier to keep an eye on you in owl form. I've been...concerned." He caressed her cheek with his warm hand, and she closed her eyes at his touch.

Chance broke out of his serious mood and laughed out loud.

"What?"

"I just remembered before I met you, Mom thought there was something seriously wrong, drugs or something." He waved his hand. "I stopped hanging out with my friends after I...changed. Grandfather told her I was just going through a *phase*. Which was the truth, sort of. She was relieved when I started working at Kenny's shop, and for *her* sake I made an effort with my old friends. She was *so* happy when I met you. I think she was worried she'd never see grandchildren."

Ana burst out giggling.

"What?"

"My mom was worried too. I didn't date or hang out with friends. The first time I brought *you* home, I thought my mom wouldn't care if I brought the frog prince home. She was just happy I wasn't alone anymore." She lifted her brow coyly at him. "You can't turn into a frog, can you?"

He laughed with her and then paused. "Will you kiss me, even if I don't turn into a prince?" Chance leaned forward, and she met him in a passionate kiss.

Chance groaned and pulled back as Ana's elevated heartbeat pounded in her ears. Then he grew serious and stared into her eyes.

Was she responsible for his sadness? Hastily, she distracted herself with another question. "So, umm...that reminds me. Was I carried by an animal after passing out?"

"Riiigght. Well, the fastest way I could get you back without hurting you was to shift into a mustang."

Ana put her hand up to her mouth in surprise. He rushed ahead. "I've never shifted into one before. I've observed their energy mapping, but I've never been able to create that form. It's a larger animal and takes more power. I guess I had the incentive when you turned purple." Chance shuddered and said, "Grandfather lifted you over my back, and I hauled you home. Ruined another pair of jeans though. Luckily I had a pair stashed behind the wood pile I threw on before getting Mom."

Ana didn't follow. What was he talking about now?

Chance blushed and said, "Like I said before, when I shift, my clothes don't come with me. When I change form my clothes fall off, or get torn, depending on how large I become.

I normally take them off *first* so they aren't ruined and well, when I change back, I'm in my birthday suit. That's why I've stashed clothing around on the property — in case of emergencies."

It all fell into place for Ana, as Chance's chiseled form flashed in her thoughts and her cheeks flushed.

A light knock came from Ana's door. Lost in the moment, she had forgotten where she was. The door swung open to reveal Aiyana in her blue nurse's uniform. Her long hair was pulled into a tidy braid which fell to the middle of her back.

Aiyana folded her arms and grinned at Chance, who was sitting on the edge of the bed. "Hold on now. Aren't you supposed to be *recovering*? Off the bed Mr. Morgan — give the patient some breathing space."

Chance flushed and cleared his throat. He walked over and gave his mother a peck on the cheek, then went to the door. "I know some people who've been waiting for you to wake up. Let me go get your family. They left to grab some lunch down in the cafeteria."

"Hurry back?" she asked.

"Wild horses couldn't keep me away."

***

"What were you thinking?!" Melissa questioned her daughter, tears welling in her eyes.

A wave of guilt engulfed Ana. She had caused her family anguish. Her foolishness could have killed her.

"I'm so sorry, Mom. I thought Chance was in danger. I heard a cougar and rushed off thinking he'd get hurt. Turns out he was fine. I'm *sooo* sorry. I won't be so thoughtless again. I promise." She hugged her mother, who held her so close, Ana wasn't sure she was going to let go.

"Well, at least you're okay now. I've been at my wits end. Thank goodness Aiyana's a nurse. She kept your heart going until the ambulance arrived." Melissa leaned back and tucked her hair behind her ear. "I've been sitting with Chance's family in the waiting room. They're very nice people. I want to have them over for dinner to properly thank them for everything." She held Ana's face in the palms of her hands, as tears welled up in her eyes again.

"Just, please. Take *care* of yourself. You don't get a do-over, Ana. You don't have nine lives."

Regret submerged her. Ana couldn't remember ever feeling so bad. Not even when she broke the crystal vase that was Nana's. Mere minutes earlier she was euphoric after the simple words, *I love you*. *What a day for highs and lows*. She stared at her hands as they clutched at the fuzzy blue blanket. Unable to meet her mother's face, she simply nodded her head and closed her eyes, fighting back apologetic tears as Melissa's lips brushed against her forehead.

CHAPTER 30

"Finally."

Ana inhaled a welcome breath of fresh air as she was wheeled out of Sandpoint Hospital.

Chance asked to push her out, and the nurse relinquished her patient to hurry down the hallway when alarms sounded from a nearby room.

"You're free," Chance whispered in her ear.

His warm breath breezed by the hairs of her neck and raised goose bumps.

"And wiser too. *Now* I know I don't need to worry about mountain lions."

Ana extended her hand to his, as he growled in her ear. "That's what *you* think." Her eyes widened, and then she smiled.

"Oh, look – there's Mom." Ana was stiff as she rose from the wheelchair. She gained her balance and walked to the curb with Chance's arm around her as she reached the car. The door was opened for her before she could reach out.

Melissa and Eva sat in the front. A large balloon in the shape of a fish floated against the ceiling. Melissa gave it an annoyed glance.

Eva held Ana's large bouquet of flowers that Chance's parents had brought. They billowed before her, and she had to tilt to the side just to peer out the window. A small stuffed frog waited for Ana on the back seat. Melissa's gift was part of a tradition her mother started long ago – a small stuffed animal for each hospital stay. Most were kept in a basket in her closet since her fondness for stuffed animals faded when she turned twelve, but she clung to the memories. Even if they were painful.

Ana had a hard time listening to her mother's chit chat. She was too excited to delve into the political situation at Melissa's work. What would it be like to see Chance shapeshift? *I hope he's ready to show me*. While she held him hostage in her arms at the hospital, she made him promise to show her as soon as possible.

After two days of observation, Ana was happy to come back to her own bedroom in the little blue house at the edge of the forest. Their home seemed cheerful despite the rain that trickled down its gutters, the soft lights within exposing its dry warm interior.

Melissa parked beside Chance's truck, and everyone hurried to the front stoop and out of the rain. They tumbled into the warm, ambient living room.

Across the fireplace, a long stretch of papers were taped together into a banner with the words *Welcome Home Ana* written across it. A shower of hand-drawn hearts were scattered across the sign with Eva's signature along the bottom.

"Aww, thanks Eva. It's great! I *love* it." Ana drew her sister into a bear hug, and Eva beamed happily.

"Eva started a pot roast in the crock pot before we left. It should be ready soon – right Eva?" Melissa asked.

"It should be ready in half an hour," Eva said, after she craned at the wall clock.

"Great. So, that means I have time to show her my surprise." Chance led Ana toward the stairs as her mother and sister shared secretive smiles.

"What surprise? You didn't need to do anything for me." It was awkward accepting anything from Chance. Ana dragged her tired feet and allowed him to usher her upstairs to her room. The wood door was closed. Chance stopped in front of it and said, "Okay, shut your eyes."

Ana obliged after she gave a suspicious grin. The door opened, and she was guided into the center of her room. Chance left her side for a moment, then his strong hand gripped hers, and after a quick squeeze, he said, "Okay, open up."

Was she amongst the stars? Soft points of light glimmered around her. An array of Christmas lights shone from the ceiling, gleaming bright.

"Your own night sky, and these are for you, too." Chance handed her a large bunch of Heartleaf Arnica tied with a red ribbon.

"Chance, it's wonderful." Ana leapt into his arms, her hands rested at the back of his neck. She dragged her fingers up to the base of his hairline, and he shivered in her arms.

"Now, don't go distracting me. I had something I wanted to ask you."

She pulled away puzzled, unsure of what he could possibly want to ask.

"Well, I just wanted to lock it in. I don't want any vampires or wizards cutting in line – Ana, would you be my date for prom?"

Ana laughed at the unexpected invitation. She stopped short when Chance frowned. She didn't want him to think she was laughing at him.

"Definitely. It's what? Three weeks away?" Ana pulled back, and squinted at a calendar pinned to her wall. The joy of the moment was almost too much. She always dreamt of going to the prom, although she never would have admitted it. But there was one thing she didn't look forward to. "Hmmm…"

"What?"

"Oh, well…It's nothing for you to worry about. It's just going to be a pain trying to find a dress that covers my scar." She lifted her hand to her chest and dropped her head.

"Don't worry about that. You're beautiful." He touched her chin. "I've seen you in a hospital gown and ratty sweats. You're like a star shining through it all – beautiful. Get one you like, and don't worry about your scar. It'll be your badge of courage. Be proud.

"I'm going to kiss that frown away," Chance said and

kissed her forehead. After the fifth kiss, she laughed and shook her head. "Fine. Okay."

Rain drops tapped on the roof like small pebbles scattering as they wandered down to dinner.

"Well Ana, you still have to go back to school tomorrow," Melissa said as she removed dishes from the table after they finished eating.

"Right." School was something Ana had purposefully forgotten about.

Chance stood, stretched, and helped remove the remaining items off the table. "Well, I guess I should get going."

Ana whipped her head around to glare at him.

He put his finger to his lips and waved her toward the door. She followed him to the entry as they both grabbed their jackets and slipped them on.

Melissa popped her head around the corner and said, "Bye Chance, thanks for everything. You've been a big help. And thank your parents again for me."

Eva jumped up and gave him a giant hug. "Bye, Chance – see you later."

Ana followed Chance to his truck and said in an audible whisper, "You said you'd show me – why are you leaving?!"

Chance stopped, opened his door, and pulled something from the cab. He held it out to her with a grin.

"What's this?" Ana asked and grabbed the green duffle bag from his hands. She unzipped it and peered inside with a scowl. Folded jeans and a sweatshirt poked out. A slow grin crept across her face.

"Where do you want me to hide it?" she said as she bit her lip in excitement.

Chance hesitated and shook his head. "Ana, I don't think tonight's a good night...you just got home from the hospital." He touched the dark bags under her eyes and then her plum colored lips.

"No way! I've been looking forward to it. I'm sitting outside tonight if you come or not – and I suggest you come." Ana huffed and pulled the duffle from his hands. Her agitation roiled below the surface, like a serpent rising up from the murky depths.

Chance sighed in defeat and said, "Okay, but I don't think you should stay up late tonight." He thrust his hands into his pockets and shook his head. "Go ahead and stash the bag behind a tree, next to your rock. Looks like the rain's stopped for the night so give me twenty to get home and check in with the folks and ten to fly back." He kissed her forehead then added, "See you soon."

Ana decided to place the bag out at the trees near her gazing rock before she returned to the house, not wanting to answer any questions about where the duffle came from.

Ana sat and watched TV with Eva to pass the time. She tapped her foot against the floor, shaking everything in a close radius. Eva glared at her from the opposite side of the couch, groaned, and slid off the couch to the carpet below.

Melissa walked into the living room and said, "Hey Eva, it's time to go brush your teeth. And Ana, were you going to bed early tonight?"

"Um, no. I think I'm gonna head out to the rock since its stopped raining." She noticed her mother's distress and added, "I'll take the waterproof picnic blanket – I'll be fine. Eva's pot roast gave me a burst of energy." She grinned, straightened up, and forced an energetic appearance.

Melissa stood still, and her face clouded over like the sky outside. "Ana, if you get yourself sick I won't be happy. Remember your promise." Melissa stared at Ana for a moment and caved in. "Okay, but not too long. It's still pretty cold out. Wear your jacket – the thick one."

Ana went to the hall closet to search for the waterproof blanket. She was confident it had wound up in one of the boxes Melissa had stuffed away, hidden from view.

Ana emerged with a red and black checkerboard blanket and threw on her jacket as she sauntered out the back door. She settled her chin and lips into the snug folds of the fleece lining to collect some needed warmth.

Within moments, she stepped into her sanctuary and tentatively called out. "Chance?"

Only sporadic drips slapped the damp forest floor, so she laid the blanket out on the rock, sat down cross-legged, and searched the darkened sky.

Although she knew it was futile, she still tried sharpening her weak human senses to peer through the evening gloom. Ana soon gave up, closed her eyes, and listened to the wet forest. Tap, tap, thud. She familiarized herself with the aqueous noises until she heard soft flapping.

Her eyes flashed open. A branch cracked, and she turned. She spotted a large owl perched on a low lying pine bough. Ana rose, her eyes glued to the regal feathered creature. Cautious in her approach, she stretched out her hand to touch it. The bird remained still and closed its eyes as her hand slid down its feathered back.

The animal turned its head with eyes wide open. Ana pointed in the direction she had hidden Chance's bag and stepped back as the large wings extended in preparation for flight. The owl swooped down into the forest and disappeared from sight.

Ana couldn't move. In suspense, her heart fluttered like the owls wings, and her breath caught as she stared into the empty space where the bird had vanished, waiting and listening in complete attention.

Ground cover rustled from the spinney covert. As though in a dream, a form emerged.

Chance pulled his sweatshirt over his head as he walked forward, and Ana noticed his muscular chest before it was covered with black cotton. He stopped before her, looked down to the ground, and avoided her eyes.

"Wow," she said in awe.

His shoulders rocked as he laughed in silence. He tilted his head back, his white teeth gleaming in the dark. He drew her in to him and held her in a tight embrace.

"So, you haven't changed your mind then?" Chance smiled at her.

"Tch, right. So, umm, does your grandfather know that I know?"

"Yeah. He kinda figured after the whole cougar catastrophe you *may* have had some questions. He's always been super protective. He made me swear I would never tell anyone, but the circumstances have changed now. Don't worry about him – he'll come around."

Ana tucked her hair behind her ear and said, "And so, do I get to watch you train?"

He laughed. "Well, how 'bout the day after tomorrow? I'll carry you there, since it's too far for you to hike. I don't want you hospitalized again."

"Really?! That would be fantastic!" Ana was elated and glanced down the path toward the house, remembering she wasn't supposed to be talking to anyone outside.

"I've always wanted to ride a horse. Can you phase into a mustang again?" Ana's voice rose in excitement.

Chance cleared his throat and gave a shy smile. "Well, I haven't tried taking horse form since the other day, but I can try – for you."

"I guess I won't need to worry about getting bucked off." She grasped his hand, led him to the blanket and sat down.

"I'm not your new *pet,* you know! I'm more than just another cute furry face!" He pushed her back onto the blanket as she giggled in response.

"I've always wanted a puppy. Do you like bows?"

The sound of muffled laughter danced around the fir trees and brambles as clouds ambled across the sky.

Chance gazed up then grew serious. "So, there's

something I've been talking to Grandfather about. Shapeshifting isn't the *only* ability my ancestors discovered. Not many have been interested in trying it because it's so risky. There have been some very powerful shifters who were able to, well...heal. It's dangerous to try, and Grandfather's told me I'm not ready yet but it's something I'm working toward."

What did he mean? Then she understood. "Chance, you don't need to..."

Chance touched his finger to her lips and silenced her. "It requires the kind of power I don't have – yet. To heal, I would link my energy to another's. I guess it would kinda get sucked out of me. It's dangerous to test, because it takes twice as much energy to change something outside of myself than it does to change my *own* body. If there was some condition I wasn't aware of it could get bad. Like if I set out to heal a cut, but the injured person had cancer, then I've overcommitted myself.

"Grandfather explained it this way – imagine a big jug of water, flipped upside down over a basin. If the jug is filled, representing a powerful shifter and the basin below only requires a small amount of water, then the shifter isn't in danger. If the situation is flipped and the shifter has less energy than needed to fill the patient, then disconnecting before you're totally drained is near impossible. Which could mean the shifter would...die."

His jaw clenched and he rushed to finish, as Ana shook her head vigorously. "I *want* to help you. I've been training hard to increase my power. That's what we were doing when you found us on the mountain. But grandfather hasn't exactly volunteered more information about it." Chance frowned, clearly frustrated.

Ana grasped his hands, and said, "Chance! I don't want you *hurting yourself* trying to help me. Have faith everything will work out. I do."

She saw his expression, identifying her own stubbornness reflected in his eyes. He nodded in agreement, but she didn't buy it. What if he's only agreeing to stop the discussion?

Obviously, the matter wasn't resolved. Ana would have to keep an eye on him.

CHAPTER 31

Ana followed Chance down the walkway. As they approached the porch they spotted Niyol, who stood in wait on the top stair. She stopped and greeted him warmly. "Hello, sir."

Chance leapt up the steps and rested his hand on his grandfather's shoulder and asked, "Are we ready?"

Niyol nodded with a serious expression and began to lead the way. His steady form was far more solid than she previously thought. She hadn't realized he was as tall as Chance. His clothing hung away from his broad shoulders, which disguised his true form. He didn't seem as elderly as she first thought either. The hunched figure engulfed by the comfy chair didn't represent the person walking before her now.

Niyol paused at the mouth of a trail near the driveway and faced Chance. Ana noticed a woven blanket clutched under his arm and wondered what it was for.

"Time to hop on." Chance stepped in front of Ana and leaned down.

She wrapped her arms around his neck and jumped on his back, while Chance caught and held her legs around his abdomen.

He squeezed her tight and started up the trail. Without a sound, he and Niyol moved along the path.

Ana was stunned by their speed. They moved more swiftly than she ever would have guessed. Chance followed in his grandfather's steps with ease, even with the extra load on his back.

Once they reached the top of the ridge, they descended into the meadow where she had discovered them less than a week ago. Gravity pushed her forward and into his back as they descended the trail, and she savored the closeness.

They entered the center of the grassy field, and Ana slid from Chance's back but kept her hands on his shoulders for support. Once she was stable, she let go.

Niyol stepped between her and Chance and stared intently into her eyes. He spoke in his deep, melodic voice. "Ana, I know Chance trusts you. But the knowledge you hold now has the power to destroy this family – and most of all, Chance. I can see you care for him – but no matter what happens between you two, you must promise to never speak of his powers to anyone."

Ana answered immediately, without a thought. "Of course. I swear on my life I will never say anything to anyone. I wouldn't do that to him, or you."

The lines around his eyes creased as he squinted at her. "I was taught sacrifice is a true way to make a bond."

A glint of silver shone from his palm as Ana realized he held a knife.

"Whoa, grandfather! It's cool. She said she wouldn't tell anyone. I trust her." Chance lowered Niyol's hand and cushioned himself between them. Niyol grumbled and backed off, tucking his weapon into a sheath on his belt.

Ana swallowed hard and held her palm out. "I don't mind. I'll do it."

Some blood was an easy payment to display her intention to keep the family secret.

Chance shook his head and met her eyes. "No. It's not necessary. Let's just get started. You can watch from over there." He pointed to a fallen log about ten paces away. "I was going to try the mustang again for you. And I *still* need to perfect the cougar." Chance led her to her perch. He placed a soft kiss on her neck before walking back to where Niyol stood. A few whispers were passed between the men.

Ana watched as Chance waved to her with a smile, and Niyol stepped away from his grandson. Chance pulled off his shirt and sat down cross legged before his grandfather and closed his eyes. Niyol unfolded the blanket he had carried and waited with it in his arms. After a few minutes, Chance reopened his eyes, stood, and stared intently at his grandfather.

She held her breath. The exhilaration was almost too much for her to take. Completely still, she didn't want to miss a moment.

Niyol opened the blanket, holding it in his outstretched arms. Chance disappeared behind the screen, and Ana realized what it was for.

She heard Niyol say softly, "Focus. Close your eyes and visualize it. Touch it with your mind. Your body knows its form. You *can* do it again. It will be easier this time. There you go..."

Niyol dropped the blanket to expose a beautiful chestnut mustang with a dark brown mane. It tossed its head uneasily and snorted.

Ana stood and began to move forward, but Niyol met her gaze and held his hand up. She remained in place as the animal before her adjusted to its body.

The brown stallion began to walk, occasionally catching its hoof on the earth. The snorting continued, its head whipping around as though it had an itchy nose. After a long wet blast from its muzzle, the creature seemed to calm and began to trot in a tight circle.

She couldn't help but smile as she witnessed him explore his new form. In her amusement, she turned to Niyol and thought she noticed a reserved grin. He met her gaze and nodded.

After it bucked a few times, the horse calmed and walked towards Ana. Large russet eyes confronted her before it dipped its muzzle down to her hand. She placed her cool fingers on the beautiful creature's head. Its muscles twitched and quivered at her touch. The mustang moved sideways, and she let her hand drift down the breadth of its strong back. After a whinny, it turned to look at her.

"What – you want me to get on?" Ana said between

giggles.

It lowered its head. *Well, I guess he can understand me in animal form.*

With quivering legs, she stepped up onto the log and grabbed a handful of the horse's mane with one hand. Her other hand moved to its back as she lifted her leg up to jump on. In an awkward motion, she was able to pull and half jump her way on. She settled herself in place, gripping the mane so tight her knuckles grew white.

"I've never done this before," she said in warning.

The mustang whinnied in response and shook its head up and down. Ana imagined he would be laughing right now, if he could.

"Right – I guess you haven't either."

The horse moved forward slowly, as though it wanted to make sure she was secure on its back. After a loop in the meadow, it began to pick up speed, trotting.

Ana's happy laughter encouraged a canter. Her hair pulled back in the breeze, and the mustang's warm muscular body moved through the wilderness like it belonged there.

***

This form was comfortable. It did take a little getting used to, although after transforming into other four-legged animals, Chance adjusted easily. But his face felt strange, his nose in particular. It tingled for a while, but then it faded.

Chance slowed down, concerned Ana would tire from holding on. She leaned forward, hugged his massive neck, and said in a whisper, "I love you."

He snickered and stomped his foot twice on the ground. Chance walked her back to the log, and Ana slid off his back. She rubbed his forehead, and he leaned his long muzzle in to her. She rested her forehead to his as she held his jaw in her grasp. Then he turned to head back to his grandfather. He had too much to say and couldn't in this form.

Niyol lifted the blanket again and blocked Ana's view. After the transformation was complete, Chance wrapped it around his human form and walked over to Ana with a broad smile.

"So, you love me?" he said as he lifted her up with ease.

Ana avoided his gaze, but she couldn't for long. Chance absorbed her hands within his and stared into her eyes. Time stood still for a long moment until he kissed her nose, chuckled, and said, "Any other wishes I can fulfill?"

He kissed her on the forehead. She accepted him so openly it baffled him, but he didn't linger on it. He enjoyed her hands on his skin, and his flesh burned below her fingertips.

"And here I was thinking *I* was the lucky one."

He pulled back, uncomfortable with Niyol's gaze on them.

Chance continued to train and phased into his cougar form. It was easier for him to revisit this shape, compared to last time. Repetition made it more comfortable to phase because it didn't require the same amount of focus when he grew familiar with an animal's structure. The more accustomed he was with a mapping, the easier it was. It didn't burn up as much energy.

As a giant cat, he stalked around the meadow. He didn't screech this time. The unpleasant outcome from his growling the other day remained bitter in his thoughts. But he did creep through the tall grasses in the field, enjoying his lanky, sinuous body. The large feline provided claws which he used to scale an evergreen. He swayed high up in the treetops, recalling his struggle with shifting into the cougar for the first time. Shifting seemed so much harder before he met Ana. Now his energy flowed with purpose.

After each practice session, his power reserve increased. His focus intensified as his confidence grew. Chance wanted to continue so he could begin experimenting with healing.

It was his priority now – training. Nothing else mattered.

Chance practiced at least once every day. Power expansion was his singular focus.

Niyol's composed and quiet demeanor agitated Chance. "It is something that takes time. Do not rush. To truly understand the way your abilities work, it requires focus and attention. This can't be measured in a week, month or even a year."

Niyol warned Chance. "Healing isn't something you should try yet. It's too dangerous. It requires more energy than you have. Remember, Chance – things can go wrong fast."

Then he said the word Chance had begun to loathe, "Patience."

However, Chance had very little of it, if any.

He was anxious. Time wasn't on his side. He knew Ana's health could decline at any time, and he didn't want her to suffer through a transplant.

He listened to his grandfather's warnings, but it only pushed Chance to train harder. He needed more energy to heal. Like training for a weight lifting competition, he needed to bulk up, and fast. Unfortunately, there was no special drink or exercise he could take to speed the process.

He had to do it the hard way.

CHAPTER 32

Chance slipped up to Ana at lunch period and pulled her away from any listening ears.

"Can you come over tonight?" he asked with a slight squeeze of her hand.

His bright eyes and wide smile made her heart patter. What is he was so enthusiastic about?

"Sure, what's up? Something special going on tonight?"

He tugged her against his chest, and with an arched eyebrow, he said mysteriously, "We're supposed to have a lightning storm later."

"And why would I want to come over in a lightning storm? You aren't training, are you?" She wasn't quite sure if this was a safe idea.

"Uh, that's right — I haven't told you yet." He gave her another mysterious grin. "When electricity's in the air, I can pull from it. It helps me expand my own energy." He released his hold on her and made sweeping gestures, clearly enthusiastic at his plans. "It's perfect for training. It lets me phase into larger forms I couldn't do otherwise. The larger the form, the more power it requires. Along with the first time you try to take a new form — that also sucks a lot out of you." He whispered into Ana's ear, holding her against him, "Tonight I'm going to try a bear."

"Wow, I wouldn't miss it. But are you sure it's safe?"

"You'll be fine. You'll be with me. But don't forget to dress warm — don't want you catching a cold."

"Okay, Mom."

He kissed her forehead and zipped her jacket all the way up to her chin.

***

After Melissa returned home from work that night, Ana

grabbed a coat and headed to Chance's house.

The clouded sky left the landscape gray and bleak. Statuesque pines reached upwards into the dry static air and stretched for a dewy drink in the clouds.

Ana's bright yellow van cut through the shadowed forest and crept its way to the dimly lit home at the end of the drive. She snuggled her face into the fuzzy lining of her coat as she walked around the house to the front door. She rang the bell and moved her feet up and down, trying to keep warm. A moment later Chase opened the door and waved her in.

She darted through the entryway into the ambient warmth. Chance closed the door and sealed out the bitter cold.

Chance led her to the dining room. Metallic clangs tinkled inside. Ben was at the table with his fork poised above his dinner. There were two empty place settings and one plate with half eaten food.

"Hi, Ana. How're you tonight?" Ben welcomed her with a smile as he wiped his mouth with a napkin.

"Oh, I'm fine. I've been busy studying for finals though. I'm ready for a break."

Chance invited her to sit down at the table and asked, "Did you eat yet? I was just finishing up. Grandfather's already done and getting ready."

"Oh, no. I ran out of the house too quickly."

"Let me grab you a plate, real quick." Chance walked out of the dining room and through the archway.

Ben balanced his fork in his hand, ready to take another bite. "Chance has been busy studying too. I hope he didn't drag you out here if you should be resting or studying instead."

"Oh, no, not at all. I'm burnt out for today. I couldn't study if my brain allowed it."

Chance walked back in with a full plate of steaming rice,

green beans and roast beef. Aiyana followed him, her hands sheathed in a pair of dripping yellow gloves and gave Ana a careful hug before going back into the kitchen.

Ben asked, "So, you guys are going out for the lightning show? Now, we're responsible for Ana while she's here. I don't want to make a habit of taking her to the hospital. You take care of her tonight – you hear me?"

"Of course, Dad. Grandfather will be with us. Trust me, I wouldn't put her in danger."

They ate their meal as fast as they could and rinsed their empty plates at the sink and put them in the dishwasher. Chance went upstairs and came back with a folded blanket.

"Won't you get cold shifting in the storm?" Ana said in a quiet whisper.

"I don't really experience the cold so much anymore. My body seems to regulate my temperature no matter what it's like outside. Must have to do with adapting survival skills to my human form. I still don't get it, but I certainly won't complain – makes things easy. Anyway, I'll be fine. This blanket's for you to wrap around your jacket. Grandfather's bringing another for me."

She zipped up her jacket and flipped her hood up. He opened the blanket and enveloped her in its folds.

He pulled on a rain slicker just as his parents came into the entryway.

"What should I say...have fun? And keep an eye on Ana, we don't want her getting sick," Aiyana said and rubbed Ana's shoulder, hidden somewhere in the depths of the blanket.

"No one has her interest more at heart than I do, Mom. Don't worry."

Niyol came downstairs with folded woven fabric in his arms. This time Ana knew what it was for.

"Goodbye, Father," Aiyana said and kissed his lined cheek. Niyol nodded and returned a kiss to her youthful face.

The three left the house and moved briskly down the

driveway. Ana took her familiar place on Chance's back and rocked around as they sprinted through the wilderness. She was snug and warm, like a baby carried by her mother.

They arrived at the field just as a resonant rumble touched everything in the valley. Ana sat on her log and tried to settle in. She understood the importance of staying out of the way, so Chance wouldn't get distracted. Sometimes, he had a hard time controlling his form. It could be dangerous being near him while he occupied a shape that had the potential to hurt her.

Another thunderous explosion reverberated through the landscape. Ana hunched down under the blanket, tucked her hands into the folds around her, and peered out at the two forms in the meadow.

CHAPTER 33

Chance checked on Ana, worried she was frightened. Instead, he found her stooped over in a lumpy pile on the log. He laughed. The only thing that appeared to be affecting her was the cold.

Niyol said from behind, "Are you ready? It's time to sit." Niyol held up the blanket shield.

Chance listened to his grandfather, stopped smiling, and focused his energy. He pulled off his shirt and pants, sat at his grandfather's feet, and closed his eyes. The blanket was draped across his lap. He opened his mind to the natural world around him, sensing wildlife skittering behind the tree wall. The hairs on his arms lifted as he manipulated the electricity in the earth and in the crisp evening air. Movement stilled in the clearing, and a quiet fell in the forest. Chance could see small watchful eyes peer out from the dark.

His grandfather's voice broke the silence. "Now feel yourself pushing outward. Absorb what's around you; focus on your core expanding, growing."

Chance recognized the static within himself, collected it in a smooth radius, and pulled in the available current outside of his body. The energy in the air and earth coalesced with his power, mounting and enlarging within, while he maintained control.

"Remember the bear." His grandfather's voice intones. "Think of the time you observed it, mapping its imprint. See him in your mind... and welcome the form to your body."

Chance reflected on the time he hiked through the mountains and discovered a grizzly amongst the pines. He held the animal's attention long enough to study its intricate mapping before it grew agitated, and he was forced to phase into eagle form and fly to safety.

His thoughts tangled with the wet black nose, the large bulky body and sharp intelligent eyes. Chance breathed in, opened up his senses to meld with the bear and needle-like prickles coursed through his body.

***

From Ana's vantage point she saw Chance one minute, then in the next, fur erupted across his body as he grew into a huge beast that reached far above his grandfather. She drew in a sharp breath. She had never witnessed the moment of transformation. She sat in awe when the bear stumbled and tried to keep balance. A strange moan rumbled from the bear's chest as it swayed in place.

***

Chance struggled to keep balance, grasping at his new form. He pulled at his blurred senses and attempted to sharpen his foggy eyes, like the focus on a camera. He stared ahead at his grandfather's face; his eyes honed in on Niyol's nose. Disappointed his eyesight wasn't better, he hoped the other senses would compensate.

He sniffed the air around him. He recognized Ana's and Niyol's familiar scents and then thought he caught the faint smell of a buck that must have passed hours earlier. He lifted his long snout and pulled in the thick smells of rotted pine needles, damp earth and a Fire Ant colony that layered around him, delicious like a custard filled trifle. He was excited by his new ability. This was the best sense of smell he had experienced yet.

A brilliant burst of lightning rocked him from his reverie, and he sought his grandfather's face once again. Chance grumbled and put a tentative foot forward to test the range of movement in his new hulking form.

Niyol held his arm out toward the forest and said, "Go try it out, Chance. We'll be waiting for you here."

***

Ana stared at the huge bear stumbling through the murky field. It slowly gained its footing before dissolving into the forests architecture.

Niyol joined her on the log.

"He needs to get used to this new form. The extra power from the lightning storm helped him gain the bear. The first step is changing form, the next is keeping control." Niyol's face was turned toward the place his grandson had disappeared.

"So, I've been wondering..." Ana fidgeted with her hands for a moment before she said, "I'm not sure I understand what Chance said about the Thunderbird. Was it a real animal, or what?" She wasn't sure if Niyol was protective of these matters, and hoped she wouldn't make him mad asking.

Niyol took a slow breath and said, "Well, the form goes back. Far back. One of my ancestors created it. Powerful shifters can safely create shapes they can only imagine. It is dangerous experimenting."

"So, it wasn't a *real* animal then?"

"No. Only real to those who witnessed it."

Ana became more comfortable in their conversation and settled onto the bumpy log. She pointed toward the forest where she last saw the bear and said, "It's amazing to watch him shift – I wish I could do something like that." Ana and Niyol scanned the dense forest line.

He faced her in the darkness. When their eyes locked, she was held by a light that shone through his eyes. Although it was dark, she could see he seemed to be searching for something.

"You let yourself be guided by fear. So you can never reach your full potential."

The words hit her with force. *What does he mean I'm guided by fear?* "You are no different from any other yet different in every way. Everyone dies – in this, you are no different. What you do while you're alive *IS* the difference." Niyol held his hand inches away from her chest and said, "*This* is what makes you different, and *that* is the blessing. You have a deep strength you haven't used. You have the power in you – you are unique."

Time stood still as each word pounded into her chest, as though the words themselves cracked it open. Pain flooded out from an emotional hole inside, and she realized her face was wet with tears.

He sat still beside her as he stared intently into the ebony woodland.

When she couldn't cry anymore and the last of the pain trickled out of her, a cool electric breath filled her lungs and radiated out to her body.

This was the moment. The moment she chose to leave all the angst she had clung to. She didn't want to die in fear. Niyol was right, everyone would die. She needed to live while she could. An entirely different attitude began to surface. Choices appeared that had been invisible but were now so clear. Her life was waiting.

"Thank you." Ana whispered to Niyol.

"I've led a good life. I met my love and lived happily for a long time. But I've learned, that if you have a power – you're obligated to use it. *Everyone* has a power, Ana."

Bushes rustled at the forests edge. Chance's immense body crashed through the shrubbery. He tucked into a roll and flopped onto the ground in the field.

Ana giggled, and Niyol smiled, clearly amused by Chance's attention grabbing performance.

The bear's form lifted up and loped toward the two figures on the log. He stopped before them and gave a soft growl, his lips extending in articulation.

"Did you enjoy scaring Thumper and Bambi?"

CHAPTER 34

"Now, that one's pretty. It brings out your cans." Aunt Tera's voice rose over Ana's shoulder.

She flinched, trying to block out her aunt's voice, unsure how she finessed her way into the shopping trip. It may have had to do with Tera boasting to Melissa about knowing all the best dress shops around the lake.

A wall of mirrors stretched before Ana as she pivoted in place, frowning at the flashy turquoise dress. Her scar screamed for her attention, peeking out from the lacey bodice. She let her eyes blur, and its sharp line faded. Her new attitude told her to pick the prettiest dress and proudly display the line that ran down her chest, but it challenged her natural instincts to cover herself up.

Melissa walked up with two more dresses. "I think you're going to LOVE this one. Don't think — just put it on." She pointed at a dark green dress that was obscured by a black one. The fact it had a drop neck didn't get past Ana.

Ana's eyebrows rose, but she held her hand out anyway, grabbed the dresses and sailed into her dressing room. She zipped and fastened the dress and pushed open the changing room door, then peered around the edge.

"What are you waiting for?"

"Come on out and show us how beautiful you are," the women chorused.

Ana sighed, straightened as though someone was pulling her strings and glided out in front of the mirrors, walking tall.

"Ooooh, I *like* that one. You look like a movie star!" Eva exclaimed and jumped forward in her seat.

"Oh, Ana. You look...well...beautiful." Melissa dabbed at her tears with the edge of her shirt.

"Lovely. Truly, Sweetie," Aunt Tera said, clearly at a loss, as though all of her embarrassing comments had been used up.

Ana appraised herself. The green satin dress clung to her figure and dropped in a swirl of fabric at her feet. The neckline plummeted down, exposing her pale skin. The thin white scar screamed at her, *Look at me*, as it plunged beneath the silken fabric. She shook her head and forced the voice away. A tall, proud girl reflected back at her.

"You look so grown up. A real adult." Melissa raised an eyebrow. "That dress could stop traffic. I'm not sure I should let you go out looking so pretty…"

Ana inspected her mother's proud grin through the mirror.

"I bet we could find a drape or scarf for you to cover yourself with," Melissa said.

"But that would cover my scar…" Ana pulled her shoulders back and gazed at her badge of honor. She challenged herself to shy away from her reflection and stood tall.

Her mother's brows knitted together. "That doesn't sound like you. You aren't trying to cover your scar anymore?"

Ana lifted her chin. "No. I've decided its time to move forward. I don't care who knows. I won't let it affect me from living my life."

Aunt Tera and Eva exchanged surprised glances, both raised their eyebrows and shrugged.

"I'm proud of you, baby," Melissa whispered. "That makes me happy to hear. So… does that mean you want the dress?" She opened her purse.

Ana turned in the mirror and assessed her glamorous reflection. She thought about going to the prom with Chance in a black tux. How handsome he would be. The inner vault labeled 'wishful thinking' had been thrown open. She was living the daydream she had kept locked away from herself.

She blinked, her throat tightened, and she had a hard time swallowing.

"This is the one." She smiled up at her mother's emotional face.

***

A light knock came from Ana's door.

Small twinkling lights glowed softly. Ana saw her reflection in the window; a ghostlike apparition overlaid the dark shadows of trees outside. Green satin shimmered on the contours of her body. Her dark hair was swept up her head with a pretty hair clip Melissa lent her, and a few stray strands curled their way down her exposed back. She put mascara on to lengthen her already long eyelashes, and colored lip gloss shined on her lips. She was uncertain what else to do, so she didn't add anything more.

"Come in," she said, too anxious to face the door.

She saw the door open through the reflection.

"Close your eyes," Chance's golden toned voice said.

Her feet settled onto the floor, and she breathed out unhurriedly, letting her lids slide shut.

A moment later something cold was draped around her neck. The surprise left her chest frozen. She breathed in a stilted breath as she opened her eyes, laid her hand on her chest, and dropped her head to inspect a new sparkling necklace.

"I had Dad make it for you. Rainbow Moonstones. I thought they'd be perfect for you. I hope you like it. It's not the *traditional* corsage, but…"

Strands of pale stones entwined her neck in a decorative bramble. The small, faceted tear shapes encircled her neck and shone iridescently.

"It's perfect. Thank you, Chance." Ana turned around and faced her Prince Charming.

Formal in black, he *was* a prince, and her eyes stung as Chance's eyes widened. He lifted his eyebrow in response and shook his head. *Just breathe, Ana.* Her heart grew in her chest, which left little room for her deflated lungs.

"Speaking of perfect. You're amazing, Ana."

Her cheeks heated, and she turned her eyes down to the wood floor. "Thanks, and you look perfectly handsome."

"Well, there's a camera attached to a really excited mother downstairs. She's waiting for us; we should go. Anyway, if we don't leave now I may have second thoughts about taking you out looking *so beautiful*. I may need to take bear form to fight off all the guys who'll be staring at you," he said with a chuckle.

Chance offered her his elbow, and she reached out, happy to anchor herself to him. She took a deep breath before they started downstairs.

"Oh, baby! You two look *wonderful*. Okay, stand together so I can get a picture!" Melissa struggled with Ana's camera and seemed confused. Ana set it on automatic and instructed her to just hit the button, but in her excitement she must have forgotten Ana's simple instructions.

"Oh, right." Melissa held the camera up to her eye, and a blinding flash burst through the room.

After a series of photos, Ana and Chance finally escaped the little blue house and walked out into the night.

They drove to Clark Bend High School, and Chance escorted Ana to the gym. Students dressed to impress lined up and waited to enter. The sound of music and laughter filled the air as they drew closer to the party.

The prom photographer was set up at the door and took photos of couples as they entered. A tall, white trellis stood with fake roses entwining its base, and a backdrop of the ocean hung from behind.

Ana stared at the scene and tried to piece together what the theme was supposed to be. When it was their turn in front of the camera, she held a nervous smile and forced her eyes wide.

"That'll be one for the mantle," Ana said as they entered the gym.

Chance laughed at her, pulled her close, and kissed the

top of her head. "You want me to go maul the camera? I'll leave *no* trace."

"Oh, my hero!" Ana laughed, half mockingly.

Through the night they danced and rested until Ana's burdensome heart left her wilted. Chance pulled her to a bench to rest while he went to retrieve her coat and his parked truck.

They arrived back home just past midnight. Ana peeked through the living room window to confirm her mother wasn't up waiting. She stood on her toes then Chance lifted her, and their eyes locked. As was ritual now, he lingered in anticipation of the awaited kiss. It started slowly, but when their lips moved more fervently they paused in their embrace, both clearly sensing Ana's pounding heart.

Ana groaned and said, "I hope someday I can kiss you *without* worrying about my heart stopping." She gave an uncomfortable giggle, leaned her head against his chest, and listened to his strong heartbeat.

Chance remained silent. He held her until she pulled away. And still as a guardian, he watched her enter the darkened blue house. Ana peeked out the window. Chance stared into the sky until a shooting star streaked across the vaulted expanse.

A moment later his figure was gone.

CHAPTER 35

Finals week was over in a flurry.

Ana and Chance studied every day after school. There was no time for lessons with his grandfather. It had to wait for the following week. Chance was annoyed and agitated about the delay to his training, but he supposed it was a good thing to keep an eye on Ana, who was totally depleted of energy.

He anxiously took her to her routine doctor's visit. He was disappointed to learn her condition had continued to deteriorate since the heart procedure. Chance didn't expect a miracle, but it still stung.

After Ana scheduled another checkup for four weeks away, they left, eager to escape the white walled fortress for the fresh air outside.

They drove back home to Clark Bend early enough in the afternoon to allow time for Chance to train. At his house, they found Niyol in a wooden chair on the porch.

Chance sauntered up and said, "Hello, grandfather. Feel like going out?"

In response, Niyol stood and nodded. After retrieving a blanket, they set out to their private training ground.

The sun shone, warming the swaying grass in the meadow. A raven cawed at them as they entered the valley. Perched on Ana's log, it flicked its tail in agitation. As they approached, it flew away, clearly perturbed to lose its sun spot, squawking and scolding as it arched through the sky.

Ana walked to her regular station and sat on the log.

"Do you want to do the bear again today?" Niyol asked, as he opened the blanket to screen Chance from Ana.

"Sure. It's getting easier for me to take its shape."

Chance settled at his grandfather's feet after he stripped his clothing off and set them in a pile. He covered himself with the blanket so Ana could watch the transformation. He closed his eyes in silent meditation. His skin prickled and his body arched. The tingle from his fur in the breeze gave him chills. Chance stared down at his immense shadow and rose high on his rear feet. He towered above Niyol and stretched his club-like arms out.

Chance enjoyed the bear shape. His strength surpassed any other form, and his sense of smell was immeasurably effective. It was quickly becoming his favorite embodiment.

He paraded around the meadow to test his senses and then returned to his grandfather who held out the blanket. Chance shrank behind it as he returned to his human form, wrapped the blanket around his waist, and sat down at Niyol's feet.

"Grandfather, I can take bear form. My power has grown, and I wanted to know if I could start working with healing now." He glanced up at Niyol's softened eyes.

"I know why you're working so hard, son. I understand the pressure you have put on yourself. But it is still unsafe for you to practice. Testing on yourself will not give you the benefit you seek. It will only offer a false sense of security. Unfortunately, you can't practice on me or Ana either. I am an old man, and Ana has structural...imperfections. We would pull every last spark of your essence from you. My knowledge on the subject is vague, but I do know it is something deadly to try. Only the masters would bother with it, because there was no risk of dying."

"So, is there a master shapeshifter I can ask? Are there others around like me?"

Niyol sighed and said, "Now is not the time for that talk."

Chance dropped his head into his hands and bellowed loudly. The sound reverberated through the open meadow.

"Look at me," his grandfather said.

Chance returned his gaze to his grandfather's.

"You need to listen closely to me. This is very important. Healing takes more than *twice* as much power than transformation. You are taking your energy and changing something outside of yourself. It is *very* different from changing your own cells. When you extend your own power to heal someone, a vacuum is created between yourself and the patient. Your energy gets drawn into the subject. And depending on the sickness or injury, it can be a gentle pull or a forceful vacuum. If you commit to a healing beyond your power, it can kill you if you can't break the connection. Remember this, Chance. Frustrating, I know. But anything worth learning takes time. Some individuals take what isn't theirs, but they never really *own* it, because *they* didn't *earn* it. Do you understand?"

Chance nodded his head vaguely.

"I know you want to help Ana. I care about her fate as well – but is it worth your life?"

Chance sat in silence.

Ana rose and walked cautiously toward them. She stopped beside Chance and studied his face.

"What's wrong?" Ana's eyes narrowed.

"For now, let's work on cultivating your power. You still haven't achieved Thunderbird. It's a true challenge, taking a unique form that you can *only* envision in your mind," Niyol said, patting Chance's arm.

Chance nodded. His torment and anger roiled inside his belly and radiated throughout his body. He shrugged his shoulders and lifted himself off the ground without any effort.

"Fine. Thunderbird. Let's do it."

Niyol seemed to appraise his grandson's new façade. Chance's recklessness seeped in and partnered with a desperation that deadened him.

"It would be best to work with the Bald Eagle first. It's a large bird, and it should help you take Thunderbird form."

"*Should* help me?" Chance sneered, his shoulders tensed as his fists balled. "Why is it you're so vague about such important things? So many questions I ask you, you just ignore. Don't you trust me enough to tell me the truth, or don't you know?"

"Chance!" Ana whispered disapprovingly.

As though he was snapped with a rubber band, Chance jerked his eyes to Ana. He had forgotten she was there. Shame trickled down like icy fingers along his flesh, and he shook his head.

"I'm sorry, Grandfather. Forgive me. I don't mean to be unkind or ungrateful."

"I understand, Chance." Niyol never flinched through his grandson's tantrum. "Now, I believe you have the eagle mapped already, am I right?"

Chance nodded shamefaced, unable to speak.

"I know you weren't interested in it before because you didn't favor flying. I believe you are more...familiar now? Getting more practice recently?" Niyol stared at Chance.

Ana and Chance exchanged grins, and Chance broke down and chuckled.

"I'm pretty good now. I have the horned owl down pat."

Chance sank back into the billowing grass at Niyol's feet, shook his head, and closed his eyes.

***

Ana departed his side and settled on her perch. *He's tenacious, to say the least.* Far from being a quitter. Admirable. But a little reckless too.

CHAPTER 36

Chance sat before Niyol in their grassy field.

Bright spots of color splashed through the long stalks. Wildflowers were rushing to bloom, seeking the warm sunlight.

Chance's eyes were closed in meditation as Niyol guided him through an unfamiliar transformation.

"Listen carefully, Chance. You need to envision this in your mind. Your ancestors cultivated the power of a great bird with a body the size of a human being, its wingspan up to thirty feet. The wings were said to be the color of cinnamon with tips as if dipped in snow. Its large talons are used for ripping and tearing. Yellow eyes view the world so clearly; there is no match to its vision.

"Now Chance, imagine this great animal...feel yourself soaring through the skies. Feel the wind through your wings, lifting you, taking you where you wish to go."

Chance's energy pulsed, ready at his bidding. His body tingled as he imagined a great raptor so large it could cut through the Earth's atmosphere as though it were made solely for him, existing only for him.

His pores burned and prickled. He pushed past it and clung to his vision. A screeching cry erupted from his chest. His lungs and organs burned, and then the acute pain ended as he finalized his form.

Chance immediately knew it had gone wrong when he zeroed in on his grandfather's face. From his height, he knew he wasn't as big as he should have been. He stretched himself out and looked from side to side, trying not to lose balance.

Long feathers draped his arms, where he should have had wings. He lifted his hands to his face. A beak extended where his nose once was, his skin was layered with soft downy feathers, although his eyes seemed unaltered.

He was frightened. It had been a long time since a

transformation went so wrong, and he was thankful he couldn't see himself. His grandfather's reaction was enough.

Niyol cleared his throat, his eyes wide and asked, "Does it hurt?"

Chance shook his head. It didn't feel *good* either. He would have to describe the pins and needles of discomfort later. It was probably the feathers that tugged at his flesh.

"Okay, that didn't go well. It can take some trial and error. Don't get discouraged Chance, this is the hardest form to take, especially if you don't have an example to study. Times have changed. My father learned the form from his father. The generations would pass it down." Niyol seemed sad as he continued and said, "I'm sorry I can't personally teach you the shape. It's my place as your teacher. But there *is* something I may be able to give you to help…" His eyes drifted to the skies as though he could see the great Thunderbird flying overhead.

Chance tried to stand still to center his energy enough to change back into his human form. Were his legs different lengths? He wobbled and teetered uncontrollably. Finally able to focus enough, he returned to his normal shape.

He cleared his throat. "Was it as bad as I think?" Chance asked halfheartedly, not entirely sure he wanted to hear the answer.

"I shouldn't have encouraged you to try it – that was dangerous." Niyol's frown accentuated the lines on his face.

"Can we try again later?"

"Not sure. You should take some forms that are familiar before attempting it again. What do you feel like right now?"

Chance grinned and said, "Bear. It's my favorite."

"Very well. Let's work on expanding your energy. You can start with bear and work your way down the chain. Let's see how many transformations you can do before you run out of power. Remember, leave enough strength to change back or we'll be stuck out here a while. I don't think your mother would take it well if you went home for dinner in squirrel form."

***

On Friday afternoon, Ana stood in her room shrouded in yellow polyester grasping a blue graduation cap. Her reflection in a small star shaped mirror revealed her light rose cheeks, which outshone even her robes.

She floated out of the room and met her sister in the hallway.

"I forgot my sweater." Eva blew by like a hummingbird and entered her cactus flower pink room.

Ana was halfway down the stairs before Eva buzzed by her again.

"Oh, don't you two look pretty. Stand together and let me get a picture."

Melissa waited for them in the living room with Ana's large black camera around her neck. This time she remembered what to do and held her finger on the button as she waited for the girls to hug.

After Melissa swapped places with Eva for a photo with Ana, they gathered their belongings and headed to Clark Bend High School.

When they arrived, Ana left her mother and sister to meet up with the senior class in the auditorium. As she approached the room of excited graduates, suddenly arms wrapped around her waist and warm breath tickled her neck. She spun too quickly to place her hands on Chance's face, and he held her steady as her head rush passed.

"Hello, beautiful. Ready to graduate?"

"More than ready. How 'bout you?"

"I'm ready to spend my free time with you." He leaned forward and placed a gentle kiss on her lips. Ana's mind went blank while she forgot her surroundings.

A throat cleared, and they paused. Ana opened her eyes. Laura stood grinning at the two of them, slightly embarrassed.

"Hey guys – just wanted to say congrats!" she smiled brightly.

Ana gave Laura a hug. "Thanks, Laura! I owe my B+ in calc to you!"

The three of them joined the rest of their group and listened to the principal, who came to talk before the ceremony. They tried to pay attention to the endless instructions that followed and were relieved when he left to begin the proceedings.

Clark Bend High School had seventy nine graduating students; the event took under an hour.

When Ana walked across the stage to accept her diploma a loud shout, which only could have originated from Uncle Jace, rang through the auditorium. As she turned to smile and wave, a blinding flash left her staggering off the stage. "Mom," she said to herself and chuckled.

After the last graduate crossed the platform, the principal thanked the audience and the air filled with spinning blue caps and loud shouts.

Chance and Ana met up among the tangle of folding chairs. Then the customary sound of familial embarrassment caught up to her.

"Ana, I thought you were going to fall on your face up there. Your mother sure has timing. I saw the picture though, it turned out nicely. You'd never have known you were about to fall over on the stairs!"

Aunt Tera rushed to give her a tight squeeze, and her curls tickled Ana's nose. Ana pulled away just in time to get swept up in Uncle Jace's arms.

"That was great, Ana. It felt like the time I caught a thirty inch steelhead."

"You can just say you're proud. Really Jace, I don't know

why you don't just say it." Aunt Tera seemed embarrassed by her husband.

Ana patted his arm. "It's okay, Uncle Jace. I know you're proud."

More voices joined their group as Chance's parents approached them with smiling faces. Aiyana's arms opened and entwined her son. "Congratulations, Honey. You too, Ana. You guys looked great up there."

Melissa and Ben gave each other a warm hug. While the group chatted, Aunt Tera slapped Uncle Jace's belly with the back of her hand and said, "Go on. Give it to her."

Uncle Jace widened his eyes and tucked his hand into his back pocket and pulled out a wrinkled blue envelope.

"I see I should have put it in my purse." Tera winked at Ana.

He handed the card to Ana, who was only too familiar with the humiliation of Aunt Tera's scorching spotlight. "It's okay, Uncle Jace. It's the thought that counts."

She accepted it and unsealed the envelope. As she opened the card something slipped free and fluttered to the ground. Before she could reach the floor, Chance snagged it and delivered it to Ana.

"Thanks."

Ana glanced at what Chance handed to her and faced her aunt and uncle.

"Thank you *sooo* much. That's *very* generous of you." She clung to them both as she held the check they had gifted her.

"Well, we thought you could use the money for school or whatever it was you planned on doing. We know you want to travel. You're welcome." Aunt Tera blushed and grew quiet.

Melissa appeared to be on cloud nine, her eyes aglow and overjoyed about her daughter's accomplishment. Ana achieved more than a diploma. She was alive.

They headed toward the parking lot, greeting and receiving congratulations along the way.

After Ana thanked her aunt and uncle again for their gift, she waved goodbye and climbed into Chance's truck. "Bye, Mom. See you in a minute."

***

When Chance and Ana entered his house, they were welcomed with balloons and ribbons. Food was laid out on the dining table buffet style, and a burst of colorful flowers centered the ambrosia.

Aiyana walked in from the kitchen with a bowl in her hands. "Hi, guys. What do you think?"

"It's great. I can't wait to try...everything," Ana said as her eyes passed hungrily over the table.

A voice rose from behind the graduates, which startled Ana. Chance appeared unsurprised. "Congratulations to you both."

They turned to face Niyol, who greeted them with his hands held out to each.

"Thank you," Ana said, as she accepted what he placed into her palm.

Chance held his gift and began to study it.

"Chance, this is something that was passed to me from my father," he said as he caught Chance's eye. "Something that has been passed through many generations. Keep it *protected*. I believe it will prove to be useful...somehow."

A huge claw-like nail extended from Chance's hand, like a scythe. He inspected it, puzzled. Was it a fossil? It was far too large to belong to anything he had ever seen.

Niyol rounded his attention to Ana, and his eyes softened. "Ana. This is something I've had a long time. I gave it to my wife a lifetime ago, but now I think it belongs to you."

As he spoke, she held the silver ring between her fingertips and slid it onto her finger; a perfect fit. It was a simple band, but had an intricate feather design.

"It's an eagle feather." He continued. "Something sacred. Eagles hear and see all. They represent courage and guidance. Eagle feathers were used by shamans as tools in healing because of their power. This reminder may bring you closer to your potential."

Chance wondered what his grandfather meant but didn't want to interrupt.

"Thank you, Niyol – it's beautiful. Are you sure?" Ana admired it with wide eyes.

She was family now. Chance knew Niyol had accepted Ana enough to let her in on their family secret. A secret he had never shared with Aiyana.

"It's yours."

A loud knock at the front door drew their attention. Melissa's loud compliments rose from the entry. "Isn't this a beautiful home? And so big. I *love* how you've decorated it."

Melissa and Eva were welcomed into the living room. Eva's eyes went right to the food.

Aiyana carried in a stack of plates and set them on the table. "Well, if you're ready we can begin eating."

Everyone milled toward the table and the piles of steaming meat, potatoes and grilled vegetables. Eva stood with a plate in her hands, eyes closed, as she inhaled the aroma from each tray. Aiyana stood beside her with an appreciative grin.

Ana and Chance sat beside each other on the brown suede couch while they tucked into their food.

Eva placed herself beside Aiyana and quizzed her about ingredients. "Is there rosemary in the beef? And orange?"

Aiyana answered in appreciation for her new little friend. "Why, yes, Eva. You have excellent taste buds. You must like to cook?"

The phone rang from the kitchen, which interrupted their conversation. Aiyana jumped to answer it. Melissa and Ben continued their discussion as the soft melody of classical music danced through the air.

A moment later, Aiyana wandered into the living room with a confused look. "Father, you have a phone call. It's George."

Niyol's eyes shot to the doorway where Aiyana had just appeared. He rose from his chair and proceeded to the kitchen as though something unwelcome lay ahead.

Chance turned his head and caught his mother's eye. "George, the ranch manager? Did he say why he was calling?"

Aiyana shrugged and said, "No. You'll have to ask when he's off the phone."

He ate in silence until his grandfather reentered the room. Chance followed him with his eyes and sniffed the air. Was it fear he smelled? Niyol lowered himself into his recliner and stared at the Thunderbird weaving on the wall.

Chance walked over to his grandfather and squatted beside him.

"What's wrong?" Chance whispered.

"Not now, Chance."

Chance raised his eyebrow and snorted.

"Not now." Niyol avoided eye contact with Chance. Without consolation, Chance returned to his place next to Ana.

"What's up?" Ana had watched the entire interaction with interest.

He turned his head toward his grandfather, whose stoic, hardened expression worried Chance. "I don't know. Something's wrong. Stay after dinner – I'll offer to drive you home," he said casually to Ana, and she nodded back.

Niyol seemed aware he was being monitored throughout the evening. He kept his eyes averted.

When Melissa gathered her coat, Ana went to talk to her quietly. "Mom, do you mind if Chance drops me off a little later?"

"Oh, sure I guess that's fine. You deserve it." Melissa

picked her purse up and flung it over her shoulder. "Eva, it's time to go."

Eva dragged herself off the couch and grabbed her stomach. "Thank you so much for that delicious food."

Aiyana smiled proudly and handed Eva some note cards.

Eva read them and leapt to hug Aiyana. "Thank you so much. I can't wait to make the beef recipe. It was sooo good!"

"Thank you, Ben and Aiyana for your wonderful hospitality. I look forward to seeing you again soon." Melissa made her way toward the front door with Eva on her trail.

CHAPTER 37

After Melissa's headlights wove down the drive and disappeared into the night, Chance approached his grandfather again. Niyol shook his head and said, "Not in front of your parents. Let's go stargaze on the porch."

Ana grabbed her jacket for warmth. Chance didn't require any extra clothing and followed his grandfather out the back door to the deck. Before Niyol slipped outside, he said to Aiyana, who was doing dishes with Ben, "I'm going to teach the kids some constellations out back. It'll be a little while."

Aiyana waved her dripping gloved hand as they dissolved into the darkness.

Chance followed close behind Niyol as though he thought his grandfather might escape.

Niyol settled onto the wooden stairs.

Ana and Chance flanked him, waiting for him to speak.

"First, Chance, I recommend you take Ana home. If you love her, and want to protect her, she shouldn't hear this. She shouldn't get involved."

"Well, you can tell me, and I tell her later, or you just tell us both now." Chance shrugged.

Niyol faced Ana and asked, "Are you sure you want to hear this? It could risk your safety."

"If Chance is in danger, I want to know about it. My life is already balanced on a knife," she said and took a shaky breath. "I'd rather know what's happening."

"Very well." Niyol focused on the stars above and avoided eye contact with either of them.

"This story begins a long time ago, but I'll start when I was a young teenager," he said. "I lived on the reservation in Arizona with my brothers, my mother and father. My father was a shapeshifter. We came from the direct line of the *original one*. Stories of our ancestors were passed down by every generation, something our family was proud of and careful to protect.

"My father always taught us that the power was to be used to keep balance in the universe. There were other shifters who chose the path of imbalance and destruction. It was these evil doers who forever ruined the name of shapeshifters, and that was why we were never to reveal what my father truly was to *anyone*.

"When my two older brothers started behaving differently they were older teenagers. I didn't know what was happening – but my father did.

"One day my middle brother phased right in front of me into a small bobcat. I was surprised and envious. At first, I looked up to them in admiration. They both were honored with having the *gift*. My father, he was so proud – two of his sons had the rare ability." Niyol stared at the night sky before continuing.

"Well, then things started happening. Bad things. A girl was found killed by an animal, a sweet girl my brother had shown favor towards. Then, my older brother disappeared. Gone without a trace. My remaining brother became very dark and frightening." Niyol shook his head as though he were trying to shake the memory from his mind. "After my eldest brother disappeared, my father seemed to understand what was happening. He confronted my brother. They argued, and fought, and my brother disappeared. A couple days later, while my father slept, my brother returned and killed him."

Ana gasped and put her hand to her mouth. Chance's foot slipped from its resting place.

"My brother disappeared, but before he left, he made me promise I'd never return or threaten his power. I didn't have the family talent, so I wasn't a threat. I was as useless as dirt, he said. He thought I was pathetic and that was what saved my life. I fled and never returned. I'm not sure where he settled, if he did at all.

"The pact I made with my brother applies to my kin as well. To you, Chance.

"This gift has only been passed to the males in the family. So I knew your mother wouldn't show the skill. When you began to show talent, I knew I'd have to train you and keep you hidden. I decided using the gift for good was a responsibility and necessary to continue the honor of our blood line. I've had to be so careful teaching you."

Niyol sat stone still as he gazed at the stars. "Now, the phone call. George, my ranch manager, he called to say a young man came through asking for me. He had Native American bloodlines, and George thought he might be one of my grandchildren."

Niyol stared Chance in the eyes. "I might be jumping to conclusions, but my brother's blood line may have survived. And maybe his kin is asking questions about me and about where I live. If I am right, he will come searching for us – here.

"No one can know you've been given the gift. Too dangerous for all of us. Your parents can't know about our family history. They need to be sheltered from this. They have no way to protect themselves. Son, you must stop ALL use of your powers for the time being."

Ana's mouth hung open. She squinted and scanned the forest. Her body slid closer to Chance's.

"Well, if you insist. I'll lay low." Chance glared into the wilderness as his mind reeled with questions.

"Yes, I do. For everyone's sake. Be normal for a while. This boy could be here already – the ranch isn't that far as the bird flies. He could be watching us right now," Niyol said while he surveyed the black profiles of the evergreens that loomed above. "We have to show there are no powers on this side of the family. None." Niyol leaned forward to look his grandson in the eye. His face remained like stone, unmoving.

"Why do you think this guy's bad news anyway? Just because his grandfather or whatever was some crazy shapeshifter?"

"Listen to me, Chance! It's *important* – you can't give your cousin any reason to kill you. I *can't* let that happen."

"Kill?!" Chance said with a yell and whipped his head around to search his grandfather's solemn profile. "What's going *on*, Grandfather?! Is there anything you're not telling me?!" Chance stood and gripped the stair rail. His jaw clenched, and his gaze was forceful. "Why can't I just fight, then? Let me end it now. I'm strong; I have bear form." His mind spun. What was his grandfather talking about? Why would anyone want to kill him?

"Chance, settle down. Understand this. You have no experience fighting your own. There is *much* you don't know. You can't enter a fight with an unknown enemy. What if you're outmatched?!" Niyol shook his head. "You need to stop all use of your powers. Now. Once he sees our family is powerless, he should move on. Please, Chance. I don't want anything happening to you. Promise me you'll stop practicing for now. Until we determine it's safe." Niyol pleaded with him.

Ana broke her silence and said, "Chance, maybe you should listen to your grandfather. Really, he only wants what's best for you. I don't want anything happening to you either. It'll just be for a little while. Try not to think about it."

"*Fine*. I don't like just sitting idle. But I'll stop using my 'special abilities'." Chance made finger brackets and spoke mockingly. His anger was framed in his locked jaw and tensed muscles. Why hadn't his grandfather told him any of this before? Agitated, he glared at Niyol.

Ana rose and laid her hands on his shoulders. His stone body grew tighter under her touch, almost in defiance. She leaned in and nuzzled her face into his back. Like butter, his muscles melted at her soft caress.

He growled and turned. "Okay, okay, I guess we'll do something like the movies *instead*. I'll take you out to dinner, too. A real date. We'll stay out of the forest – for once."

Niyol stood and patted his grandson's head. "Thanks, Chance." He retreated to the confines of the house and left the teenagers outside on the stairs.

"Come on. It can't be that bad. I'm sure we can find *some* things to do together that don't involve you turning into an animal. And if it keeps us safe, let's do it." Ana kissed him, and he knew she was trying to distract him.

He pulled away smoothly not to hurt Ana's feelings and gazed into her shaded eyes. "Ana, but I do it all for you. I want to protect you even more now. If I need to be just a little stronger to heal you, or to fight some crazy nut, then I want to be ready."

"Chance, what would your family and I do without you? Please, just listen to him for now. Patience...*please*." Ana grabbed the front of his shirt in desperation. "I *can't* lose you."

"I'm right here." He lifted her to the next step, and they clung to each other as though it were their last night together.

"Want to look at the stars for a while before you take me home?"

"Sure." Chance lowered himself onto a stair ledge and pulled Ana into his lap. She giggled and leaned her head against his chest.

While Ana stared up at the stars, Chance's mind wandered. He began to speculate. If there were stories about brave protectors, could there be other stories, ones about terrible animals haunting various tribes through history?

Of course there were. It dawned on him. All Native American tribes have stories about animal spirits. Some good and some bad.

Chance decided after he took Ana home, he would do some research on his laptop. There would have to be a multitude of stories that could answer his questions. If his grandfather wasn't going to talk, then he would have to use another resource.

He enjoyed being with Ana and he hated being away from her, but tonight he was too anxious about the mysterious information from his grandfather. Questions bubbled up that he needed to find answers to. He wanted to get her home so he could begin his private studies.

Chance stroked her face and said, "I bet you're exhausted after today. You look a little tired. Should I take you home so you can get some rest? Maybe tomorrow we can do the real date thing. Dinner and a movie. What do you think?"

Ana stretched while yawning and said, "Yeah. What a day. I guess I *am* tired. You're so good to me. I'm so lucky to have you in my life."

Ana dropped down to the next stair while Chance rose and jumped in front of her with his hand outstretched.

After he pulled her up, they walked into the house and tracked down Chance's parents who were half-asleep on the couch. Ben was reading the newspaper, and Aiyana's eyes were closed.

"I'm going to take Ana home now. I'll be back soon."

"Oh, okay. See you later Ana – and congratulations." Ben lowered the paper as he spoke, clearly trying not to disturb his wife who was propped against him.

"Thanks for everything tonight. The food was wonderful. Will you let her know for me? I'll see you soon." Ana waved, then Chance tugged her out of the house by the hand.

"Geez, where's the fire? You trying to get rid of me?" Ana said with a laugh, but her eyes narrowed with suspicion.

"No way. I wouldn't do that. I just don't want you passing out. You're *always* my first priority." Chance put on his best poker face. He wasn't lying about caring for her, but he didn't want her to know he was going to poke around for more information, especially after he promised he'd let it go.

On the way to her house, Ana chatted about the different

movies they could go to the next night. Chance's black truck pulled up the gravel driveway to the welcoming little blue house with the shining light.

"I'll call you in the morning and check on you. Oh, hey, could you stay in the house right now; no more star gazing for a while?"

"Yeah, no problem – I'll stay in the house. And Chance, remember *your* promise." Ana kissed his forehead, grazing his frown lines. His eyes followed her as she walked into the house.

He sped home. Along the way he realized he wasn't as discreet as he thought. That or Ana had begun to understand him so well he'd be hard pressed lying to her in the future.

When he arrived in his driveway, most of the lights were out in the house. He sped upstairs to collect his laptop, unsure if using his accelerated abilities was included in the whole no-special-powers ban. His speed, hearing, sight and smell were things he had grown accustomed to. And didn't want to give them up.

He opened his computer. The screen flashed blue as it came to life. Chance typed in, *Navajo animal attacks.*

The first couple of results summarized superstitions Navajo have about dead animals. The next seemed promising, titled *Skinwalkers- Navajo Shapeshifters.*

He clicked on the link and read the first paragraph.

The Navajo yee naaldlooshii ("with it, he goes on all fours") use their powers to travel in animal form. When a priest, or shaman, has achieved the highest level of power and commits the act of killing an immediate member of the family, they thus gain the evil powers associated with skinwalkers. They have the ability to assume the form of any animal they choose, depending on what they need. Also utilizing the power to hurt victims by simple touch, they become the culmination of every bad character imaginable – put together. Many attempts have reportedly been made to shoot or kill one but are usually not successful. Native People do not speak of them, for fear they will be attacked in retribution.

Chance rubbed his eyes and whistled. Although he was sure some of the information couldn't be totally accurate, it revealed a lot. Especially the part about the murder of family members – that fell into line with what Grandfather told him. What *little* he had said.

Frustrated, he pounded his fist onto his desk and then glanced to his door.

He had only heard positive stories and legends from his family. It could fall to reason that there would be ones who sought power at the highest cost – human life. *But what power did they seek? Were they just evil, getting gratification from hurting others?*

What did he need to know to kill or stop another shapeshifter? From his research, he gathered Native Americans thought shapeshifters were near impossible to kill. He remembered the countless times he had injured himself. Chance had healed himself countless times after shifting back to human form. A shapeshifter would have to be *severely* incapacitated if they were unable to heal themselves from phasing. There was no way to know for sure. Not without getting into a fight with another like himself. Or asking his grandfather. And both were out of the question.

The gravity of the situation weighed on him. There was nothing he wanted more than to keep Ana safe. If he could protect her. If only he was stronger – if he had Thunderbird. He snapped his laptop shut and glared out the window.

Patience was not his strong suit.

CHAPTER 38

"So hey, want to go out tonight? Dinner and a movie?" Chance's voice asked over the phone line.

"That depends, is it a comedy, a chic flick, horror or action movie? Let's see how well you know me." Ana curled her hair around her finger and smiled coyly.

"Hmmm, guess horror is out. I don't think you'd go for action. And a chick flick would make you laugh more than cry, and our time would be better spent watching a *real* comedy. How 'bout it? You want to go laugh with me?" Chance paused and added, "What do you want to eat? Burgers or pizza? I'm going to go with hamburgers. Well, judge – how'd I do?"

"Eh, I'll let you slip by with a B. Yes, to the movie, but I'm in the mood for burritos, feeling kinda nostalgic today." Her thoughts tumbled over their first kiss when Chance rowed them to picnic on the island.

"Of course, your wish is my command." His voice growled.

"Okay, I command you to stay out of trouble," she said with a laugh, then turned serious. "So, what did *you* do last night?" She waited to see if he would try to lie.

"Oh, just did some reading and then went to bed."

Although he kept his tone casual, she knew he wasn't being forthright. "Ummm-hmmm, good one. Well, as long as you're staying out of danger. Okay, when are we going?"

"How 'bout I swing by around five?"

"Sure. You going to hang out with your grandfather 'til then?" Ana suggested not so subtly.

"Uhh, you trying to get a babysitter for me?" He laughed into the phone, but she could tell he was agitated.

"I don't know what you're talking about. Alright, I'm gonna hang with Eva for a bit, and I'll see *you* later."

***

After he snapped the phone shut, Chance leapt up the stairs four at a time and reached the top landing in just two and a half strides. He grinned. It never got old. He loved his powers.

He ducked into his room and closed the door without a sound. His blinds were open; his mother must have come in earlier to let in the light. Chance craved a cave-like space right now. It would serve him better.

Darkness encompassed the room as he moved from one window to the next and twisted the blinds shut. His shirt dropped to the floor. Soon his pants followed.

He poised himself at the edge of his bed and closed his eyes. The radiant energy held within his body fluxed at his attention. The static blue power listened eagerly, waiting for his next impulse.

Had his grandfather been in the room he would have seen Chance flash from fox, to squirrel and back again. In an energy conserving exercise, he tried to move from form to form to build up endurance. Every shape shift depleted his reserve.

He sat in his room while his family was unaware of his activities for over an hour. Tired after he expended all of his strength, he went downstairs to make a snack. His body required constant sustenance, and with the effort he put out, he was ravenous.

Once he ransacked the fridge, he went to take a nap on the couch and slept for a couple hours, exhausted after his secret training.

He woke from his slumber when a light beam, from a nearby window, crept across his face. Chance rubbed his eyes, disoriented.

Ben walked through the room and chuckled. "Enjoying your school-free day?"

Chance frowned and said, "No, actually. I'm bored."

"You could always go by Kenny's," Ben said. "I worked at a

gas station when I was in school. Wasn't the best money, but it was something to do. Kept me out of trouble. Well, for the most part." Ben's eyes glazed over, and an impish grin broke across his face.

"That's great, Dad." Chance yawned and stretched. "I think I'm gonna enjoy a couple more days of boredom before heading back in. Kenny told me to take some free time – his graduation gift to me."

Ben nodded and said, "Enjoy. Okay, well, I'm off to the shop. I need to deliver a custom order. Mom should be off her shift late tonight. I'll be back later." He wandered out of the room carrying a leather briefcase.

Chance sat up and stared out the window. The trees swayed in the breeze and rumbled like a distant freight train. Cotton white clouds slid across the sky like pads of butter on a griddle.

He headed back to his room and shut the door like a bear reentering his cave. Most of his energy had returned, but it was like sap – sticky and resistant. He sat again on his bed and reached for the claw his grandfather gave him. It sat innocently on his side table. He held it at each end and stared intently at it. What animal could it belong to? It seemed too long to be a claw. What if it were a Thunderbird talon? There was no way of knowing.

Electricity surged within him, charged and hot. It coalesced and grew in intensity; a tentative pulse of power reached down his arms and pooled in his hands. Surprised, his eyes flared open as he stared at the gigantic claw. Blue threads wove across its surface and met in the center. He had never seen anything mapped that wasn't part of a living animal before. His heart pounded in his chest.

A light knock came from his closed door. His head jerked to the side, and his eyes flashed in shock. So absorbed with his new exploration, it took a moment for him to remember his surroundings.

The sound of his grandfather's voice met his ears. "Chance, I was going to sit on the porch. Do you want to join me?"

"Yeah. Let me get my shoes on," he answered as he moved to open his door. He turned, sat on his bed, and laced his sneakers up with shaky fingers.

Niyol peered into the room observantly, and Chance noticed his eyes sweep over every corner.

"Did you take a nap?" Niyol asked and squinted at Chance.

"Uh, yeah. Why?"

"Your blinds are shut. Well, let's wake you up before your date with Ana."

"Sounds like a plan."

The two generations of men sat out on the porch together. Niyol filled the quiet with stories of his childhood. His deep voice painted pictures of another time while Chance closed his eyes and imagined his grandfather as a youth.

Niyol's melodic tone was so soft and low, it diffused as it rose to the evergreens. A large black crow sat on a high branch and cocked its head.

CHAPTER 39

Chance pulled up into Kenny's Auto Shop and sauntered over to the side of the building. Kenny was stacking some loose tires against the back of the brick wall.

"Hey, Kenny. I was wondering if that heater hose came in yet?" Chance asked and leaned against the edge of the lime green wall while he listened to cars zoom down the road. His eyes combed past some finches scavenging near a grassy meadow. They scurried onto the oily gravel and darted back and forth in a hungry relay race. He looked back at Kenny who had stopped and stared at him.

"Something on your mind?" Kenny asked, looking amused.

Chance shook his head and said, "Naw, it's nothing."

"Sorry, man. I just got a call from Arney and he said the shipment was delayed – maybe a couple more days."

"Oh, okay. Yeah, I gotta take off. When did you want me back?"

Kenny scratched his head and smiled. "You that eager to get back to work? Like I said – enjoy some time off, and I'll see you in a week, say."

Chance shrugged and turned. "Kay, see ya."

He jogged back to his truck, and as he fired up the engine, a black form flew overhead and landed on Kenny's sign.

He shook his head. Now he was on the lookout, and every animal was suspicious. This was going to be a challenge.

The shiny black truck crawled onto the highway and sped to Ana's house. Blurred wilderness fell behind until he crawled onto her driveway. A cloud of dust stirred a hazy veil around his windows, and he waited for it to settle before he opened his door.

He darted up the walk and counted five squirrels that clamored around a grove of firs, and he detected some kind of small furry mammal hidden in the nearby field. His senses were on fire; everything threw an alarm.

Before he realized, Ana was by his side, looking curiously at him.

"So, what did you do today?" she asked as they walked out to his black truck.

"Not much. I was totally bored, so I caught a good two hour nap on the couch. How 'bout you?"

"Oh, Eva and I played a couple card games. Then I finished my portfolio. Mom wants to take it to work. I guess she knows some people who may need a photographer. We'll see."

"That'd be cool. Hungry? Ready for some burritos?"

"Yeah, I didn't eat lunch, so I'm starving."

They drove to a Mexican restaurant in Sandpoint and were seated at a corner booth. Soft Mariachi music filled the air. A waitress approached. She wore a red shirt, and her hair was slicked back into a bun.

"Hi, can we have two iced teas to start? Thanks."

Chance peered at Ana over the top of his menu. "So, was it hard not stargazing last night?"

"No way. When I thought about some guy out there watching me, I was more than happy staying indoors. I'll be relieved when your grandfather thinks he's gone, or that it's safe again," she said, as she stared at the menu. "I'm a little freaked out. Your grandfather said his *own brother* killed their father and probably his brother too. Who knows what kind of nut job is out there looking for you?"

Goosebumps rose on her arms, and she appeared to try to smooth them down with her hands. "I hope you're taking his advice seriously, Chance. You aren't using your powers anymore...right?"

He reached his hand out to hers and warmed her cool fingers. "Don't worry, Ana. I don't want you hurting yourself from the stress. Try not to think about it."

"Yeah, right. That's easy to say. And that isn't an answer. Are *you* keeping your mind off of it?" she asked, and her shoulders lifted.

The waitress walked up, placed their drinks on the table and waited with her book ready to take their order.

"I'll have the smothered chicken burrito." Ana snapped her menu shut.

"And the beef taco dinner platter. Thanks." Chance handed their menus to the waitress and waited for her to walk away before he addressed Ana.

"Look – I understand. You're worried. I think everything should be fine. Let's just try not to think about it tonight. Let's just enjoy our time out together." His hands crept across the table and cradled hers delicately. "Hey, you know you look really pretty tonight. It'll be hard sitting next to you in the dark theater. I'm not sure which I'll be watching more." He lifted her hand and kissed each finger.

Small goose pimples rose on her skin again, and she brushed her hair behind her shoulder.

"Smooth talker. I can't resist you." She rolled her eyes.

Chance chuckled in victory, lifted his eyebrow and kissed the top of her hand.

Their first dinner date seemed to move them past their worries and concerns. Ana walked out of the restaurant with a yawn. Chance was happy to lead her to the truck, and she leaned her head against his shoulder as they went. The setting sun made the sky glow azure, and thin clouds streaked across like pulled taffy.

"Now, what movie were we seeing again? I forgot."

"You know, that one about the self taught rocket scientist. With that guy you like…"

"Riiiight. I hope I can keep my eyes open; that food made me sleepy."

"Your *normal* tired?"

"For the most part. There was a really noisy bird outside my window early this morning. It wasn't you, was it?" Ana asked and cocked her head.

"Innocent." He lifted his hands up.

Caw, caw.

They walked down the gray street to the parking lot. A couple of ravens pecked at a pile of crumbs beside the street corner. Perched on the bed of Chance's truck was a solitary crow.

Chance was gone from Ana's side in a flash as he used inhuman speed to dart through the lot. With a triumphant smile, he stood beside his truck and held the surprised crow in his hands. It began to peck at his fingers and caw in surprise.

"Chance?! What are you *doing*?!"

"It could be him...the...the guy!"

The bird stared wide-eyed and turned its head around, clearly unsure about what was happening. It continued to caw, and Chance pinched its beak shut, silencing it.

Ana glanced from the bird to Chance and said, "Um, it looks *just* like a frightened bird to me..."

"You said this morning a bird was cawing outside your window, and I've noticed crows around," Chance said.

"Um, I may not be as knowledgeable as you about animals, but I *do* know that crows are like the most common bird, *riiight*?"

Heat radiated from his cheeks as the wind let out of his sails, and he grew embarrassed. He examined the frightened bird in his clenched hands then Ana's bewildered look.

He threw the bird into the air, and it flew into the nebulous sky. Chance rubbed his temple and stared at the ground.

"That was embarrassing. Okay, so maybe it's been bothering me more than I've let on. It can't hurt to be observant and cautious."

Ana hugged him and said, "Don't be embarrassed. I agree. It can't hurt that you're trying to look out for us. At least you didn't hurt the bird."

"I guess I ate *crow* tonight."

Their laughter rose through the dim parking lot, as a nearby light flickered and went out. The dark flying form had since disappeared, but its noisy protest could still be heard.

CHAPTER 40

"Come over." Chance's voice pleaded through the phone.

Ana stretched on their couch, comfortable in the ratty shirt and flannel pants she had slept in. Cartoons were on and Eva was eating dry cereal from the box.

"But I'm not even dressed."

"Perfect."

"Ugh. Well, I could drive over after a shower. Give me an hour or so."

"I love you even when you're dirty. Okay, okay, I'll wait and try to be *patient*."

"Me, too. See you soon," Ana laughed and shut the phone.

It took another ten minutes to get enough motivation to pull herself off the couch. She slunk through the house like she was a member of the Adam's Family.

Later, her erect figure reemerged from the bathroom with wet hair and a rejuvenated step. She tugged through her empty drawers and realized it was time to do laundry. After she found a fresh pair of jeans and a plain white tee, she brushed out her tangled chestnut locks and lumbered down the stairs, shoes in hand.

Melissa greeted her in the kitchen. "Decided to scrape yourself off the couch? You look freshened up. Guess the shower did the trick. What are you up to today?"

"I'm headed to Chance's now. I get the feeling we're just going to wind up bored together. But that's better than being bored alone."

Ana sat on the edge of her seat and leaned over to slip on her shoes. Halfway through she had to sit up when too much blood rushed to her head, making her dizzy.

"Well, I hope you have a nice time together being bored. If you're looking for something to do, you could always help me organize my closet," Melissa half joked.

"Have fun with that," Ana said, and rose to her feet. "Oh, I think I need to stop for gas. Can I please have some gas money?" Ana batted her eyes.

"Oh, and you're ready to leave me high and dry when it comes to my closet? Thanks." Melissa said as she grabbed her purse off a kitchen chair and pulled out her wallet. She handed Ana some folded bills and added before she let go. "I have a couple photography job prospects lining up for you. I'm getting to know lots of people from working at the bank. Anyway, soon you'll be covering your *own* gas bills." Melissa smirked and released the money.

"I guess that's fair," Ana said . "I appreciate it all Mom. Thanks."

"Well, you know I'd do anything for you." Melissa pecked her cheek, and Ana searched for her keys and wallet.

After she found her things, she began the drive to Chance's house. A mile or two past the city limits, she pulled off into a gas station that butted up against the base of a pine forest.

Ana leaned against the side of her van while she pumped gas. Across the highway, a wide grassy stretch extended up to a cluster of birch trees that shielded the dark windy river.

Out of the corner of her eye, she saw a dark form walk towards her.

CHAPTER 41

From the porch, Chance could see ominous clouds tumbling through the atmosphere. Electricity was in the air and raised the hair on his arms. His impatience was palpable and made him pace, unable to keep still. He wished he were in the meadow training and not on restriction.

If Ana were here, at least his attention would be more readily engaged. Where was she anyway?

He held the claw-like token his grandfather gave him as he paced. His thumb traced along the arch and created friction. Blue light glinted.

His back pocket rang, and he flipped his phone open. "Where have you been?! You said you were coming over after a shower? It's been over *three hours*!"

Silence.

Chance squinted his eyes as his pores tingled in warning. "Hello? Ana?"

A voice answered him, but it wasn't Ana's.

"I'm sorry. Ana's busy right now...busy turning blue. I think she needs a doctor." The pubescent voice chuckled.

"What?! Who is this?! What's happened to Ana?!" The veins in Chance's neck throbbed as he roared into the phone.

"Is that how you talk to family? Play nice, Chance." It sounded like the voice was being thrown to stay deep and smooth, but a couple high pitched tones broke through the condescension. A young teenager, definitely.

His body released its tension except for the hand that held the phone, which was coiled so tight his fingertips tingled. "What do you want?"

"To meet you. Come join us. We're at the top of the mountain just north of your home. You can't miss us. Not with *your* eyesight. Oh, and uh...you might want to hurry, she *really* isn't looking good."

Chance could hear the smirk through the phone, and his

temper flared. His energy no longer blue, burned into a red inferno and licked at the air around him as it radiated beyond his body.

"If you hurt her..." Chance said through pursed lips.

"I don't think you're in a position to threaten me."

The connection went dead as Chance frantically yelled into the phone.

Birds burst high from their perches as a howl tore across the mountainside.

Chance tore through the house and ran upstairs to his grandfather's room. Without knocking, he burst through the door.

Niyol sat at the end of his bed. His face was pale, his eyes wide.

"He has her, Grandfather! They're at the top of the mountain just north of the house! I have to get her – save her!" Chance said in one breath.

Niyol stood and opened his mouth to speak, but Chance brushed past him to his bedroom window. The curtains were yanked off the rod as Chance shoved the window open. In one smooth movement he flung himself from the window and dropped down.

"Chance! No!" Niyol called out as a large bald eagle rose into the sky.

CHAPTER 42

Ana had a hard time focusing. She couldn't see. Similar to when she had passed out in the meadow with Chance, she was removed from everything. Detached, simply an observer.

Her body lay limp on a rocky outcropping. Pine and fir trees huddled around the rocks.

A cold wind whipped through the woods and sliced through the branches like icy knives. Ana couldn't feel the cold. She was numb, dulled, trapped in her own body. She tried to open the curtains of her eyes so she could see outward, but someone had boarded the windows shut.

She imagined a fire inside her; the red flames kept her warm, even if just in her thoughts. Her attention on the pyre made images flash through her mind. Images of driving, then of stopping.

There was a gas station at the base of the forest. Yes. That was right; she remembered that. She stopped for gas. Then…something was said, someone spoke to her and she turned to face…what?

A young man's body sauntered toward her, but instead of a boy's face, a distorted beast sneered at her. The hideous maw with sharp, knifelike teeth opened menacingly. Grey eyes narrowed and focused on her while pointed ears pulled back. If it was the head of a wolf, she would hate to meet one like this in the forest. The monstrous head was now too clear, now too close. Its musty odor was laced with such a putrid stench, it turned her stomach. She tried to move her thoughts to something else.

She saw his hand lift up and rest on her chest. Pain – so much pain.

Her bruised arms and legs ached. She had tumbled around on the back bench of her van. It must have been an uphill drive on a rutted road, because her body was repeatedly slammed against the back hatch.

Fear entered her. Ana flung her eyes open.

Everything was sideways and blurry. She felt her body again and then wished she couldn't. Every inch screamed in pain; her heart sloshed around like a boat taking on water. Her veins burned along with her lungs and arms. She closed her eyes for a moment as the pressure in her head became too much.

She slid her eyes open again, still unsure of where she was. It was so dark she couldn't tell if it was day or night. The sun and moon were absent. She could barely see anything, but the air smelled like rain and pine trees and something electric.

Tall trees swayed around her. A burst of wind blew her hair from her face, and she saw a tall form standing near.

Her eyes lifted.

"Finally. Decided to join me?" a low voice said.

A tall boy, a couple years her junior, sneered down at her broken body. He had a pockmarked face and colorless eyes. They were so indistinct she thought they could be gray or made of stone. His oily hair was a limp tangled mass that hung to his shoulders, and his clothes were dirty and disheveled. He cleared his throat, pushed his hands into his dark jeans, and flexed his undeveloped biceps. "Didn't think you were gonna wake up." His voice came out deeper this time, controlled.

There was no trace of kindness in his eyes. She recoiled from his glare. He seemed pleased with her response, puffed his chest out, and lilted his head to the side with a sneer.

"Your boyfriend will be here soon. I wonder, will he fly or run? Wanna bet?" He stared at her as she lay soundless on the callous stone. "Maybe you'd prefer a different bet. How fast I'll kill him? If he's a *good* boy," he said like he tasted something sour. "Then he's been wasting his time learning from scratch. If he was smart he woulda done it the way *I* did." He sniffed and rubbed the end of his nose with his thumb. "I'm gonna go with ten minutes. I'm feeling generous."

What was this guy talking about? She couldn't figure it out.

Enflamed by her reaction, he lost control of his voice, and it wobbled in anger. "What are you looking at? I'm sorry, *sweetheart*, but I'm not on the market," he said and turned away from her to stare into the dark forest.

Ana's eyes widened. Was this guy insane? Mentally fragile, at the very least.

He whipped around to reveal his deep frown that crept upward into a frightening grimace. "I thought this-" he waved to the trees, "would be *much* more exciting than killing him in his sleep. Whad'ya think?" He didn't appear to require an answer, so he said without another glance, "I put a lot of thought into it, which says a lot, 'cause I *really hate* waiting. I'm so glad Chance has powers. Starting with family – just seems right." Then he laughed to himself. "Well, maybe he isn't the *first*..."

She couldn't believe her ears. What had happened? Was she going to die here with Chance? And where was he?

Her eyes fluttered as her heart rested in her chest. She used her last reserve of strength to reflect on Chance's face, and her useless heart jumped to life again. She kept him in her thoughts as a lifeline, unwilling to give in so easily. She would fight to stay alive.

"Don't die...yet, it'd be *so much better* if he hears your heart stop for himself."

Unable to speak, for fear it would take her breath away, she glared up at the cocky kid who stood triumphantly over her.

He chuckled, amused with her frown and crossed his arms in front of his sweat stained shirt. Then his attention snapped upward, and his face grew rigid. "He chose to fly. That's okay. It'll drain his energy *much* quicker." His back was turned to

Ana, and her line of sight became obscured by his body.

A long minute passed, which seemed like hours as she waited to hear Chance's voice. She wanted to hear him again, feel him near her. She didn't want to die alone.

"Where is she?" a scathing voice spat, so unrecognizable at first she couldn't believe it was Chance's.

"Right here. She's been *dying* to see you. Not very talkative though."

"Why are you *doing* this?!"

"You don't *know*?" Mocking laughter filled the air.

The boy's lanky body rocked back, and then her eyes were locked behind the blackened veil again. She clung to the sound of Chance's voice and the unsteady beat of her heart.

No matter how hard she tried, she couldn't grasp what was happening around her. Her consciousness faded to black.

***

"What do you mean?" Chance scowled at the boy before him. He measured him up and figured he could take him in a fist fight. Easy. They were around the same height, but Chance was broader and more muscular.

"Interesting. You don't have *any idea* what I want with you? Fine, guess *grandpa* kept you in the dark. Works for me." The boy shrugged and said, "It'll be fun and easy this way."

"Hold on, aren't you here to stop my grandfather's bloodline? To keep your family power?" Chance wanted to keep him engaged, to give him more time to figure out what to do. He peered around the boy and saw Ana sprawled on the rocks behind him. He sensed a faint heartbeat. At least she was still alive, for now.

"You could say that. I am here for power. To *take* it." The boy groaned with a smile. "Man, I'm younger than you, but *you're* the innocent retard." He chuckled, amused and clapped lazily, putting on a performance that would have offended anyone. "Duh. You probably don't even know there's others like us all around the world. Not many. Gotta breed and mature naturally. We can't just be created like that!" He snapped his fingers with a grin. "We live *long* lives – as long as we aren't killed first!" He struck his chest out, looked away and bobbed his head.

Chance was annoyed with this cocky punk, but tried keeping his cool. He didn't want to fan the fire.

"Got your powers around sixteen, right? That's average. Well, hey you've had two years to work at it. I imagine your grandpa's been teaching you slowly. There are ways around *that*. I got my powers only six months ago. I bet I'm *still* better than you. Thanks to my grandfather I've got *plenty* of skills. Can't wait to see what you can do. I can feel the draw – can't wait to kill you too."

He tightened his arms with a sneer, and suddenly his lanky form shivered down into a snapping crocodile. Its thick hide tore apart the dirty clothing so it hung by threads. The muddy colored beast lunged forward and showed its white pointy teeth in a broad smile. Chance stepped back in surprise. *What?!*

The large armored crocodilian morphed into a towering bleached white polar bear, and the remains of tattered clothing drifted down to the pine needles. It grumbled raucously and swayed in place. Chance guessed he wasn't familiar with this form and recognized his disorientation. He also recognized the sheer power put into these animal forms. *He's so powerful and has so many fierce forms. Hopefully his inexperience will help me.*

Promptly, the ghostly white shape dropped down into a serpentine rope. The dark brown body was innocent enough until its hood opened to reveal its true majesty. A forked tongue tasted the air, and its muscles flexed and lifted up to meet Chance's gaze.

They stared at each other for a long moment before the cobra lifted into the boy's human form. He smirked at Chance and reached down to grab his shredded clothing. "And I've *still* got plenty of energy..."

Why didn't Grandfather teach me to fight shifters?!. He had no idea what to do to win a fight with one of his kind. This kid was more powerful and knowledgeable. The only thing on Chance's side was the boy's inexperience.

He checked on Ana discreetly. She needed a doctor quick; her blue lips signaled trouble. He needed to move things along even if he didn't have a plan. "Nice show." Chance cleared his throat and said, "How'd you know I had powers? I haven't used them for the last two days – or did you assume?"

His counterpart shrugged. "You had it right, dumb-bo. I thought you had me...until you let me fly free." A smile spread across his face as he watched Chance's jaw drop open in realization.

"The *crow*? I was *right*?!" Chance could have screamed. If he had trusted his instincts, this demon wouldn't be standing before him now.

"If you had an *ounce* of guts, you'd have just killed the bird, but you're one of the nice guys. And you know what? Like they say, nice guys always finish last."

Chance wanted to tear every limb off the boy's body. He snapped his jaw shut and tasted salty blood after he caught his tongue by accident. The distraction drew his focus inward and things began to fall into place. A clear blue outline appeared in his mind, then he heard his grandfather's voice counsel him, *Keep your focus Chance; collect your energy*.

Again, to keep the boy's mind away from what he was doing, he asked, "You gonna to tell me your name before you kill me?"

Chance dropped his hand to his side and recaptured the electricity he experienced from the large talon. His fingers prickled with sensation.

"My name's Markus. Got any last words?"

In wide eyed meditation Chance drew from the electromagnetic current in the air around him and pulled it in like a sieve. He was thankful it was a stormy day, although if it boosted him, it would equally help his opponent – an opponent who seemed to understand their abilities better than he did.

Chance sucked in one last breath and an explosion of power burst outward; blue light radiated up from his hand. He backed up to the edge of the cliff, turned, and jumped.

He fell heavily for a moment. *Please work...please...*

CHAPTER 43

Thunder clapped in the absence of lightning. A massive flying shape soared into the clouds, and swooped back around to meet Markus, who stood with his mouth open.

Chance dove in and then swept across the ledge, his talons open, ready to grab his enemy.

In a flash Markus was gone from the top of the ridge, as he flung himself from the crag Ana lay upon.

Chance was joined in the skies. He examined his doppelganger with his new sharpened vision, able to target his eyesight at a whim. The enormous bird had no living equal, frightful in size with large clenched claws and a sharp beak used to tear and rip. Cinnamon feathers rippled in the air current, the tips snow white.

Chance's yellow eyes flashed as he swooped toward the other bird. Their talons met in a violent tangle, and they spiraled down toward the earth. Neither would let go.

Their eyes locked and their powerful nails released at the last moment, and they began an upward ascension, just avoiding a collision into the forest below.

The two huge bodies circled in the sky and sought an opportunity to attack. Chance studied Markus teeter sloppily and wobble through the air. Even if he was powerful, he wasn't experienced.

Chance kept a close eye on his opponent's erratic flight pattern. Slowly as he gained altitude he sensed a point of weakness and dove through the sky, his wings tucked against his body. Markus saw him coming and pivoted his talons ready to take a swipe.

Their bodies connected, and agonizing pain seized Chance's leg. His sharpened claws met Markus's chest and tore downwards. Their weapons connected, and they fell into another coiled plunge toward the earth. They broke free from each other and flew in opposite directions.

Chance's wings rippled in the wind dangerously and threatened to thrust him downward. He had never been hurt in animal form and didn't know how to handle a flying shape while injured. He was weakened. He would have winced if he could. His leg stung in pain, unable to tell how bad the wound was. He knew his claw sank into the flesh of his assailant's chest and hoped he had done damage.

A memory visited him. His grandfather told him that the Thunderbird could direct lightning. He skimmed through the air, careful his rival was not near and pulled in the electricity, which made his pores throb. It collected and arched between the ground and clouds.

His beak tickled when a bright burst of light blinded him. At first he thought he was successful. Then his body fell through the gloom. He hadn't been quick enough. Markus used his own plan against him. Electricity ravaged him. Everything hurt. He struggled to glide downward, but his body bent in pain. Chance spiraled in a wide circle, and his wings did their best to guide him to the earth.

He tried to level out, reaching his legs ahead of himself, and braced for his landing. As his feet hit the ground, his gashed leg collapsed, and he tumbled into a feathery heap. Unable to move, his body could not follow directions. It was busy short circuiting. Dirt and needles settled around him, and he drew his wobbly body upright. The pain was unreal. Bursts of flame seared his muscles and joints.

As he lay in the dust cloud, fear bled through him. *How's Markus so powerful?* Chance's energy was half depleted from taking Thunderbird, and that was with the benefit of the electricity in the air to aid him. His thoughts scrambled wildly. *How can Markus take Thunderbird form? He said he's only had abilities for six months... that's impossible! How can this be?*

Chance pulled himself up and faltered, crumbling back into his dirty resting place.

He knew what he needed to do.

The gigantic bird circled above and screamed in exultation.

Chance's chocolate brown fur bristled as Markus dove through the air to hit him. Erect and now pain free after taking grizzly bear form, Chance's energy reserve was sapped, but it was worth it. He towered over nine feet tall on his hind legs and readied his long razor claws for the oncoming Thunderbird.

The bird grew near with its legs extended, aiming for the grizzly's chest. In one sweeping motion, Chance cleaved his arm downward and razed a deep gash across the bird's legs, which sent the creature crashing into the dark trees. Branch tips swayed violently from the impact and dropped green immature pinecones to the ground like grenades.

A large cloud of dust and pine needles lifted, and Chance turned his upright body to survey the scene. While the dust settled, another tall form materialized through the disturbed air.

A black bear emerged with a roar, silencing the forest creatures and lifted onto its hind legs. White teeth glinted beneath its lips which curled back in an ominous reproach.

Chance was larger than the black bear that stood before him, but he guessed Markus had an ample power supply, capable of many animal forms. He was in a fight with a boy who should be weaker and less experienced than he was.

He strained his attention and listened for Ana's heartbeat. A soft rhythm sputtered from her direction. It sloshed recklessly, like a bucket filled too high. Time bore down on him. He had to stop this madness quickly to get her help.

A loud roar snapped him back to his current situation. He feared he was at a disadvantage, so he moved to the safety of the pines and left a tree trunk as a barrier. Markus moved forward and Chance wove from side to side, careful to keep the shield between them.

The odd dance continued until Markus swiped around the

tree and hit Chance on the arm. Chance was bigger, but he was also slower. The cuts stung, and he knew it left a mark. He needed to hurt Markus enough to force him to take another shape. He would have to attack relentlessly until Markus couldn't phase anymore and end his life swiftly.

Chance dodged from behind the tree and struck out at the smaller bear, but his body moved sluggishly and missed. The black bear beat him to it and pain seared his chest. The bear's paw impaled in Chance's sternum. The agony came from more than just the claws that sank into him - they radiated what felt like poison. A pea green glow stained his fur at the point of contact. His energy leached away like a bike tire deflating.

With a sudden explosion of power, Chance's grizzly form retracted from Markus's grasp and staggered back onto all fours. The shaky exhalation that sputtered from the grizzly's lips brought a macabre smirk to the black bear's maw.

A burst of tan fur shivered across Chance's grizzly's form. He sank down into a mountain lion, crouched on the forest floor.

The black bear stumbled backwards surprised and ducked down with its paws ready for a low attack.

Power built in Chance's front and hind legs. His body was free of pain and ready to inflict it. His lean form shot forward, ears pulled back. Powerful jaws and claws reached for flesh. They found purchase on the bear's arms, rupturing the onyx carpet of fur, staining it red.

Markus fell forward in an effort to tackle the large cat. Chance backed up as the bear crashed towards him.

Chance jumped up, clung to a tree trunk and began to scale a pine. It began to sway as the bear shook the base, trying to rattle him free.

Markus stopped and took another approach, and began to climb the neighboring pine.

Chance ascended high up the trunk and stopped before it

could arch from his weight. In amazement, he saw Markus's stocky black form claw up the tree beside him. As the furry form paralleled his, he lashed out. His paw pummeled the bear. Claws met flesh again, and Markus let out a roar in pain.

While they fought, their respective trees swayed fitfully. Markus knocked Chance's head with a heavy blow and caused him to slip four feet down the trunk. Bark rained down, which joined the needles on the forest floor.

In a quick decision, Chance leapt up and across to cling from the black bear's legs. His jaws and claws sank into the black fur, as blood oozed down his muzzle.

Markus, unable to hold on any longer, dropped them both to the earth. Claws raked down the trunk, and bits of tree bark tapped onto the ground.

The bear's heavy body crushed Chance when they impacted. Then the bear rolled off and to the side. It lay there unmoving.

The background noise of Ana's soft heartbeats stammered and changed as they became feeble and weak.

Chance grumbled, looked reproachfully over his shoulder and limped out of the forest. He neared Ana's weakened body and nestled his bloody muzzle into her chest to check for a heartbeat.

"Chance." A whisper broke from her lips, and then a spasm of pain ripped through her and she went limp.

He lifted a paw to touch her chest and sensed movement, spontaneously turned and leapt through the air, colliding with another cougar. They fell into the dirt and sprang to their feet, backing away like repelling magnets.

Low rumbling growls twisted and tangled together. Their ears laid flat against their heads, their haunches dropped to the ground, ready to launch.

Markus sprang first, his claw sank into Chance's neck. The force knocked him to the side, as his head rang from the blow.

Markus sauntered toward Ana. Chance snapped out of his daze and clawed his opponent's rear. Markus feigned to the side, avoided injury and swiped Chance across the face, putting out his left eye.

Chance stood tall and swayed for a moment as vertigo hit. With only one eye he tilted his head to the side to see. The mountain lion watched him wobble and pulled his lips back into a sneer.

Chance knew he had to make this count. His energy was waning, and he wouldn't have more than one or two shifts left. A fox wouldn't be able to incapacitate a cougar. This was his last powerful form.

He crouched and waited to see what Markus would do next.

The rival cat tilted its head back to look at Ana, Chance followed his gaze. Without hesitation, Markus leapt onto Chance and sank his teeth in his neck. Chance used the last of his strength to pull his claws back and sink them into Markus's face. The teeth released their hold on Chance as his body dropped to the ground.

Chance's blood seeped from his body. The electric blue energy within him wanted to find a more powerful shape. To save energy, he utilized the static power from the air to phase form yet again.

He jumped to his feet, defeated. A red fox now sat at the foot of the mountain lion.

Chance's attention was drawn behind the cougar, and his eyes widened. Markus, clearly thought it was a ruse, identical to the one he had just pulled and kept his eyes on the red furry body in front of him.

An elderly man stood at the edge of the forest. His familiar face brought Chance relief and then fear sank in. He didn't want his grandfather injured trying to save him.

While Chance frantically thought about what to do next, he watched in wide-eyed wonder as Niyol's clothing dropped to the ground.

There, among the fabric, a large wolverine emerged.

Like a rocket, it dove under the unsuspecting cougar, clawing and tearing at its stomach. A wet ripping sound alerted Markus as he jumped straight up. The wolverine clung fast as it was lifted through the air and was dropped again.

Chance's body jumped to action, as he bit at the cougar, although his mind remained stunned. He didn't understand. How could his grandfather change form?

Niyol's dark body came out from underneath the cougar and clawed the cougar's eyes.

The mountain lion tried to back into the forest, but Chance positioned himself around his backside. The cat gave one last cry before it shifted into something smaller.

A fawn bobcat with pointed ears crouched between Niyol and Chance. No one moved.

The bobcat mewed, and then the wolverine pelted the cat with successive blows, rendering it blind. The fox and his partner continued their relentless attack until it shivered and shrank into a prairie dog.

The slightest movement drew Chance's attention to Ana. A raspy breath caught in her throat, then released with a slow hiss. Then silence. She lay still.

Chance listened closely, unable to detect a heartbeat.

No.

Chance glanced over and saw his grandfather with the prairie dog in his mouth. He immediately came back to his human form and blazed to Ana's side.

The clouds condensed and a loud clap shook the earth with a bright flash, striking in unison. The air thickened and mist descended the mountains. The forest grew quiet and still as though it could hold its breath and regard the drama in the clearing.

"No! Ana! Stay with me! Don't die. You *can't* die!" Chance gripped at her shirt and pulled her up in desperation. Her body hung lifeless from his hands.

A dark expression crossed his face. He set her on the ground, closed his eyes, and reached out his hands to her chest.

His power was now minimal. To pull his sluggish energy back to center was like a tug of war. Static in the air raised the hairs on his arms, and it melted into his skin. He absorbed as much as possible. He flexed the growing sphere of power within. Frustration built as he tried to manipulate his sticky life force. It dragged down his arms into his hands.

One more glance over to his grandfather told him Niyol had the situation under control with Markus. The wolverine batted the prairie dog with his claws, but then seemed to notice Chance wasn't with him any longer. Niyol pressed his foot into the small animal, which gave a shudder and disappeared.

The wolverine paused with its foot in the air as it gazed at Chance and Ana. In a smooth transition, the wild animal turned into an elderly man.

At that precise moment, Chance initiated the connection between himself and Ana. Energy pulled through his hands and into her with such force his head dropped back, his life ebbing. Like water pulled down a swirling maelstrom, he was sucked in, unable to brace against the force.

"NO! Chance, wait!" Niyol ran to his grandson with his arms outstretched.

Chance was oblivious of his surroundings and couldn't hear his grandfather's call. His thoughts were only for Ana – to protect her, heal her. He couldn't lose her and didn't want to live in a world without her. And if necessary he would settle for her living without him.

The last essence of life was leaving his body. He smiled as he sensed her heart stir below his hands. A sapphire glow emanated from her chest and radiated from his hands.

With his last breath he whispered, "For always...my love."

His body slumped over Ana's with a victorious grin across his lips.

CHAPTER 44

Among billowy clouds, Ana soared above an expansive landscape. Sun tipped grasses waved as air currents massaged their stalks. Tall evergreens stretched to reach her heights but looked like plastic toys from her altitude. A breeze rippled her hair and caressed her cheeks, then it turned more violent. Something struck her. Nothing slowed the unpleasant poking. She flinched as wet beads slapped her cool face and wrenched her from the dream.

Ana's mind was fuzzy as her eyes flickered. As though she was woken from a deep hibernation, she struggled with her comatose body.

Steady rhythmic chanting filled her ears as Chance came into focus beside her. When she saw him, joy filled her heart.

It dissolved into horror when she saw Niyol 's hands rest on Chance's chest. Chance was lifeless.

Her were eyes wide with terror as the chanting slowed and ended in a whisper. Blue light radiated and pulsed from Niyol's hands and burst into Chance's body. It blasted with such force, the air moved around it, and rustled the ground cover along with Chance's hair. The light faded into Chance's chest, and Niyol swayed and tipped to the ground. Chance's skin glowed like starlight for a moment before it faded and dissipated into an afterglow.

Ana gasped and sat upright. "Niyol?!"

Chance sputtered. Light droplets tapped on his almond skin, and his hands reached up in a defensive posture.

His eyes flashed open as he sucked in a sharp breath. He rolled his head and met her gaze. Chance's eyes brightened, and he reached across to touch her cheek. "Ana... Ana, it worked," he said as he stroked her face with the tips of his fingers and stared at her in adoration.

Ana's frantic gaze reached past him to the still form lying in the dirt. Confused, Chance followed her gaze and shouted,

"Grandfather!" He turned to Ana and said with a shout, "What happened?!"

Her raspy voice said, "I don't know. When I woke up...he was chanting beside you with his hands over your chest...and then blue light went from his hands into you, and he just...fell over." Ana's eyes combed down Chance's body, noticed his lack of clothing under the woven cloth and turned to give him privacy as he jumped up to wrap the blanket around his waist.

Chance squatted down over Niyol's body, grasped his shoulders and stared intently at his face.

"Is he breathing?"

"No..." Chance said hoarsely.

CHAPTER 45

Chance knew he couldn't save his grandfather. His energy was too low. To try it again would be a death sentence. He knew that now.

He straightened up and scanned the forest line as he remembered Markus. Then he recalled his grandfather ended that pathetic life and shook his head in relief.

He looked down at his grandfather's peaceful face, and his body grew rigid as a flash of images passed through his mind.

They were like memories, but they weren't his.

As though he viewed the scene through the bottom of a glass, the focal point was clear, but faded into an unfocused haze around the periphery. It was very different from his own memories.

A forest entered his vision as a cloudy panorama came into view. A fox cowered before a cougar. The observer turned to see a girl lying on the stony ground.

"No, way!" Chance gasped.

Ana tilted her head in confusion and frowned at Chance. She was about to speak when he held his hand up to signal her to wait.

The anomalous memories continued, and he heard a voice, a familiar voice. *Grandfather!* It was Niyol's memory. But how was that possible?

You can do it...you have to. Niyol's deep tone echoed in his head, and he felt his grandfather struggle with his own power inside himself. A tiny static ball at his core ignited into blue fire as Niyol watched Chance back away from the cougar. *I must save him! NOW!*

His skin prickled as the perspective changed to that of a shorter creature. *It's been sooo long...I never thought...I could ever again...I thought the light had gone out.* Chance closed his eyes to concentrate on the real life movie playing itself out in his head.

The scene continued in a flurry. From Niyol's perspective, Chance saw himself rip and claw at the cougar. Go *for the stomach; it's vulnerable*. Niyol's voice echoed in his head. He heard his grandfather's thoughts as though they were his own. He had an intense need to destroy the cougar, to end the creature's life, so it could never hurt or kill again. His muzzle was wet with blood, ready to finish the fight. The wolverine was voracious, intense.

Chance gazed at his grandfather lying on the pine needles and continued to reflect on this new unfamiliar memory. Maybe it would reveal something he had missed.

He pummeled the bobcat with repetitive blows to the face, and the cat tipped to its side in blindness. The cat shrank into a defenseless prairie dog.

The prairie dog turned to escape, but Chance heard his grandfather's thoughts echo through his mind, *Go ahead and run – I'm faster than you*. The small animal scurried a couple feet before his body dove into it and smashed it into the ground.

His powerful jaws picked the limp animal up and shook it fiercely. He dropped it to the dirt, leapt into the air, and dropped down on the small creature. It trembled and disappeared. His instincts triggered and his attention shifted. *Where's Chance?* His view moved upward and searched the landscape. He saw himself through his grandfather's eyes, leaning over Ana.

He felt Ana stare at him. She seemed disturbed. But now wasn't the time to explain, whatever was happening.

He entered the point in the timeline that was missing for him. He saw his body give a subtle jolt as his hands hovered over Ana's lifeless form and heard his grandfather's voice call out. "NO! Chance, *wait*!" His grandfather had returned to his human shape and ran toward Chance. "Wait!"

Chance's eyes glazed over. He experienced his grandfather's anxiety. *He's going to kill himself. He doesn't have enough power to heal her and live. He won't be able to pull away in time!*

Thoughts sped through his mind. He saw a slow smile creep across his own face as his body slumped over Ana's.

"No! What have you done, Chance?!" The words flew out of his mouth, and Ana appeared deeply rattled.

"Chance? What's going *on*? You're freaking me out!" Ana said, her eyes opened wide.

Chance couldn't believe what was happening, but continued to observe the scene in his head. Niyol heard Ana's heartbeat from a distance and knew there was no sign of life within Chance. Niyol moved to his pile of clothes and pulled them on, ending with his shoes. He withdrew a blanket from a backpack near the clothes. It chilled Chance to see his own lifeless body and was relieved when his grandfather covered him with a blanket and looked away from his hollow eyes.

The vision continued as Niyol lowered himself beside Chance and stretched out his hands. *Chance. It is a responsibility to use your gifts for good. I know you will do the right thing. It will soon make sense, I hope. I chose to turn away from my power and grow old, to live a simple life with your grandmother. I loved her, like you love Ana...and it pained me not to grow old with her. I'm sorry I wasn't able to stay with you longer. There was so much more...to teach and tell you. I will always be with you...joined in spirit and power. There is one you can trust for guidance, family. You will find him. He was always meant to be your true teacher.*

Niyol's rhythmic chanting filled his senses as he stared wide-eyed at his grandfather's peaceful face. Soon the deep voice faded, and a blue light generated from his grandfather's fingertips and shot into his own body as Niyol's thoughts faded into a soft whisper until there was silence.

The memory slipped from his mind, and he was left with his own stricken thoughts.

Why didn't his grandfather ever tell him any of this? Too

many questions were left unanswered. He was alone in a foreign world. His grandfather was the only link to this secret life. Now he was without a guide. Alone.

Or was he?

Wet drops continued to fall from the sky, like tears, saying goodbye to Niyol's peaceful spirit.

A bright burst of lightning shot down into the carpeted forest below, with a simultaneous deafening rumble.

Chance and Ana arched their faces to the sky as a flock of birds lifted from the strike point. They scattered and swooped back down within the trees for shelter from the rain.

"Chance, what did I miss? What happened?!" Ana said, clearly desperate for information.

Chance stood entirely caught in his own thoughts. Ana touched his shoulder. With blinding speed, he wrapped her in his arms, picked her off the ground, and grasped at her like a life line.

Her body was alive and real against him. While he caressed her hair, his raspy breath breezed past her ear.

"He saved me. He gave his life for mine…"

"What do you mean? What happened to you? Did that boy…*hurt* you?" she said, and her eyes widened.

He pulled her away from him so he could gaze at her. His face remained tense, but softened as he said, "He arrived in time to save me from being killed by Markus, but then, your heart stopped." He choked out.

Ana sucked in air, alarmed.

"I couldn't let you die – there's no point without you."

Ana's eyes welled up, and she said, "Chance, you didn't…"

"I had to, Ana. You have to live."

"But Chance, I'm confused. If you died then how are you here? I thought Niyol didn't have powers?"

"I guess there's a lot he never told me, but I think I'll be learning more. Soon."

"What do you mean?" She shook her head in disbelief.

"Ana, you probably have a lot of questions, but I need to take Grandfather home. He needs to be taken care of. My mom…"

"Wait, what about that guy? Where is he?" Her eyes widened in fright.

"Oh, Markus. Grandfather took care of him – he's gone. He'll never hurt you again. Let's get going," he said. "It's getting late." Chance glanced at the ominous cloud cover and rain pelted down and laid his hair against his head. Droplets curled down his exposed chest and back and cooled his warm skin.

He walked over to the discarded backpack and noticed how it still appeared full. He pulled out a pair of his pants and a shirt and shook his head. *Grandfather, always thinking ahead*. Pain scalded his throat, and he pinched off the instinct to scream or cry. He tugged on his clothes, and unwound the blanket from his waist, and laid it on the ground. Without effort, he lifted Niyol, placed him on the woven fabric and enveloped him. In a smooth movement, he picked up his grandfather and laid him over his shoulder.

Sad and numb, he turned to Ana and asked with a frown, "Will you be able to climb down? I spotted your van down the mountain a ways on the road. You think you can make it? Or, I can come back for you…"

He stopped to look at her and checked to see if she was hurt. She appeared disoriented for a moment, and then as if a switch was flipped, she blinked and was spurred to action.

***

So absorbed was Ana with Chance and his grandfather, she had forgotten about her own health. She stretched out her arms and legs to check for injuries and then listened to her heartbeat. She felt fine. A little tired, cold and achy, but healthy.

"I'm okay, let's go. If I need to stop, I will. Don't worry about me, Chance. Just take care of *him*." She glanced at the form draped over Chance's shoulder and walked forward.

Chance led the way from the small clearing. Through a wall of pines, he descended the hillside, slow and deliberate, and wove through the lanky trees. Ana stayed close on his trail. He seemed to be aware of her short distance from him, and he moved more rapidly down the slippery pine needle laden slopes.

Ana remained close behind.

Steady footing was hard to find until they reached spongier ground. The rain eased, and a soft mist filled their lungs. A low fog searched the hillside.

He quickened his pace as they grew closer to Ana's van.

Through the dense growth, a gray windy road emerged. A bright yellow beacon shone through the dingy dark and called to them. Even with its dull paint job, it still broke through the grey shroud.

Glad to see her banana colored van again, Ana said a silent prayer of gratitude. For everything. Chance jogged up to the driver's side door and wrenched it open. With a sigh of relief, he said, "The keys are still in it. Okay, can you open the hatch?"

She opened the back of the van where she had so recently rolled around unconscious.

He gently tipped the wrapped body off his shoulder and set Niyol on the back bench. With a sideways glance, he shut the hatch.

Ana moved forward and embraced Chance. He clung to her. Their sodden bodies stood in silence.

Ana pulled away. "I'm so sorry, Chance. If I hadn't been there – it's my fault," she said and stared at her feet.

Like a slap in the face, Chance grabbed her shoulders. "What are you talking about?! Ana! *None* of this was your fault. If anything, it's mine. I should have kept you safe. It was *me* Markus was after. It was *me* Grandfather was saving." His jaw clenched, and his face grew dark.

It was Ana's turn, who shook her head vigorously. "Chance, it wasn't your fault. You were just trying to save me. I'm not very happy about you choosing my life over yours, but your grandfather knew what he was doing. It was his choice. It was the way he wanted it."

Chance's face softened as he searched her eyes. "You know – I feel *so* empty, devastated about Grandfather. And I'm just *so happy* you're alive. I can't believe it. You were so lifeless...I thought I'd never see your beautiful green eyes again." He dropped his head.

Ana lifted her gaze to meet his. His face lowered, and their lips met in a soft caress, which built in intensity. Her heart sped in excitement, and Chance pulled away. His hand reached for hers and placed it over her heart.

"Something's changed – your rhythm, it sounds...different."

Ana found it hard to focus on anything but his body held so close to her own and his hand on hers. The beat of her heart *did* seem altered. It wasn't a fluttery, syncopated beat. Plus, she wasn't lightheaded. She felt strong.

"Yes," Ana said and closed her eyes.

He lowered his ear to her chest.

In response Ana wrapped her arms around him and stood in shock. Now that he mentioned it, she did feel different. She had moved down the mountain completely at ease, without even a rest and her chest wasn't poised to explode in hysterics, although with Chance against her chest, her body was animated in *other* ways.

Chance listened to the cadence of her heart. "Hmmm, strange. I could pick you out of a crowd by the sound of your heart. But now, you sound different."

He seemed preoccupied with her skin so close to his and released her in hesitation. He kissed her moist forehead and led her to the passenger side of the van.

On the drive down the mountain, he reminded her. "Grandfather didn't want my parents to know about Markus or any other details. I need to figure out a story that doesn't involve being attacked by a shapeshifter."

Ana stared at the misty hillside they had just descended, took in a shaky breath and said, "What if you say you were out hiking when it happened? Like he had a heart attack or just sat down and went to sleep?" She closed her eyes and forced the image of Niyol's death from her mind.

"Yeah, I guess that could work," he said. "I'm going to park your van up the road above our driveway so they don't see it. I'll carry him into the house so they don't know we drove him here. Ana, it's best you go home; you were never here. I'll call you later, after…everything."

"Alright, I'll be waiting. If there's anything I can do to help." After a moment Ana asked, "Oh, right, what should I tell *my* mom? I've been gone all day, and I said I was going to your house."

"Just say, that on the way to meet me I called you and changed plans because I needed to do something with my grandfather. So then you decided to go to Sandpoint for something – shopping?"

"I can say I went to window shop. Eva's birthday is coming up, so that works," she said. She really hated lying to her mother. She was so bad at it.

They neared Chance's driveway, and he slowed down, cautious. He pulled into a clearing and parked.

The spot was unfamiliar to Ana. She had never ventured past his house and never would have known they were close to his home. The grove of Western red cedars and dogwoods offered a different view.

They both moved from the car and opened the back hatch. The rolled up shroud that encased Niyol lay before them. Before Chance picked him up, he gave Ana a bear hug which squeezed the air from her lungs. After she recovered, she said, "I love you, Chance."

They parted and Ana turned her head to face Niyol's tranquil body. As she fidgeted with the silver ring on her finger, a stream of tears journeyed down her rosy cheeks. The salty river continued as her muscles jerked in a fitful spasm. Her fingers rested on the geometric patterned fabric of his cocoon. "Thank you, Niyol...for everything." Her voice pinched off, and she ran around the van and jumped into the driver's seat.

She turned on the engine as soon as Chance removed Niyol from the back and slammed the door shut. Through the window his tall form moved lithely down the gravel road until it disappeared below the sloped grade.

Ana dropped her head against the wheel and keened mournfully.

CHAPTER 46

After she cried herself dry, Ana pulled herself together and drove home. By the time she arrived, it was dinner time.

The expansive gray sky had begun to break up and exposed cracks in its mantle. Dark blue hues peeked through, and a nebulous moon tinged the edges of the clouds with a magical silver glow.

Ana sauntered up the front walk, brushed the dirt from her face and hair as the smell of dinner wafted out to meet her. Gratitude filled her. Her eyes began to blur and sting. She pinched her lips together fiercely, painfully tight, and then swallowed hard. She forced the emotional turmoil back down to deal with later.

There was a time, just a couple hours ago, when she thought she would never see her family again or the little blue house huddled among the firs. Happiness mingled with bitter sadness. If she were a compass, her needle would spin in circles.

A draft of cold air from outside blew in as she tumbled into the house. She shut the door with a thud.

"Ana? Is that you?" Melissa's voice rang from the kitchen.

"Yeah, it's me." She dropped her keys on the dining table and flipped up her slicker's hood to cover her dirty, tangled hair. She took a cleansing breath and popped her head into the kitchen.

Eva was stirring something in a saucepan. Melissa sat at the kitchen table. She chopped a green herb with one hand as she raised a glass of white wine to her lips with the other.

"Try to chop it *finely,* Mom," Eva said over her shoulder. "Hey, Ana. I'm making pot roast tonight. I hope you're hungry."

"Yeah, sure."

"So, what did you do today?" Melissa asked as she took another sip from her wine glass.

"Oh, well Chance had to cancel last minute because of some plans with his grandfather. So, I decided to run over to Sandpoint to go window shopping. Someone's birthday's coming up." She forced a smile at her sister who raised her eyebrows in enthusiasm.

"It was pretty nasty out today. I hope you didn't get too wet."

"No, I stayed indoors. I sat in a coffee shop for a bit when it really let loose. Um, I feel like a shower – to warm up. I'll be back down for dinner."

Ana ran upstairs anxious to avoid further conversation. She was hollow inside from crying so much. She imagined what was happening at Chance's house, and it made her depressed. Poor Aiyana wouldn't have any warning before she found out her father was dead.

Heat penetrated her cool, damp body as she stepped into the shower. Dirt, bits of leaves and pine needles swirled down the drain. Her hair was so filthy it looked like she had bathed in dirt, and her clothes were stained and streaked. She was thankful her mother hadn't noticed when she came in.

Pine and earth no longer scented her body, but instead rose infused shampoo clung to her pores. The welcomed fragrance enveloped her while she forced the image of the boy with a monster's head out of her mind. The vision frightened her. Nightmares were inevitable.

Ana's soft clean bed supported her when she sat down in delayed shock. She put on her fresh clothing and curled up to rest. Had it only been a day? It seemed like a lifetime.

"Ana?! Dinner!"

She sat up and found her favorite slippers. The soft scritch-scratch from her shuffling feet went silent once she descended the carpeted stairs.

The three of them ate Eva's dinner in silence as they appreciated the hot food. Ana surprised herself by eating so much. She had skipped lunch when she left to meet Chance, and with the tumultuous day, she was famished. She cleaned her plate and drank all of her water.

"You seem awfully quiet tonight, is there something wrong?" Melissa asked.

"Well, actually, I got a call just a bit ago from Chance. His grandfather died this afternoon," she said and bit her lip.

Melissa rested her hand at her throat in surprise. "Oh, no! Is that why he canceled your plans? Do you know what happened?"

"Not sure. I haven't been told any details yet. But when he canceled our plans he said he was heading out on a hike with him."

"Well, we'll make some food to bring by for Aiyana. She must be devastated. They seemed close."

Eva nodded and picked up her plate to deposit in the kitchen. She returned with a cook book and flipped through the pages in search of a suitable recipe.

Ana's phone rang, and she answered it as she walked out of the room for privacy.

As she left, Melissa called out. "Give our condolences."

"Chance?! What's happening?" Ana ran up to her room and shut the door behind her.

A brief moment of silence followed. "Well, they have no reason to doubt me. I told them Grandfather collapsed when we were out hiking. It was normal to them that we were out in the rain storm, because we do it all the time." His took a raspy breath and said, "Since Mom's a nurse she knew who to call. She's trying to move this along fast. It's Navajo tradition to bury the dead quickly. She's looking into burying him here on the property. I guess there's no law against it. Looks like we can put him to rest tomorrow, once Mom takes care of the paperwork. Good thing she has connections."

"Chance, I'm so sorry. How did your mother react?"

"She seemed prepared for it. She hasn't cried at all, from

what I've seen, anyway. Grandfather once told me, it's expected to stay in control of emotions when a loved one dies. Navajo accept death in silence. It's the way Grandfather would have wanted it," he said.

"Do you want to be alone, or if you want, I can come over?"

"No, I don't want to be here *or* alone. Can I come to your house?"

"Of course, are you driving or flying?"

"Well, I figure we'll be talking, and I don't want you sitting outside in this weather. Think you could ask your mom if I can come over?"

"Of course, let me check." Ana reemerged from her room and trotted down the stairs as she said, "I told Mom that your grandfather died today but said I didn't know the details yet. She was really sad and offered her condolences. So, she knows that much."

"Good to know."

Ana found her mother and sister around the dining table playing a board game. Melissa glanced up when her daughter entered the room.

Ana lowered the phone and asked, "Hey, Mom. Is it okay if Chance comes over tonight?"

"Of course, baby. But shouldn't he stay with his family tonight?"

"No, I don't think he wants to be home, but he doesn't want to be alone either..."

"That's fine, we're happy to have him as long as his mother doesn't object. Anytime – he's family."

"Thanks, Mom." Ana glided back out of the room and returned upstairs.

"It's fine with her, of course. Say, your mom doesn't mind? She doesn't want you home?"

"She'll understand. She knows how much Grandfather meant to me and that I'm closer to you than anyone."

"Okay, head over any time."

"Thank you, my love."

"I love you, too."

Ana flipped her phone shut and sat on her bed, staring out her blackened window.

CHAPTER 47

Chance passed by his grandfather's room before he went downstairs. He nudged the door open with the back of his hand and walked inside.

The window remained up from when he thrust it open earlier in his hurry to save Ana. The curtains hung in a tangle. Moisture dewed around the sill, and Chance walked over to shut it. He hung the curtains back up.

At the foot of the bed, a sunken indentation lingered in the blankets from his grandfather. He had sat in that very spot when Chance launched himself into the room and put into motion the series of events that led to his death. All three of theirs.

Only Chance and Ana had survived.

He traced his fingers along the crater and walked to a simple wooden chair in the corner of the room. He surveyed his grandfather's belongings. Dirty clothing was piled in his hamper, a book sat on his bedside table, all were as Niyol left them.

Traces of recent memories flavored his thoughts. On graduation night when Chance received the talon, he had no idea what it was. It lay cradled in his palm now. He regarded it soberly. It had been the key to unlock his Thunderbird form. He wondered if his grandfather had known at the time what it was and why he had given it to him.

Then almost as though a balled up piece of paper getting smoothed out, another unfamiliar vision came into focus. He sat erect as though movement would change the reception.

A man stood before him with long dark hair and deep copper skin. He held a large hooked talon. Two young boys flanked him as they sat on the smooth chalky ground in shaded darkness. Chance gauged from his own stature that he was an adolescent as well. It looked like they were in a large make-shift room. Bright light flooded in from a nearby doorway and through gaps in the wood and sticks that made the walls. He took in these odd surroundings and realized he was in a simple home, of sorts.

A deep voice emanated from the man. "Sons, listen. For many generations this has been passed down in our family. It is a link to our ancestors. Honorable ancestors – servants of our people. But remember there are others, the evil skin walkers who we must not speak of – who will seek your power and do harm for pleasure." His face darkened, and he held up the talon. "If you are given the power by the Holy People, it is only to keep balance and harmony. It is my will, that someday, one of you will earn this through perseverance and honor. It must be protected and respected."

Although the man spoke a language he never heard before, Chance was able to understand him. The words flowed through his thoughts.

Chance felt the boy's excitement. *I hope I can earn it.*

The vividness of that vision faded and another formed.

He sensed he was back in the small rustic home, although it was nighttime now. Bright moonlight gave everything a hazy film. The shaded silhouette of a man, who Chance assumed was his grandfather's father, stood before him, lean and gray. Time had passed. Chance knew his grandfather was older now, he was taller and his muscular arm, reached out deftly to receive something.

Chance's ancestor dropped a satchel into Niyol's hand and spoke in a soft whisper – so low that anyone without heightened abilities wouldn't hear. "Niyol, this is now yours to protect. It is our connection to the ancestors – sacred. And is now *your* duty to keep it safe." His hands rested on Niyol's shoulders. "Son, you must keep your secret from your brother. You can *not* have him know you have been given the gift. *Protect* your secret."

The scene dissolved and another unraveled.

It was nighttime. The scene remained the same, inside his

simple home, but he was alone now.

A lumpy cloth sat in his hand as he tucked it into his back pocket. He snuck to the doorway and peered out to examine the rolling hills gleam in the moonlight. Lanky grass arched pale and fluid toward the low hills in the distance. Bright stars shone with the waning moon; sheep bleated from a simple wooden enclosure.

He stepped out and darted around the house. A backpack was flung over his shoulder and he began to run. *I will keep the secret safe, Father.*

The realistic hallucination dimmed and ended. His grandfather's still room came back into view. Pain throbbed from Chance's hand. He looked down in surprise. He had grasped the talon so tight, the point had pressed into his palm, drawing blood.

A huge sigh erupted from his lungs. Without being aware of it, he had been holding his breath as well.

Chance was overcome with the strange new information. So much of what Markus had said gave him pause. These new bizarre 'memories' or hallucinations must mean something. Somehow. They must be part of an even bigger picture. But what?

He thought he had the answer. His temples and head hurt.

He wanted to sit with Ana, needed to talk it out, and figure out what was happening.

With a heavy heart, he stood. His shoulders slouched as he left the room. He shut the door without a sound.

Chance walked away with a saddened backward glance and ambled to the kitchen where Aiyana was on the phone. His dad stood beside her and held out a pad and pen.

"Dad? I don't feel like being home tonight...I...if it's too..." Chance broke off and scratched his head, then cleared his throat. "Melissa said it was okay for me to head over there. I feel like I need to be with Ana right now to talk. That okay?"

Ben faced Aiyana shook her head as she continued her

phone conversation.

"Don't think so, Bud, why don't you stay here with us? Maybe you can see Ana tomorrow. How are you holding up?" his dad asked in concern. "You were so close. It must have been hard seeing him...Well, if you need to talk at all, Mom and I are here."

"I'll be fine."

Ben approached his son with his arms open and wrenched him into a tight squeeze. "Want to go sit in the living room with me?"

"Naw. I'm leaving. Sorry, I just can't be here right now."

He turned away and ran from the house with shouts from his parents chasing him down the front walk.

He didn't want to think any more, so he put in one of his favorite CD's and turned the volume all the way up. Music filled the air while he sat, numb and dazed. He sped down his driveway and made his way to Ana's house.

When the little blue home came into view, warmth cracked through his hardened exterior. His heart picked up a beat as Ana's face skimmed his thoughts.

Ana.

She was the one good thing through all of it. The moment he met her, she took up residence in his heart. Home was wherever Ana was.

He was home. She was right through the wooden door before him. Before he could lift his hand, she was there.

Soft yellow light glowed behind her, which only made her more angelic. She held her hand out to him, and he allowed himself to be led inside.

Ana leaned in and said, "Let Mom say 'hi' first, then we can go to my room and talk."

Melissa entered the living room with her arms outstretched. "Ohh, Chance — let me give you a hug. I'm *so* sorry about your grandfather. You two were close, weren't you? You're so lucky. Ana never had a relationship like that with her grandparents before they passed."

"Yeah, we were. I'm going to miss him." Chance pulled back and glanced down to the ground, and Melissa took the hint.

"I bet you two want to be alone to talk then. Go ahead. We'll stay out of your way." Melissa rubbed his shoulder before they walked past her to go upstairs.

Ana switched on the twinkle lights Chance had tacked to her ceiling during her last hospital visit and shut the door to her room.

Chance pulled out her desk chair and sat on it backwards, facing Ana who flopped onto her bed.

"Well, I've been experiencing something kinda odd," Chance said.

"What?"

"Remember earlier – after everything? I was spaced out staring at Grandfather?" Chance raised his eyes anxiously while his head remained lowered.

"Yeah, what was happening?" Ana said as she cocked her head.

"Umm, since I woke from Grandfather saving my life, I've been...seeing things."

"Seeing things? What kind of things?"

"Don't think I'm crazy, but they're like visions or memories, or something, but they aren't mine. They must be Grandfather's. Weird, huh?"

"Maybe, maybe not. Chance, there's nothing normal about any of this. Since I met you, I've seen things no one would believe. It's not weird; it just is. Go on, I'm listening."

"After Grandfather saved me, giving me his life – I saw *his* memories leading up to his death. Like a hallucination or a vision. I heard *his* thoughts and saw everything from his point of view. And before I came over here I was in his room holding his gift to me. Remember that huge claw?"

Ana nodded in response.

"Well, I flashed to a memory when he was a boy. And his father was telling him and his brothers about the talon, how it'd been passed down through generations. He said it was earned through hard work and integrity. Then I had another memory of his." Chance pushed on without looking up. "He must have been older. He was bigger, maybe just a little younger than me. His dad secretively gave him the talon but warned him to keep it and his powers a secret."

He sighed and paused as he recalled the last vision. "Right after that, I had another memory of him throwing a backpack over his shoulder and running away from home." Chance shook his head and stared out the window at the clear darkened sky.

"Remember Grandfather telling us about his family? How his brother became dark and killed their father and probably his other brother, too? Good thing he hid his powers from him, or I don't think I'd be alive right now."

"Wow," Ana said in a whisper, as she sat up, eyes wide.

"Yeah."

"Why's the talon important though?"

So much had happened since he discovered the mapping in the talon he hadn't been able to tell Ana.

"Right, you don't know." He grinned sadly and said, "Before Markus showed up, I discovered blue mapping all over it. That was a first. I've never tried to map a creature from bones… or any kind of fragment. I tried to become Thunderbird, and it didn't work." Chance shuddered as he remembered the sensation of feathers tugging out from his skin when the transformation went horribly wrong. "Well, when I was on the mountaintop with Markus I chanced it. I had a feeling about the claw. Hoped it was the connection I needed for Thunderbird…and it worked." Chance shrugged.

"Wait, you were able to phase into Thunderbird?!" Ana asked and gripped the edge of her bed. "And I missed it?!"

"Sorry, you were busy trying to stay alive." Chance

scratched his head. "Yeah, it was pretty cool. So now I'm guessing the claw is a special talisman passed down, who knows how far back, for generations. I guess, so Thunderbird was never lost, or forgotten."

Ana seemed to consider her next question. "That makes sense. But why do you think you're having his memories?"

"Okay, I've been thinking about this constantly. Before we fought, Markus bragged. He said my grandfather hadn't told me much about the shapeshifting world. And even though he'd only been phasing for a couple months, he was sure he was stronger. Thanks to his grandfather...

"Ana, what if somehow when Grandfather died, he passed part of himself to me? Into me. Maybe Markus had a similar thing. I looked up some stuff on the computer when I was supposed to be *behaving*. Navajos believe evil shapeshifters get their powers from killing family members. What if that's true? Not just family members but other shifters. Markus probably killed his grandfather for *his* powers. That could be why he was so powerful. Ana, what if I got Grandfather's powers along with his memories?"

Chance groaned and dropped his head onto his arms. He said, "I don't know though – I haven't used my powers since everything happened! It's real frustrating. I wish he'd just been honest with me! There's a lot more to this than I know. It could risk our safety, for sure, especially if more power nuts are out there like Markus. Anyway, now I know there are others like me. Markus said it – all over the world." Chance's eyes squinted at the prospect of it.

"Wow. Really? That's great, isn't it? Maybe there's someone out there willing to help you. If there's more and if we could find one..."

"Ana, what makes you think they wouldn't just kill me like Markus wanted to? He said shifters can live long lives, if you aren't killed for your powers first. I'm sorry, that makes it sound really unfriendly out there. I don't want to die.

Grandfather probably hid from his abilities for good reasons. He lived a long happy life with my grandmother until she died. And he never would have died if it weren't for his powers!"

"Chance, your grandfather said to me that if you have a power within you, it's an obligation to use it. He inspired me to stop moping and to live without fear."

Chance stared at his hands wrapped around the chair and said, "He *did* have a message for me before he died..."

"He did? What was it?"

"He said it was my responsibility to use my powers for good, and it was my choice what to do with them. Maybe that's why he trained me. He said something else, too. There's another I could trust. Family." Ana raised her eyebrows, and her mouth fell open. Chance continued. "And he was meant to be my *true* teacher. So, I guess I'm not really alone in this. If they're still alive."

They remained silent. Chance thought about Markus. He was one who chose to walk the easy, seductive road. To take from others to gain what he wanted – power. Chance wasn't interested in going out of his way to find trouble. But if he chose not to equip himself with the power to protect his loved ones, then it would be his fault if anything happened to them. And there was no question in his mind. He had to protect Ana. He couldn't allow anything to hurt her again.

What should he do? His fighting spirit raised its head as a fire burned within him.

"Grrrrahh! You're right, he's right." He tightened his grip on the back of the chair. "I can't just let someone like Markus terrorize us again. Maybe I should find this teacher."

He loosened his hold then dropped his hands to his sides. "When I held the talon, a vision came almost in answer. It flashed in my head." He shrugged. "Maybe if I think about it I'll get an answer."

"Be patient. You'll learn more as other visions pop-up. He

probably planned on telling you everything when you were ready, or strong enough to face what was waiting for you. It just didn't go according to plan. But look, you *do* have a way to learn that lost knowledge, even if he *is* gone."

"Yeah, you're right. But I'd rather still have *him,* instead of his memories."

CHAPTER 48

The sun shone brightly the next day. Plants unfurled and reached toward their life source as the forest animals foraged through the sodden wilderness. Birds sang and praised the summer day.

Ana woke to the outdoor chorus and wiped the sleep from her eyes.

Chance left late the night before with much on his mind. He had no one else to talk to now. Ana was the only one who knew his secret.

Her toes touched the cold wood floor, which forced her to pull out a pair of socks and sweatpants.

She thudded down the stairs, confident she was the last one to wake. Sleep was precious. Her mother and sister always seemed to wake at the break of the day, but not Ana.

Eva was on the couch reading a book when Ana walked in.

"Morning," Eva said as she continued to read.

"Good morning. You eaten breakfast yet?"

"Yup."

"Mom at work?"

Eva snorted and said, "Yeah, she left hours ago."

Ana spun around and returned to the kitchen and picked a yogurt from the fridge. She sat and squinted in the blinding light, as she finished her breakfast and wondered if Chance was up yet. She grabbed her phone and called.

"Good morning."

"Morning."

Chance sounded tired and depressed.

"You talk to your mom yet?"

"Yeah, she's going downtown to fill out some papers to bury Grandfather. One of the doctors she works with is coming by. He'll do a quick look over on Grandfather, and then he'll sign something. I don't know. From what Mom said, sounds like we can bury him this afternoon. There's a spot he wanted to be buried, down the slope a ways."

"Want me to come over?"

"Well, I think it will just be us for the burial. Tradition you know, sorry. It limits it to a couple of people, but later I wanted to go up to Grandfather's favorite place on the mountain to say goodbye. I can carry you up, but you don't have to come if you don't want to."

"Of course, I want to come and be with you. I need to say goodbye, too. How about you give me a call, let me know when to head over?"

"Yeah...soon, my love."

"Love you too, Chance."

Ana closed her phone and set it on the kitchen table. It was a mild day, maybe she'd go take a brief walk in the woods or find her way down to the meadow. She was strangely effervescent. It felt so different.

She jogged upstairs to her room and pulled on her tennis shoes, then bounded back down to the kitchen.

Before opening the back door, she called out to her sister. "I'm goin' for a walk, wanna come, Eva?"

"No." Wafted from the living room.

"'Kay, just stay to the house then. Be back soon."

The scent of fresh firs almost made Ana dizzy when she walked outside. The rain from the day before had soaked into the soil and offered a soft and springy surface to walk on.

Ana strode down the damp trail to her outdoor observatory. An occasional drip fell from the moist tree canopy and sank into her scalp. It had been a while since she visited her rock.

The sun had already dried the stone and left a wisp of vapor in the air above it. Not in the mood to sit still, she continued past it into the wilderness.

The darkened forest grew lighter as she approached its boundary. A rocky slope dropped into the green field below— the very field she'd spied from her gazing rock.

Her heart fluttered with happiness. Wildflowers exploded throughout the fresh grasses. The path moved downward. It could be a challenge to climb back up, but she was up to it. She imagined herself an explorer today. Ready to approach adversity.

She hastened down the hill into the blades of grass and stared at the flowers, Monks-hood, larkspur and woodland stars. Bees buzzed from one blossom to the next. The sun heated the air, which kept the daytime occupants contented.

Inspired by the beauty around her, she picked wildflowers. It would make the perfect gift for Aiyana. In no time, she had a large bundle under her arm and decided to walk back to the house by way of the field to see if she could spot her rock from below.

Ana soon located the stone jutting out high above her and was startled by a small rabbit dashing through the undergrowth. She shook her head and continued on in search for a way back up to the house. The steep slope wrapped around and seemed to continue until she noticed a rocky embankment.

She kept on and paused as she remembered the large bouquet under her arm. A soft giggle broke from her lips when she thought about her new behavior.

She flipped the flowers backward so the stems pointed forward and began to climb the slope. Her free hand grabbed onto the rocks to pull herself up.

Past the sparse trees, Ana spotted the road back and wove through the firs. It was a short walk from the road to her driveway.

Ana entered the house with the large bouquet held in front of her.

"Hello?" Eva's asked, confused.

"It's me." Ana lowered the flowers and exposed her flushed face.

"Geez, where'd you go? You're all dirty." Eva squished up

her face.

"Oh, I went for a walk through the woods. Then, I made my way down to the meadow and picked some flowers for Aiyana. I had to climb up a slope to get home."

"You climbed?" Eva said, and her brows squished up.

"You know, I'm feeling really good today. I felt like I could do it, and I did." Ana smiled proudly.

"Well, you don't look pale. Mom's gonna freak."

Ana blew past Eva, pulled down a vase, and filled it with water. While Ana busied herself in the kitchen, Eva called from the living room. "Ana? You going to Chance's today?"

"Yeah, why?"

"I made a chicken and rice dish you can take over. It's in the fridge. And, I was hoping you could drop me by Leslie's on your way? Mom said she'd pick me up after work."

"Sure, sweetie, no problem."

Ana lowered the stems into the vase and blossoms spilled over the rim. Their sweet perfume filled the air, and she breathed in a deep lungful.

***

Chance was walking up from the gravesite when he heard the loud roar of Ana's van coming up the hill. He dug in his feet and raced through the brush and pines until he reached the gravel driveway. His breathing remained level after the dash up the mountainside.

A yellow shape materialized through the deep woods. The van stopped at Chance's feet, and Ana climbed out. She crunched across the gravel and wrapped him in her arms.

"It's done then?"

"Yeah. It was just Mom, Dad and me. He liked it there, so that's where I dug. I worked most of the afternoon making it deep enough. Mom got everything taken care of."

"I have something for your mom." Ana returned to the

270

car, opened the side and pulled out the large bundle of wildflowers and handed Chance a square Tupperware dish.

"Let's take them in to her before we go."

Chance held Ana's free hand as they wandered into the house.

"Mom? Ana's here. She brought something for you."

The scrape of a chair sliding across the wood floor came from the other room, then Aiyana floated in to meet them. Her face was drawn and her eyes seemed glassy.

"Aiyana, I picked these for you today. I'm really sorry about your father. He was a wonderful person. I'm going to miss him." Ana offered the flowers to Aiyana.

A sad smile played across Aiyana's lips, as she said, "Thank you, Ana. I know he liked you a lot. He considered you part of the family." She gave Ana a sideways embrace, careful not to disturb the flowers.

"Eva made something, too – and Mom sends her condolences."

Chance lifted the Tupperware dish and then disappeared to deposit it in the fridge.

"Please thank your family for their thoughtfulness. It was very kind."

Chance returned to Ana's side and said, "Mom, we're going up to Grandfather's favorite spot to say goodbye. Is there anything else you need from me before we go?"

Aiyana shook her head and said sadly, "Go do what you need to do." She held the vase and breathed in the sweetness.

The two left the house and returned to the driveway. Chance turned to Ana, his face blank and asked, "Okay, are you ready? You want to walk or are you going to be my koala today?"

"You know what? As enjoyable as it is being carried like a backpack, I've been feeling strangely energetic. I'll give it a try myself." Chance looked sideways at her. "I don't know what you did to me yesterday, but if you could bottle and sell it – you'd be rich," she added.

He took her hand and kissed it gently. "Makes me happy to hear that. I'll take it easy on you just in case. I don't ever want to see you in a hospital again."

They headed into the woods. The afternoon warmth had dried the leaves and rocks from the storm the day before. The air was moist and filled the forest with bold smells. Wildlife seemed determined to use every moment of daylight. Noises and movement erupted through the forest as they wandered, and Chance pointed out a family of ground squirrels hidden from view.

Ana noticed the trees change as they climbed to the top of a ridge, and the sun began its slow descent. Evergreens thinned out to make room for elderberries and a beautiful grove of maples. She could see the lake from where they stood.

"This is Grandfather's favorite spot, or...was." He flinched. "He loved coming here to watch the sun come up and go down. We'd come here and talk."

At that moment, something clicked, shifted and changed inside Ana. Everything seemed so familiar, like she had been there before.

"Weird. Déjà vu," she said, and shook her head.

Chance pulled his brows together. "Huh?"

"It's like...I've been here before."

"I've never taken you here – did Markus?" His eyes flared.

"No, no. It's like...wait...you hear that?" Ana trailed off, as she began to hear voices and stood stock still.

Chance craned his neck and shook his head. "Ana, you okay? I don't hear a thing..."

Ana clearly heard people talking. She plugged her ears to give herself better clarity. The voices become recognizable. And they echoed in her head.

"...It's like I see everything differently now...I don't know

what to do…"

"Don't question it. There's nothing to do, but love her."

"I love her more than I thought possible. I just met her…and I feel like she's meant to be with me…I'd do anything for her…"

A ghostly form materialized in her thoughts and stared at a sunset. Niyol turned to look at her before dissolving away.

What a relief to see Niyol again. It brought tears to her eyes. She lowered her hands to her side.

"What's wrong?!" Chance said, scrutinizing her closely.

"I just saw your grandfather."

"Ana, what are you talking about?!"

"He was talking and turned to look at me before disappearing." She gazed out at the distant lake through her tears.

"What could it mean?" he asked in confusion.

"Maybe he was saying goodbye…"

"Maybe." But he didn't sound sure.

Ana stared at the horizon in silence before she said, "So, have you had any more memories or visions or whatever from your grandfather since last night?"

Chance nodded and answered distractedly. "Earlier today when I was digging my grandfather's grave, I had one. In the vision, I was digging a hole, too. A deep hole. Then Grandfather buried a carved wooden box. The funny thing is…" Chance scratched his forehead. "I know where it is. Grandfather took me there. He went out of his way to show me the area. It was the exact place I saw in the vision. It's on his ranch in Montana," he said.

Ana tilted her head and looked at Chance, who continued to gaze at the lake shimmering in the distance.

"But I don't know what's in it. I didn't see him take anything like that from his father when he left home. And his home just looked like it was made of sticks, wood and mud. So I'm guessing he didn't bring any valuables with him when he left Arizona, besides the talon."

"Hmmmm. Okay, so, what do you think your grandfather could have buried? That's kinda exciting. You think he wanted you to find it?"

"I guess so. It was our special spot we went when I visited him."

"Wow. A *real life* adventure! I wonder what would happen if you thought about Sasquatch," she said.

"Maybe I should think about dragons too." Chance tousled Ana's hair.

He gave a big sigh and faced the setting sun. "I'm going to miss Grandfather. And um, tonight, I think I need to be alone – to think things out and to say goodbye." He glanced sideways. "I'm going to head back up to the top of the mountain."

Ana shrank back and said, "Are you *sure*?"

He nodded numbly. "Yeah, I'm sure."

CHAPTER 49

When Ana got home from Chance's, she found her mom in the kitchen washing dishes.

"Hey, your sister tells me you were out walking today? Feeling good?"

Ana dropped her keys and wallet on the table and plopped herself onto a kitchen chair. "Yeah. It's funny. I'm feeling really good. I didn't even get tired."

Melissa surveyed her daughter closely. Suspicion clouded her face, and she squinted her eyes.

Ana saw her mother's reaction and stood up. To demonstrate, she faced the stairs and dashed to the second floor and returned just as quickly.

Melissa's eyes widened, and her mouth dropped open. She appeared to wait to see if Ana grew faint from the exercise. When she didn't, Melissa put her hand to her lips.

"You're face has color, and you look...good...healthy. Did this suddenly happen, or have you been feeling it come on slow?"

Ana thought lying right now would be best. The truth was far less believable. "I've been feeling better throughout the last week, and today I just felt fantastic!"

"When's your next doctor's appointment?"

"In a week and a half, I think."

"Want to see if you can get in earlier? Just to see. I don't want you falling down when your heart...I'd feel better if the doctor checked you out before you start climbing any mountains. *Got it*?" Melissa's eyes narrowed.

A wave of guilt washed through Ana as she recalled her carefree day. If her mother saw her hike up the mountainside with Chance, she might just reconsider her trust in him and her.

She didn't need the doctor to tell her she was fine. She knew it.

How it would be explained, she didn't know. Miracles seemed few and far between, but that was the best term to describe it. A miracle.

"'Kay, I'll call tomorrow. Maybe there'll be a cancellation."

"So, how are they doing?"

Ana knew who her mother was referring to. "They seem okay. I picked a bouquet of wildflowers to take to Aiyana. She seems a little shell-shocked. Chance's having a hard time with it." She paused in consideration. "But they're moving forward. They're a strong family. Survivors – like us," Ana said.

Melissa nodded. "Good people." She combed her hands through her hair, and pulled it on top of her head.

"So where's Eva? You feel like a game tonight?"

Melissa wrinkled her nose. "Ah, it's a work night." Then she added wickedly. "I think I could squeeze one game in though – I'll go get your sister." She scampered up the stairs in search of Eva.

The three of them played a vigorous game of Uno, which Ana nearly won twice. Eva eventually won, as she always did.

"You're lucky Miss. D. If I wasn't so tired, I'd throw down the gauntlet," Ana said as they lumbered upstairs to bed.

CHAPTER 50

Trees blurred past Chance as he flashed through the wilderness. The wind on his face made him feel free. He pushed his body to the point of exhaustion, his legs aching from the distance and speed. Muscle burn didn't stop him; he only pushed harder until he mounted the outlook that was so graphically seared in his memories.

He stopped at the rocky crag where Ana had lain so recently. He could still visualize her lying there, lifeless and unmoving. Like death.

Right beside the crag was his grandfather's final resting spot. He dropped his backpack to the ground and stood in a daze, like he had just been given emotional anesthesia.

It was dark. The sun had dropped behind the mountains hours ago, but his inhuman eyesight allowed him to see clearly. He pushed himself to unpack his one person tent. His camp was set up, and he sat on the pine needles and stared at the open sky.

Unanswered questions and a profound sadness filled him. With a deep breath, he stared out at the tall pines and sought understanding.

A memory crept into his thoughts, as though it had a life of its own, willing itself to be remembered. A familiar open field materialized. He would know it anywhere – his training grounds. And there, before him was Grandfather guiding him through a transformation. It was all so vivid and colorful. Grief washed over him, and he knew he would never share another time with his beloved Grandfather.

Like a radio frequency being adjusted, the sounds, colors and tone changed.

An unfamiliar vision filled his mind and stilled his misery. His body froze, and he watched in silence.

A beautiful coastline stretched out before him. Soft blue waters lapped at a pale sandy beach, and large gray rocks broke the smooth lines and created a private cove. Lush tropical plants flourished all around him.

As Chance sat rigid, engrossed with his new vision, a pair of small eyes stared out at him from a bracken covered branch. Silence and stillness settled around the campsite.

A gasp broke from Chance's lips and his jaw dropped open. "No way..."

The yellow eyes above blinked, and a bat flitted across the sky hungrily in search of dinner.

Chance's form relaxed, and he shook his head, bewildered.

Now I know who taught Grandfather.

CHAPTER 51

Ana woke early the next morning when she heard her mother's car door slam. Alert and refreshed, she hopped out of bed.

It was another beautiful day. The sun was bright, and there wasn't a cloud in the sky.

From the lack of noise in the house, Ana assumed her sister wasn't up yet. That was a first. As Ana walked past Eva's door, she heard soft snores.

Hunger pangs hit her when she descended the stairs. Scrambled eggs sounded good, so she cracked the fridge open to retrieve the ingredients. Normally too tired in the morning, she didn't prepare a breakfast that required more than two steps to complete. Cereal and frozen waffles were common and easy.

A door creaked upstairs, and Eva slunk down to the kitchen, her eyes droopy and tired.

"Ooooh, you making eggs? Can I have some?"

"Sure. Go ahead and sit down – they'll be ready in a sec."

After breakfast, Ana did a load of laundry and dishes until it was late enough to call her doctor's office. She lucked out and got an appointment on Friday, only three days away.

Ana knew Chance was probably still up on the mountain and decided to look around. It was time to vacuum and mop, she noted, as dust bunnies floated across the floors. She whipped out a rag and dusted everything within reach.

While she shook a floor rug outside, her phone rang. She dropped the rug on the shaded deck so she could answer.

"Hey, you back?"

"Yeah."

"How was it?"

Silence.

"Well, I had another memory-thing. I need to talk to you about it. Can I come over?"

"Sure. See you soon."

"Bye, my love."

Twenty minutes later, Chance's black truck pulled into Ana's driveway with a dust plume trailing behind it.

"Hey," Ana said as she rushed up to welcome him. She leaned forward and kissed him on the cheek.

"Why don't we go out to the rock for privacy?"

"Sure." She grabbed his hand, and they sauntered down the trail together.

"Man, what a night."

Chance sat down upon the granite slab and Ana joined him, frowning in concern.

"Tell me." Ana took hold of his hands with hers. She enjoyed the electricity they still shared when they touched.

Chance cleared his throat and said, "It was weird going back. Lots of ghosts up there." He paled and continued. "I had another vision triggered when I remembered training with Grandfather. It was the one I've been waiting for. I think he was my age and he was traveling along the ocean – probably avoiding the US after his dad's death. I think he could have been in Mexico 'cause it just makes sense – that's where he met Grandma. So, he's cruisin' along the beach and finds this young beached whale. He decides to try and save it and then after a full day of trying, he gets it back in the bay. He realizes he's hungry and turns into a parrot and goes to eat some bugs. That was nasty. *I've* never eaten in animal form, never wanted to..." Chance said and trailed off when he glanced up to see Ana's impatient frown and smiled. "Well, then, bam! He looks over and, surprise...the orca phases into a man!"

"What?! Are you serious?!" Ana's eyes grew wide.

Chance continued in a daze and said, "Yeah, the guy told Grandfather his name was Balam. Guess he trusted Grandfather after he saved him, but it took a while for Grandfather to trust *him*. Although, he must have, because in another vision I saw them in the jungle together training,"

Chance mumbled.

"Really?! Do you think this is the guy your grandfather mentioned?"

"Probably, but I don't know for sure."

"Mexico," she said softly.

"Yeah."

They sat in silence awhile, each absorbed in their own thoughts.

An eagle glided over a distant field. Ana could almost see the air currents ripple through the sky like silk or smoke. The summer day was so bright and colorful. *I feel alive.*

"Um, you feel like heading to Spokane with me again on Friday? I think I'll have big news."

"Oh, yeah? How so?" Chance asked, distractedly.

"Oh, just a feeling. Will you come?"

"Couldn't keep me away."

CHAPTER 52

On Friday afternoon, Ana and Chance walked back into the medical center.

Ana went through the same series of tests she was used to. Chance waited beside her for the doctor to come in. It took almost an hour until a faint knock came from the door.

Dr. Tilgan's curly hair emerged first followed by her flustered face. She immediately launched into an apology and said, "I'm sorry to keep you waiting, but we seem to have some sort of mix-up. The ultrasound you had earlier seems to have been switched. We're trying to find the right one."

"Why? What do you mean?"

"Well, the one labeled with your name isn't your heart's anatomy."

"Well, how does the EKG and x-ray look?"

Dr. Tilgan frowned and opened the manila folder she had tucked under her arm. "I actually haven't looked at them yet because of the whole sonogram mix-up."

The doctor sat down while she reviewed the results. Her frown deepened, and her head rolled to the side as she scratched her temple.

Ana spoke up and said, "Um, I'm not so sure the ultrasound results *were* switched. I've been feeling...um...*different* recently. Actually, really great. I feel energetic and healthy, and I no longer get faint or winded. No more dizzy spells..."

Dr. Tilgan stared at Ana. "All of the test results reveal a healthy heart. I don't understand it. Just a couple weeks ago your heart was enlarged and hardening, and now it appears you're fine. I have no explanation for it. Has *anything happened* since your last visit?" Dr. Tilgan peered questioningly at Ana.

Ana shrugged and said, "Nope, it's weird. I just kinda started feeling better. No explanation."

"Well, there's no way I can let you leave the clinic without me *personally* double checking the results. You are going to get tired of me real quick, because this doesn't just happen. Let's head down to the ultrasound room. I hope you didn't have plans this afternoon..."

***

"You did it."

"What?"

"Healed me – it's official," Ana said and waved at the big white building across the parking lot. Its windows gleamed bright in the afternoon sunlight.

Chance rested against the side of his black truck, and Ana leaned in to hug him.

"Thank you," she whispered into his ear and pressed him close, holding her breath to slow the stinging tears.

He lifted her chin and stared into her eyes. "I'd do it again," he said seriously.

Ana frowned and said, "You won't have to. And I wouldn't want you to."

He shook his head and kept silent.

A flock of birds traveled through the cloudless sky. Ana reached up and pinched her Thunderbird talisman between her fingers and smiled.

I'm free.

CHAPTER 53

"WHAT?! That's not possible!"

Ana held out the test results to her mother who dropped her things to the floor. Too excited to wait, Ana hit her with the news as soon as she entered the door.

"What do you mean the doctor gave you a clean bill of health? Did they do an EKG, X-ray AND ultrasound?"

"All of it, and they all showed the same thing – that I'm *fine* now." Ana beamed at her mother, whose color had drained from her face in shock.

"Dr. Tilgan personally did an ultrasound to double check the results before she let me leave."

"How?" Was all Melissa could squeeze out.

"Unexplainable, really...I guess you could call it a miracle."

Melissa stumbled to the couch where Eva sat, wide eyed with a book opened in her lap. Eva watched Melissa like a frightened rabbit.

A strangled sob broke from Melissa's chest, and her head collapsed into her lap.

"Mom!" Ana ran to her mother's side and squatted down in front of her shaking body. She laid her warm fingertips on Melissa's shoulder. "It's okay. It's *really* happening."

Melissa's muffled voice found its way to Ana's ears. "How can this be? I don't understand."

Melissa lifted her face; her mascara smeared down her cheeks over a spectacular smile. She grabbed Ana in her arms and laughed as the tears continued to flow.

Eva sat still, appearing unsure how to react to the burst of emotion. The torrent of happiness that poured from their mother affected them both at once, and they joined in Melissa's teary laughter.

After they calmed down from Ana's amazing announcement, they went out to dinner to celebrate. Aunt Tera and Uncle Jace joined them, unaware of the news.

"Are you serious? Who *ever* would have thought!" Aunt Tera exclaimed, jumped up from the table, and knocked over her water glass in the process. Eva jumped from her chair and avoided the stream of icy water just in time.

Tera darted to Ana's side and pulled her into a tight embrace. The strong stranglehold around Ana's neck closed off her air supply, as she gasped for breath. "Yeah! Great, isn't it?"

Uncle Jace just sat at the table and shook his head, bewildered. "Man, didn't see *that* coming..."

Melissa was the one who spilled the news. Ana knew her mother's excitement was too great; it would have been selfish not to let her make the announcement. After all, it was Melissa who had carried the burden for eighteen years. She was the one who worked to the brink of exhaustion just to earn insurance to cover all of Ana's medical bills. She was the one who watched Ana go through so much. It was the least Ana could do for her mom. She could just imagine the next day at the bank; her mother would tell anyone who drew near enough for conversation. The thought brought a smile to Ana's lips.

"So, where's Chance? Why isn't he out celebrating with us?" Aunt Tera asked while she dabbed at the large wet spot on the table.

"He dropped me off at home and left. He said he didn't want to intrude on our moment. I tried to convince him, but..." Ana shrugged her shoulders, a little disappointed. She had wanted him to stay, although she thought she knew the reason why he left so abruptly. He wanted the three of them to have some time together, just family. He did it for Melissa. Ana suspected he knew how much the moment would mean to her. And the only reason Ana let him leave was because he promised to come back later so they could celebrate...in private.

***

True to form, Chance kept his promise. Ana was on her gazing stone admiring the North Star when something immense blocked the silvery moon. She blinked in surprise as she sat in darkness. Feathers rustled through the air as the beast swept in for a landing. Awe inspiring wings generated a burst of wind that caressed her flushed cheeks and swept loose needles and dirt back toward the trees.

The amazing specimen before her was enormous and fantastic. Something from another time, or place. Its fearsome talons made her think of the gift Chance received from his grandfather. Massive weapons so large it would be hard to contain one in the palm of her hand.

Ana whistled softly, thoroughly impressed with the display.

"Amazing," she said.

Yellow eyes flashed and met hers. Soft coos came from its open beak as it folded its huge wings against its dark feathered body.

Ana advanced slowly and kept an eye on the mythic raptor in caution. The bird watched her as she inched forward and stood still. Soft feathers brushed against her chest, and she sank into its body.

"For always..."

THE END

Fledgling

To read a 'Lost Chapter' from Fledgling, please visit-
http://www.theshapeshifterchronicles.com/free-gift
Your special password is- theprom

ABOUT THE AUTHOR

Natasha was born in Nevada City, California. An only child, she used her imagination while exploring the forest surrounding her home. Her natural interest in fantasy ignited when her parents read 'The Hobbit' to her as a youth, and from then on anything seemed possible. Once awarded with a Hershey's bar 'the size of a Buick' in her high school English class for creative writing, her passion and interest in writing has never dimmed. She now lives in Littleton, Colorado with her husband and two children.

29651872R00177

Made in the USA
Lexington, KY
02 February 2014